THE KILLER INSTINCT

KATE WILEY

Storm

This is a work of fiction. Names, characters, business, events and incidents are the products of the author's imagination. Any resemblance to actual persons, living or dead, or actual events is purely coincidental.

Copyright © Ashley MacLennan, 2024

The moral right of the author has been asserted.

All rights reserved. No part of this book may be reproduced or used in any manner without the prior written permission of the copyright owner.

To request permissions, contact the publisher at rights@stormpublishing.co

Ebook ISBN: 978-1-80508-445-7
Paperback ISBN: 978-1-80508-447-1

Cover design: Lisa Brewster
Cover images: Trevillion

Published by Storm Publishing.
For further information, visit:
www.stormpublishing.co

ALSO BY KATE WILEY

The Killer's Daughter
Her Father's Secret

As Sierra Dean

The Secret McQueen Series

Something Secret This Way Comes
A Bloody Good Secret
Deep Dark Secret
Keeping Secret
Grave Secret
Secret Unleashed
Cold Hard Secret
A Secret to Die For
Secret Lives
A Wicked Secret
Deadly Little Secret
One Last Secret

The Genie McQueen Series

Bayou Blues
Black Magic Bayou
Black-Hearted Devil
Blood in the Bayou

The Rain Chaser Series

Thunder Road

Driving Rain

Highway to Hail

The Boys of Summer Series

Pitch Perfect

Perfect Catch

High Heat

As Gretchen Rue

The Witches' Brew Mysteries

Steeped to Death

Death by Thousand Sips

The Grim Steeper

The Lucky Pie Mysteries

A Pie to Die For

This is for the two teachers who told me I could.
Anita Skene, for telling me not to become a teacher.
Miriam Toews, for every ounce of praise on my university writing.
All it takes is one positive word, and you both showed me I could get here one day.

ONE

The air in Muir Woods smelled different than anywhere in the world Detective Margot Phalen had ever been. It was cleaner, *greener* somehow, and made her feel like nature itself was embracing her with a comforting hug.

The scent also made her think of death.

It was hard to separate the environment from what had happened there, and now every time Margot came to Muir Woods, she thought about the dead.

She sat on a wooden bench, watching the sunlight shift through swaying treetops, admiring how impossible this place was. The trees were hundreds of years old, towering high above her, their trunks deceptively lean at the top, though the bases were so thick three people couldn't wrap their arms around them together. The creek babbled happily, and a persistent Pacific wren sang somewhere behind her, but the noise Margot noticed the most was *people*.

She had arrived early, not long after Muir Woods opened to the public, and the walking paths were already packed with tourists. She had come here several times in the past month.

Twice to look at bodies, and a handful more to try to understand how the bodies had *gotten* there.

In one case, the body had been located on a steeper hiking trail well out of the way of prying eyes. Since there were trails near the park that didn't require going through the main gates, they had concluded that Leanne Wu's body had been brought in from one of those paths. It wouldn't have been easy, but it would have avoided witnesses.

She sipped the iced coffee she'd brought with her, which was now more melted water than coffee thanks to the drive out here, and watched as dozens of families passed her in either direction. A few friendly souls smiled or said hello to her, but most seemed completely oblivious to her presence. One or two groups had big wagons in tow, with two or three kids on board.

The wagons were currently her team's primary theory on how the killer had brought the second body into the park. But she still wondered if someone could get away with something so brazen. An adult woman's body looked very different from a gaggle of toddlers. The math wasn't mathing as far as Margot was concerned.

Another wren joined the one behind her, and the two chirped merrily at each other, giving her something to listen to other than the din of fifteen different languages being spoken at once on the path.

So many people.

This was an age of distraction, and most of the people she watched on the path were taking selfies on their phone, or talking to each other, ignoring the signs that requested silence in certain areas. People were oblivious to their surroundings, and that could have allowed someone to pass by and dump a body here without being noticed.

Rebecca Watson's body hadn't been spotted right away. It had been left in thick underbrush a good distance from the main path, but still within sight of it. Her pink leisurewear was what had drawn a passerby to take a closer look.

Lividity in her body told them she'd died somewhere else, so she hadn't walked herself into the woods and then been murdered. And while she wasn't a big woman, she was still a grown adult, and dead weight wasn't called that for nothing. Why was she there, and not hidden more effectively?

Margot was here on her day off because this case bothered her. Two bodies found mere days apart, obviously connected, and then the killer had gone silent. That wasn't how serial killers usually operated. Typically, they started slow, often with months or years between their kills, and as they developed their skill, their thirst for blood tended to increase, as did their risky behavior.

Toward the end of a serial killer's career, they would begin to time their kills closer and closer together. It was rare for a killer to leave bodies only days apart and then see nothing from them for half a year.

Unless they'd been arrested for something else.

Or a life event required them to take a step back. Something like getting married or having a baby could put a real damper on a serial killer's activities.

Margot knew all about that.

She sighed, pulling her long copper-red hair into a ponytail as she got up from the bench to make her way back toward the main entrance. She'd hoped coming here might give her some kind of epiphany, but it had only reminded her of how cold the case was growing.

Other murders had come and gone, but these two lingered, and Margot knew that unless something had forced the killer to stop for good, then he wasn't done.

He was just biding his time.

TWO

Margot was grateful for the gym at the precinct. Sure, it smelled like feet and all the equipment had been purchased sometime in the early nineties, but it was somewhere she felt safe, where she didn't need to worry.

As a general rule, Margot didn't *do* memberships. She didn't create routines that would be easy to follow if someone wanted to know where she was at any given time. The only way she would eat out was to grab drive-thru, and even then, she was careful not to visit the same places too frequently.

Routines were dangerous.

They caused complacency. When people let their guard down, that's when bad things happened.

Her father had taught her that.

He'd taken advantage of people's complacency often enough, and it had allowed him to kill seventy-eight women. That number was currently considered a starting point by the FBI, who were actively working to get Ed Finch—the Classified Killer—to divulge more of his secrets.

Margot slammed her gloved fist into an ancient punching bag. The chain attaching it to the ceiling groaned.

Or that might have been her partner, Wes Fox, who was holding the bag for her.

"Damn, Rocky, this is just supposed to be a warm-up, not taking out your personal vendettas against Mr. Everlast himself."

Wes smirked at her, but she'd been around him long enough to know that the look in his eyes showed concern. He was worried about her.

She hit the bag again, her gloves making a satisfying *thwok* sound against the old leather. After her first visit, when she'd used the communal boxing gloves, she had gone out and bought her own pair to never have to relive that experience.

"You've got something on your mind," Wes prodded. He hadn't moved an inch, even though the last punch had come pretty close to grazing his cheek.

Margot didn't want to damage his face. She liked looking at it. Wes was in his early forties, but still carried himself like a twentysomething bachelor. He was handsome, with dark blond hair, rich brown eyes, and honest-to-God dimples when he smiled. And that smile was his greatest weapon. It was disarming, knee-shaking, and almost too much for her to resist sometimes.

It also made it difficult to cultivate a bad mood when he was aiming it at her.

"I've always got something on my mind, Wes. Unlike the airheads you date, I can actually form multiple thoughts at the same time." *Thwok.*

"Don't be anti-feminist, Margot, it doesn't suit you."

Thwok. This time intentionally closer to his pretty face. She glared at him. "OK, Gloria Steinem, please tell me more about feminism."

Wes leaned his face away, brows knitted, obviously not amused. "I'm trying to be a friend here. Let me."

Margot didn't have a lot of friends. If she discounted co-workers, she had none. Wes and Detective Leon Telly were probably the closest people in the world to her, and because they knew the truth about her and her father, she didn't need to hide that part of her life from them like she did everyone else.

Sometimes, in moments of weakness, she wondered if she and Wes might be *more* than just partners, but she knew that was a whole mess she wasn't prepared to get herself into. In the same way she didn't have friends outside work, she didn't *do* relationships. And if she and Wes stepped across that line, she knew it wouldn't be something she could keep neat and tidy and free from feelings.

It risked too much.

She unleashed a flurry of short punches on the bag then ended with a solid right uppercut, steering clear of Wes entirely. Her brow was beaded with sweat when she finished, but she did feel better, as if a demon had been exorcised.

But like all her demons, it would be back.

Wes helped her remove her gloves before handing her a bottle of water.

"I'm just thinking about the Muir Woods case," she said once she'd swallowed.

Wes arched an eyebrow. "Are you sure that's all that's bothering you?"

Yeah, dating Wes was out of the question. He knew her too well.

Her brain understood that. Her body was another matter entirely.

"What else would I be thinking about?"

Wes sat on one of the weight benches, undoing his running shoes before heading into the men's locker room to change back into his work gear. "You haven't talked about your last trip out to San Quentin," he nudged.

"There's not much to talk about."

The FBI had created a new Ed Finch task force in the past

year to investigate old cold cases that might be tied to him. Ed had been willing to talk, but his one caveat was that he'd only talk to her.

Since the previous summer they had solved two murders: Theresa Milotti, a teenage hitchhiker, and Marissa Loewen, one of the state's most famous missing persons cases. The two women had fallen victim to Ed, but at least now their families had the peace of mind of knowing justice was being served.

The cases would never go to trial. Ed was already on death row for dozens of counts of first-degree murder. He'd never be executed—not with the state's current limitations—but he was going to die behind bars in San Quentin, and that had to be some comfort to the grieving families. It was to Margot.

Ed had been hinting, ever since the Loewen girl had been found, that there were more. But the last few times Margot had made attempts to visit him on behalf of the FBI he was either cagey and unforthcoming, forcing her to cut their visits short, or he would refuse to see her at all.

When Margot had gone for her most recent visit, last week, Ed had spent fifteen minutes recounting the murder of Laura Welsh, his first victim, but giving Margot absolutely nothing new to go on. She hated hearing about the Welsh murder, not because of the details—Ed had been new to killing then, his work had been sloppy and frenzied—but because of the fact that she had been strapped into the back seat in a baby carrier at the time.

She thought often about whether or not Laura would have gotten into the car with Ed if she hadn't seen the baby in the back seat.

Margot felt like an accessory to a crime she didn't even remember happening.

Ed knew it, so he made sure to tell her over and over how Laura had said she was cute, asked her name.

"Tell me what's bothering you, Margot," Wes urged after the silence drew out too long.

"He's toying with me," she said finally. "I think he's seeing how far he can push me until it seems like I won't come back. And *then* he'll tell us something. This is a game to him. After the sniper case he called me through his lawyer and peppered me with all these sordid details of a murder he'd committed, but he was careful not to give us anything that we could actually *solve*, we just know it doesn't match any of his existing victims."

She sighed, wishing she was still in front of the heavy bag so she could throw a few aggravated punches into it.

There was no sense in telling Wes she didn't want to participate in these interviews anymore, since he wasn't the one responsible for them. And at this point she was in too deep, the key member of the FBI task force. Saying no had left the building months ago.

She had a meeting scheduled that afternoon to review their plan of attack for the next interview with Ed, and she was dreading it.

Wes leaned forward, forearms resting on his knees, and he seemed like he was on the cusp of saying something meaningful. However, Detective O'Halloran chose that moment to amble down the stairs into the gym. O'Halloran looked like every detective on 1970s cop shows, right down to the brown suit with too-short pants and socks Margot was sure needed those old-fashioned garters to stay up.

"Hey, you two are up, got a call in Chinatown."

The detectives of San Francisco's homicide department worked on a rotation, so no one team got all the easy cases, and ideally no detectives were saddled with more cases than they could handle. It was an effective system in that it forced them to keep their plates as clear as possible, because they didn't know how long they'd be waiting until their next case turned up dead.

Margot didn't like that the Muir Woods case was still

lingering on her backburner, though she was officially only helping with it. Leon Telly was primary.

She and Wes changed quickly, then got their crime scene details from dispatch and headed out to Wes's car. Margot didn't care who drove, but she knew driving to crime scenes in San Francisco fulfilled some sort of lifelong Steve McQueen *Bullitt* fantasy for Wes, so she would often let him be the wheelman of their partnership.

The midday traffic was thin, thankfully, and as they headed toward Chinatown, the bright overhead sunshine felt at odds with whatever they were driving into. Dispatch had been light on the details. Single victim, female, her son said she had missed a regularly scheduled call that morning, and he had asked for a welfare check since he lived in a different state.

As it had landed in their laps, that check obviously hadn't gone well.

Margot liked Chinatown. It was a stone's throw from her own apartment in North Beach, and on the days she did venture out on foot, she sometimes enjoyed walking down Grant Avenue.

For some reason the ever-bustling crowds made her feel safe.

It was the first week of February and the Lunar New Year was set to fall the next week. Shop windows were bedecked in red and gold, and the overhead lanterns bobbed in the afternoon breeze. Symbols of the dog—the zodiac animal for that year—were festooned everywhere Margot looked, with several of the iconic Chinatown murals having been refreshed to depict the year's token animal. As a 1980 baby, Margot knew she was year of the monkey, but she knew shockingly little about the customs of Lunar New Year beyond how *loud* they got every year.

Next week these streets would be almost impassable as shop owners and restaurateurs would try to usher in a new year of prosperity by handing out little envelopes of money to tourists and locals who were brave enough to stand shoulder to shoulder in the claustrophobic crowds.

Wes found a parking spot on Washington Street, the steep incline of the hill making him angle the car's wheels in toward the curb. As Margot stepped out of the car, she could hear laughter and conversation drifting up the hill from Grant Avenue where the heart of Chinatown stretched out for several blocks. The side streets were loaded with hidden gems, but also crammed with narrow apartments.

Margot and Wes were headed to a lean apartment complex on Washington where laundry hung from the rusted white fire escapes and many of the windows were covered over with newspaper from the inside.

The main floor of the building was a laundromat, and the smell of Peking duck wafted out into the street from the Chinese restaurants on either side. With Wes for company, Margot was feeling bold enough to stop for some lunch after the investigation.

Provided the crime scene wasn't too stomach churning.

A uniformed officer stood in the doorway that provided tenants access to the apartments overhead. They flashed their badges at him, and he stepped aside to let them through.

The stairs were narrow, scuffed, and the entire interior of the apartment building showed its age from the peeling wallpaper down to the threadbare carpet runners in the hallways. The place smelled musty, but there were brief snatches of cooking scents that came from apartments within that made the place feel homey and less abandoned.

The building had an old elevator with a metal grate that needed to be manually opened and closed. Margot had heard plenty of horror stories about old lifts getting stuck between floors, so she headed toward the stairs, gesturing for Wes to follow. She didn't trust this building's landlord to have things up to code if they couldn't even paint the yellowed walls.

Their victim's apartment was on the top floor, and Margot was out of breath and cursing her lack of cardio training by the time they got there.

Wes, unflappable, didn't even look like he'd broken a sweat.

"You're the one who wanted to take the stairs," he said, patting her on the back as she paused to catch her breath.

"Shut up," she retorted, not enough oxygen going to her brain to give her anything better.

Two more uniformed officers were outside a door at the end of the hall. As they'd passed, Margot had spotted another standing in a doorway on the floor below, chatting with one of the tenants, so initial interviews were underway. They had beaten the medical examiner's crew to the scene, so there was no protective footwear in sight, but Margot never left the station without latex gloves.

She slipped them on before they entered the crime scene, which had already been disrupted by the officer doing the wellness check—and more likely than not by a nosy super.

The room was dimly lit, with rolling blinds covering the two small windows that faced out onto Washington. The kitchen was small but exceptionally tidy, without so much as a dish in the sink, and while the tiles were old, they were spotless. Someone obviously cared for this apartment very much.

Margot's gaze passed over the joint living room dining room area, which held a two-person dining table and a love seat facing a tiny console TV atop a VCR. Margot couldn't remember the last time she'd seen a VCR. On the dining table was a small bouquet of flowers in a red vase and a stack of little red envelopes with some dollar bills on top of them waiting to be stuffed.

Money sitting right out in the open that hadn't been touched.

So, this wasn't motivated by robbery, then. Any crackhead

willing to climb all those stairs would have made off with those singles and the TV, hoping to get enough for their next fix.

Margot hadn't seen the body yet, but she'd been to her fair share of crime scenes. Everything about this told her the murder had been personal. The killer was most likely someone the victim knew.

Wes led the way down the narrow hallway to the bedroom. The walls were covered in framed photos showing an older Chinese woman in various locations, with several family photos where she was hugging two small children, while a man and woman in their thirties stood smiling on either side of her.

Margot's stomach sank.

There was no such thing as a *good* victim. Every gangbanger and sex worker had a family, had kids, had a life they left behind them that *mattered*, even if their death never made it to the front page of the newspaper.

No life was disposable.

But some victims hit hard. Kids with their whole lives ahead of them. Young mothers. People whose deaths left a crater in their wake.

Looking at the photos on the wall, Margot had a strong feeling their victim was going to be one of those.

Wes was first through the bedroom door, and he stopped in his tracks, blocking her view from whatever it was that had happened in there. He let out a low whistle.

"What?" she asked, trying to crane her neck to see over his shoulder. She was tall, but he was taller.

"I think we're going to need to wait for the ME," was all he said, stepping back so she could finally see.

Margot's mouth went dry.

The room was splattered in blood, brownish-red stains covering every wall and piece of furniture in the small space. On the center of the bed was the huddled figure of a body, curled into a ball, a pose so defensive Margot wanted to rush across the room to see if she was still alive.

But the puddle of blood congealing on the floor told her there was no need to bother.

There was nowhere to step in the room that they wouldn't leave their prints behind in the sticky blood.

Yes, it was safe to say this had been personal. Somebody wanted this lady dead.

What Margot wanted to know was *why*.

THREE

1961

Oakland, CA

Eddie couldn't figure out *why*.

He knew his mother had moods, knew to be careful what he did or said around her whenever her fury would swell up like a big dark balloon, filling their small house until no one could move or breathe without rubbing up against it.

But he didn't know why she took it out on him more than anyone.

She used to only be angry at Eddie's daddy. That was how Eddie had learned to weather a storm, by watching the way his daddy had let the lashes and barbs roll off his back. The way he'd strike back, when necessary. But Daddy had also taught Eddie that every man had his limits. He hadn't stuck around long after Mama's anger got worse. This left Eddie and his older sister Sarah all alone in the house with no one who seemed to care a lick what happened to them behind closed doors.

His neighbor to the left, Miss Shirley, was nice enough. She had a cat named Dandelion who sometimes sat on her front porch. Sarah loved that cat, and she'd spend as long as she could outside petting it—anything to avoid coming in.

Eddie didn't care much for animals, but he didn't mind Miss Shirley. Sometimes she'd give Eddie and Sarah fresh-baked cookies if she happened to see them around.

Miss Shirley liked to talk to them about Jesus a lot, which Eddie could take or leave. They didn't go to church and Miss Shirley thought this made them heathens, but she said even heathens could be saved by the grace of God, they just needed to accept Jesus as their Lord and Savior or something. She was vague on the specifics and Eddie didn't care to ask, he merely nodded, said he loved Jesus, and took his cookies.

But if Mama saw even a trace of melted chocolate on his fingers or shirt, it was all over. Eddie had to be very clean, because Mama hated dirty children. Even though he was nine, almost ten, she still insisted on bathing him regularly. Sarah was fourteen, and Mama let her bathe herself, but Eddie was dirty. She never seemed able to get him clean enough.

"It's because you have a filthy soul, like your goddamn father," she would sneer as she scrubbed his skin raw. "You can't get someone clean when they're sick in their soul."

When she looked at him, he didn't see any of the warmth he'd noticed when other moms on the block looked at their kids. She looked right through him, and Eddie didn't know why.

Eddie wished his daddy was still around, if only so there was someone else in the house Mama could fix that stare on.

Sarah didn't get off totally free and clear. Mama warned her about men, told her to keep her legs closed because otherwise she'd end up like she had, with ungrateful brats who looked like their daddy. But Eddie had heard Mama talk softly to Sarah, tell her she was pretty, and to make sure she found a husband who would take care of her, because that was probably the only way she'd get out of this place.

The nights she drank were the worst, because then she

lashed out with her hands as well as her words. On those nights Eddie would stay in his room, listening to the clatter and bang of her movements in the kitchen, and if he was quiet enough, like a little mouse, she might get drunk enough to forget he was there. That was the best he could hope for, to be forgotten. The nights she remembered he was there, things were worse.

Anything he said was an insult to her, a reason for her to retaliate. Eddie couldn't do anything right. If he agreed with her, he was being condescending. If he argued with her, he was being insolent. And simply by existing in her line of sight, he reminded her of his father, the worst insult of all. So, he got used to it, the slaps, the taunts, the way she'd twist his arm so hard it left bruises.

He told himself one day he'd get bigger.

One day she'd stop being able to hurt him.

And he'd be able to hurt her.

FOUR

The live-in building manager was a twentysomething woman named Marie who hadn't stopped crying the entire time Margot had been trying to talk to her. Marie had been the one to let the officers in for a welfare check, and had gotten the shock of her young life when she'd followed them into that bedroom to make sure they didn't touch anything.

"Sh-sh-she was s-s-such a n-nice old l-lady," she stammered as she gulped in air and blew her nose into a tissue.

Margot was sitting in one of Marie's hardback kitchen chairs, while the young woman sat on her floral sofa. Marie's apartment was nice, reminding Margot slightly of her own. All the furniture was mix-and-match second-hand stuff, and in Marie's place it created a cozy cottage vibe. In Margot's it looked like she'd moved into an apartment belonging to an old bachelor from 1964 and hadn't changed anything.

Marie seemed like the kind of woman who would live in an apartment like this. She was a little chubby, had a cute pixie-style haircut, and was wearing a billowy top that wouldn't have looked out of place on Stevie Nicks. Margot noticed a vase of flowers on her little dinette table and wondered if they were from the woman upstairs, or if Marie had given the older woman flowers. They were the same type: carnations and roses, red for the holiday.

Between sobs, Marie told Margot the woman who lived on the fifth floor was named Shuye Zhou, though many of the non-Chinese-speaking tenants apparently knew her as Susie. Shuye had dwelled in the complex longer than most of the current tenants, having been in the top-floor apartment for twenty-seven years. Longer—Marie noted—than she, herself, had been alive.

That little barb succeeded in making Margot feel about a thousand years old at the geriatric age of thirty-eight.

Shuye, according to Marie, was the best tenant in the place. Rent was always paid early and in full—usually with fresh baked goods to accompany it—and no one had ever made a single complaint about the woman in her entire time living there.

Margot asked, "Was there anyone who might harbor a grudge? An ex-husband, a neighbor who didn't like her?"

Marie shook her head, wiping away tears on her sleeve, despite the box of tissues sitting in front of her.

"Everyone loved her. Her husband passed away two years ago. Her two kids are grown up, but they come see her every few months. They live out of state. Why would *anyone* want to hurt Susie?"

That was the question, wasn't it? Because once Margot understood *why*, she'd have a better chance at unlocking *who*. Cases like this, the killer had to be someone close to the victim, but the problem with that was one major caveat: people had secrets.

There could be people in everyone's lives they wouldn't tell their friends or relatives about. Secret boyfriends, work friends who didn't typically bear mention in dinnertime chatter. Hell, the great true crime writer Ann Rule had worked right alongside Ted Bundy at a suicide hotline, never questioning for a minute that he might be a secret serial killer. Ted probably hadn't come up much in Ann's evening chitchat with her family.

So, while it was clear that Shuye had probably known her killer, it was less clear if anyone *else* in her life would know them.

What secrets was this woman hiding, and how had they led to her death?

Wes poked his head into the small living room. "Evelyn's crew is here—you ready?"

Margot nodded and passed Marie her business card. "If you think of anything else, or hear anything around the building, you can call me any time. Please don't hesitate."

Before Margot could get up, though, Marie grabbed her by the wrist. The woman's palms were clammy, and Margot recoiled, pulling her hand away. "Do you think someone in the building did this to her?" Marie didn't stammer once with that question.

"We have no way to know that at this point. But I think it's highly unlikely that whoever did this to Shuye is planning to make a habit of it." That was not entirely accurate. Margot really had no way to know what the killer would do next. But in almost all homicide cases she'd ever dealt with, slayings like these were one-and-done.

Serial killers, despite their popularity in true crime podcasts and police dramas, just weren't that common. They weren't *unheard* of. At any given time, there were dozens working in the shadows across the country, but most of them targeted high-risk populations, like sex workers and the homeless. Shuye was a grandmother. She wasn't someone who could be killed without it raising serious alarm bells.

The Chinese population of San Francisco was tight knit,

this was going to be a huge deal, especially falling at a time of year when everyone wanted to celebrate prosperity and good fortune.

Margot thought again of the little red envelopes on Shuye's dining table. The untouched singles.

Resting a hand on Marie's shoulder Margot tried for a warm smile but managed only a grimace. "You don't have anything to worry about."

Kind lies were Margot's bread and butter.

Wes was better at selling them than she was, though. She should have left Marie in his charming and capable hands.

Back on the fifth floor, once again winded and hating her distrust of old elevators, Margot joined Wes and greeted Evelyn Yao, the chief medical examiner. Her little white-suited worker bees were already buzzing around the apartment, but the queen had waited for them.

"Welcome back, kids. You ready to join the circus?" Evelyn was decked out in a full-body protective suit to keep anything from her getting on the crime scene, but also effectively keeping the crime scene off her. A box of shoe covers was waiting in her hands and Margot took them and slipped them on over her low-heeled ankle boots. She had long ago stopped feeling silly about the way they looked.

Margot had removed her original pair of gloves before speaking to Marie, not wanting to be any more off-putting than she already was, so she took a new pair from a box by the entrance, then followed Evelyn back into the apartment.

It constantly surprised her how quietly efficient the crime scene techs were. Both the SFPD crew and Evelyn's medical crew—who were collecting any human evidence—were working around each other in a well-executed dance. There was no small talk; the sound of a camera shutter was the only thing Margot could hear.

They headed back to the bedroom, which had already been photographed. The blood on the floor was mostly dry, so their footsteps wouldn't mark the scene too heavily.

Evelyn pulled her hood up to cover her short black hair. In recent months she had returned to having it dyed—currently green streaks—and Margot was happy to see that small touch brought back. Evelyn tended to cover the bright-colored streaks with black dye if she needed to testify in a trial, wanting to present a professional appearance.

Doing her day-to-day work, she had nothing to prove. Everyone she encountered knew Evelyn was the best of the best.

"You get an ID on her?" Evelyn asked, her tone serious.

Margot nodded. "Her name is Shuye Zhou. The building manager wasn't sure of her age, so we've got an officer checking the DMV records. She's got grandkids, and lived here more than twenty-five years, so I'd say seventies is a safe bet."

"You watch your tongue, Phalen." Evelyn waggled a gloved finger at her. "I'm fifty-seven and I have a grandson."

Margot was stunned she hadn't known this detail about Evelyn's personal life. They'd worked on cases together for almost a decade, and while Margot knew the basics—divorced, one daughter, voracious flirt—she rarely asked Evelyn any questions about herself.

It felt strange to stand over bodies and ask someone what their hobbies were. Plus, Margot didn't want anyone asking questions about her family life. She hated to lie, and leaving Ed out of her personal story felt like a lie by omission, even if it was to protect herself.

"I didn't know Lisa had a baby," Wes said, slapping Evelyn gamely on the shoulder. "I'd have sent something off the registry."

Wes, apparently, had no problem getting to know people.

"I'll tell her you said congratulations." The proud smile on her face said that, while Evelyn might not want to get into it here, she was obviously very pleased with her new role as cool grandma. "Maybe see if baby Charles wants a new grandpa, eh?"

Ah, there was the inappropriate Evelyn Margot knew and loved.

"Wes can teach the baby all the really vital things a little boy needs to know. How to get suits tailored and where to pick up women who aren't too discerning." Margot glanced over at her partner, checking to see if he minded the joke, but also curious to see how mentioning other women might rattle him.

"Who needs to date when I have all these beautiful women queuing up to belittle me during my working hours?" he shot back, winking.

Margot rolled her eyes and turned to Evelyn, who switched into work mode, hovering over the body. It was obvious she'd already been in to see Shuye from the way she zeroed in on the wounds.

"We know she was stabbed," Evelyn said, a gloved finger pointing at one of the slices in Shuye's pajamas. "I'll need to examine her more closely but, based on my initial observations, I'm seeing about twelve different individual wounds on her back and side alone. There are defensive wounds on the back of her hands, so I think she probably moved into the position we see her in now after an initial attack when she tried to protect her face and head." Evelyn mimicked putting her arms over her face, her hands covering the top of her head.

She dropped her hands and returned to the body, pointing at a bloody wound on the side of Shuye's head, near her ear. "While she would have died from the blood loss, regardless, this is most likely the wound that killed her. The amount of force it would take to drive a knife through the skull is incredible. I know it's your job to speculate and not mine, but whoever did this would have had a lot of adrenaline going through them at the time, because that's not the kind of thing most people are capable of. I've seen people who were attacked with hammers and the blows have to land at a precise angle to break the skull. Our heads were designed perfectly to protect our brains, and they do a good job of it. Whoever did this to her really wanted her dead." Evelyn looked down sadly at Shuye. "I hope you find this son of a bitch fast," she said quietly, almost to herself.

"Me too," Margot replied. She understood what Evelyn was feeling; she was experiencing the same thing. There was a sort of posthumous protectiveness they sometimes felt toward victims. The desire to keep them safe from harm—obviously impossible—transformed into an intense need to find them justice.

Margot wanted to solve every murder that landed on her desk.

It was just that some of them felt more urgent than others.

Maybe that wasn't good, maybe it meant her years of doing the job made her feel more for some victims than others, or some families impacted her more. But Shuye Zhao was one of those victims who seemed to immediately demand Margot's devotion.

Someone who was capable of murdering a little old grandma wasn't fit to be walking the streets. Even if Margot *did* believe what she'd told Marie, that this was most likely an isolated incident, the violence of it was so intense that the person responsible shouldn't get the opportunity to live another free day. It was that simple.

Evelyn pointed out some more superficial wounds on the body: nicks and scratches that indicated an inexperienced killer. Once she was done, Margot had a better sense of the kind of person they were looking for. This was not someone who knew what they were doing, it was someone who had let their rage overtake them. Despite the force and precision of the blow to the skull, the chances of it being someone with a violent criminal history were low.

But she was no closer to understanding why that person had chosen Shuye as his target.

FIVE

Margot was relieved to be out of Shuye's apartment, even if it did mean taking a detour into a rank-smelling alleyway.

While most of the buildings on this stretch of Washington were wedged too close together to allow passage between, Margot and Wes found that there was a narrow alley between the apartment complex and the restaurant next door. On the other side of the restaurant was the more famous Ross Alley, where tourists who longed to visit the Golden Gate Fortune Cookie Factory would find it practically hidden off the main thoroughfares.

The alley between the apartment and the restaurant, though, was a grim space where sunlight barely seemed to penetrate, and the garbage cans for the apartment complex sat alongside the larger dumpsters for the restaurant.

The space smelled of rotting vegetables and household garbage, and the ground was littered with paper and human detritus that no one bothered to pick up. A stray cat spotted Margot and Wes coming and dashed off in the direction of Jackson Street.

They continued down the alley to a small courtyard shared

by multiple apartment buildings where, aside from a few plastic chairs and an old metal coffee canister filled with cigarette butts, there wasn't much of note. It seemed like a place where people who worked in nearby businesses probably took their smoke breaks and got away from the din of the busy streets surrounding them.

Returning to the trash bins, Margot looked at their next task with no small amount of revulsion.

"Garbage day is Monday, according to our landlady, so this is about three days' worth of trash. If I were getting rid of a murder weapon, do you think I'd pick somewhere this obvious? Especially with a whole weekend between me and Monday?"

Wes wrinkled his nose, staring at the line of garbage cans while lazy flies buzzed around the big restaurant dumpster.

"A first-time killer isn't going to be experienced enough to think these things through," Wes said. "We gotta check it."

Two uniformed officers and two crime scene techs joined them, laying tarps out on the disgusting ground, and then one by one removing garbage bags from the cans. The new scents that came with each bag they opened were a putrid array of garbage greatest hits. Sour milk. Diapers. A brief reprieve from a filter filled with coffee grounds.

The crime scene technicians were meticulous, and if the smell bothered them, they were too professional to let it show. The uniformed officers, however, needed frequent breaks, which Margot could hardly blame them for. She was just grateful it was February and not July.

They checked every piece of mail that might have an address on it, but nothing they found could obviously be traced back to Shuye Zhou. Items that could immediately be dismissed were re-bagged, while others were cleaned up. Once the individual garbage cans were clear, the techs turned their attention to the dumpster.

Margot left Wes to monitor the progress of the garbage

search and made her way back to the little patio. Since they'd blocked off the alley entrances with crime scene tape, she'd expected to find the place empty and was surprised to discover a man in kitchen whites smoking a cigarette in one of the plastic chairs.

He nodded at her as if he didn't have a care in the world.

"Hey, you have a second?" she asked.

The man shrugged. "I got as long as this lasts." He tipped the half-finished cigarette in her direction. "Unless you got another one."

"I don't, but I do have this." She flashed her badge at him. The guy leaned forward, squinting at it, but showed no signs of being either impressed or fearful of it. Sometimes Margot liked to show people her badge to see if they'd start acting guilty. At a lot of crime scenes people involved in the murder would linger around, trying to get a sense for what the police knew, and they could, from time to time, give themselves away before any deeper policework needed to be done.

Margot highly doubted the cook was her killer, but she couldn't count anyone out completely.

"Someone in trouble?" he asked. The more she looked at him, the more she realized he was only a kid, maybe twenty years old at best. He held himself with the swagger and lackadaisical confidence of someone with more years under their belt.

"Someone died." She settled into a chair across from him, kicking her long legs out in front of her to show she could be just as relaxed. She was grateful she had removed the crime scene booties when they'd left the apartment. "What's your name?"

"Jin," he replied without missing a beat.

"Margot." She nodded. "You sit out here a lot, Jin?"

He shrugged, which seemed like a comfort gesture to him, something to do with his body when he wasn't necessarily sure what else to do. "Sure, when it's not raining. Don't want to be out there." He jerked his thumb in the general direction of Jackson Street.

The sound of chatter and traffic was thick even back here. Someone was arguing nearby in what Margot assumed was Chinese. She didn't speak any other languages—though she had picked up passable Spanish in school—but she could usually distinguish between Chinese and Korean, the languages she heard most in the area around where she lived.

She liked the rapid-fire cadence of both languages and the way that they could say volumes with a simple *mmm* sound sometimes.

Maybe she should learn Chinese. Everyone needed a hobby, and it wasn't like she left her apartment much in her off hours.

"How many people do you usually see back here?" She pulled her head out of the clouds and returned her focus to Jin, whose cigarette was shrinking fast.

Jin contemplated, and she appreciated that he was taking the question seriously. "There are a couple guys from my restaurant. The Golden Dragon." He looked over his shoulder to the building right behind him and pointed, in case the teal and red brick wasn't obvious. "So, like, the bussers, Teddy and Wang. The two Lis, they're servers. Sometimes the host, Sun Hee, when she's not feeling too good for us. You know how it is." The names were a mix of Chinese and Korean; most of the businesses in the area weren't strictly Chinese-owned, despite the area being called Chinatown.

Margot pulled out a notebook and jotted down the names. "The Lis you mention, are they brothers, or is that their first names?"

Jin smirked. "Li Fang and Li Wei. Brothers from other mothers, y'know?"

Margot nodded. "Anyone else?"

"Yeah, folks from the Shining Sun gift shop next door, sometimes from the Evergreen over on Washington. Couple folks from Ross will wander over to take a break."

"Anyone from this apartment complex?"

"Meh, they'll usually smoke out their windows. This kid comes down sometimes, maybe seventeen, sixteen? I dunno, not old enough to buy his own fucking smokes though, always bumming off people. He's nice enough, though, quiet, so no one gives him too much shit about it. I dunno, I think he might have a fucked-up life at home, he looks like, what's that word when people came back from war in the old days?" Jin's gaze pierced into her, expectant.

She was, after all, old enough to remember the old days.

"Shellshocked?" she offered.

He snapped his fingers. "That's it, fuck yeah. Anyway, kid looks like someone who has seen some shit, you know what I mean?"

Margot imagined how people might have described her at fifteen.

She did, indeed, know what he meant.

"Do you know his name?"

"I think it was like, Evan, or Ethan, something like that." Jin buried the butt of his cigarette in the coffee tin. "Time's up, Detective Margot, gotta go."

Margot got his full name and phone number and gave him her card in case he remembered anything else that might have been useful. She might swing into the nearby restaurants to see if anyone had been out back during the day and might have seen something, or if there were any security cameras nearby worth looking at. The Golden Dragon didn't have one, but that didn't mean there weren't others.

"Hey, Phalen?" Wes called from down the alley. "Got something here you're going to want to see."

Margot took one last look up at the apartment complex.

Dress shirts billowing in the light breeze were draped over the metal fire escape railings. Someone was listening to a political talk show too loud, the escalating voices coming out like a real argument, only the topic keeping her from getting concerned.

Was someone in that building her killer?

She headed back down the alley to where Wes was waiting.

A plastic evidence bag with a bloody knife in it was the best gift she could have hoped for today.

She took it from him, looking down at the blade which glinted in the late afternoon sunlight peeking through the two buildings.

"And it's not even my birthday."

SIX

While the crime scene techs continued to scour the restaurant dumpster for any additional clues, Margot and Wes returned to the apartment complex. The uniformed officers who had been first on the scene had already done a cursory sweep of the building, asking residents if they had seen or heard anything, and flagging anyone they thought might be worth revisiting. They'd also made note of any suites where the resident hadn't answered.

One of those was the apartment right beside Shuye's.

Margot, figuring she might as well get the worst out of the way, headed back up to the top floor. The effort of climbing so many steps in a single day made her deeply regret working out at the station that morning. Now, not only did her arms feel sore from boxing, she knew her entire body would be protesting the next day.

She might need to learn to get over her elevator thing.

They knocked on the door of apartment 5C and waited. Margot heard soft footsteps within, and light glinted out as someone peered through the peephole. For a long moment, there was no movement or response.

Margot knocked again. "SFPD. We just have a few questions for you if you don't mind opening up."

Another long, silent pause.

Rolling her eyes at Wes, Margot added, "We know you're there."

It was truly astonishing how often people thought they were being stealthy when in fact they could have installed a neon *I'm home* sign on their door and been less obvious.

The door opened, chain still affixed, and a woman's face peered through the gap at them. She was probably in her fifties, deep-set wrinkles by her eyes and mouth, her hair lank, yellowing blond at the ends with dark roots that were flecked through in gray.

She had dark eyeliner under her eyes, crusted bits of mascara clinging to her cheek like she'd slept with her makeup on and hadn't bothered to clean it up that morning. Since it was now mid-afternoon, Margot wondered what this woman did for a living.

The woman wore a thick robe and had slippers on her feet.

"Can I help you?" she asked, her voice raspy, coated with the film of decades' worth of cigarettes.

Margot and Wes showed her their badges. "I'm Detective Phalen, this is my partner Detective Fox. Would you mind if we came in for a minute to ask you a few questions?"

"Is this about Ewan?" she asked almost instantly.

Ethan, Evan, something like that. Jin's words came circling back to Margot.

"Does Ewan live with you?"

"He's my son." Not an answer, but not *not* an answer.

"We're actually here about your neighbor, Mrs. Zhou."

The woman looked momentarily confused, then asked, "Susie?"

"Shuye Zhou, yes." Margot cast a meaningful glance at the chain blocking the doorway. "Do you mind if we come in,

Ms....?" She let the greeting linger, hoping the woman would pick up the clue.

"Oh." She closed the door, then reopened it a moment later with the chain off. "I'm Toni. With an *i*. Toni Willingham." Gesturing toward the living room, she stepped out of the doorway to allow them entry.

Margot couldn't help but immediately compare the place to Shuye's. It was hard not to, considering they had almost identical layouts. Toni's apartment reeked of stale cigarette smoke. She had her curtains drawn, shutting out the afternoon light and creating an aura of disuse in the apartment that made it feel abandoned. Dust motes floated around them as they sat down. Margot took an old armchair while Toni sat on the bigger couch. Wes remained standing, pacing the apartment, trying to look disinterested.

It was one of the oldest tricks in the book. One cop does the talking, the other looks around to see if anything stands out as being suspect.

Toni watched Wes wander, her lips set in a thin line, but she said nothing.

"Did you know Mrs. Zhou well?" Margot asked.

Toni lit a cigarette, not bothering to ask if her guests minded. Based on the yellow tinge to her fingertips and nails, Margot hazarded a guess that there were very few times in life Toni *wasn't* holding a lit cigarette.

Makes a girl look cheap and disgusting, Ed had told her when she was in her early teens. *You're better than that.*

It was astonishing how much decent life advice he had given her.

Still, it was hard to get his voice out of her head sometimes, especially when someone was blowing smoke into her face.

She waved her hand back and forth and wrinkled up her nose, not bothering to hide how she felt, since it was obvious Toni didn't care a lick one way or the other.

"I mean, we weren't friends, if that's what you're asking. She would say hello, but I don't think her English was very good, so I never really stopped to chat with her."

Margot had never met Shuye when she'd been alive, but she had a very hard time believing a woman who had lived in San Francisco for over thirty years—and in this apartment for a quarter of a century—had any issues speaking English.

After explaining that Shuye had died suspiciously—avoiding the more grisly details of what had taken place on the other side of the living room wall—Margot waited for Toni's theatrical gasps of shock and despair to subside.

"Have you ever been into her apartment?" Margot's gaze raked over the living room, which radiated untidiness with dirty dishes and old newspapers on the coffee table and a pair of gym socks on the ground alongside a stained pizza box.

"I don't think so."

"How long have you lived here?"

"Just over two years."

Margot took notes. "With your son?"

"Mmhmm." Again, Toni's attention snapped back to Wes, who was lingering near the hallway that would lead to the apartment's two bedrooms. "You need the can or something, officer?"

"Detective," he corrected. "And actually, yes, if you don't mind."

"Well, second door, use your eyes. If it's got a bed in it, that ain't it."

Wes disappeared down the hallway, giving Margot a quick *How'd I get this lucky* eyebrow raise. Cheeky bastard.

"Ms. Willingham—"

"Call me Toni. Always feel like I'm in trouble for something when people call me Ms. Willingham. Like I got an overdue bill payment." She gave a half-hearted smile, and for the first time since they'd entered the apartment, Margot felt a pang of kindness toward the woman.

She reminded her a little of how her mom had been toward the end of her life. Looking the worse for wear, but trying her best. Margot's mom hadn't been able to hang on in the end. Life ground her down under its heel. For Toni's sake, and her son's, Margot hoped she was tougher than Kim had been.

Evelyn hadn't been precise on Shuye's time of death, but her preliminary estimates were that the woman had died about eight to ten hours before they first got a look at her. The blood at the scene had dried to the point of no longer being tacky, and rigor mortis had set in, suggesting the time of death was early that morning, sometime between two and six o'clock.

That was about twelve hours ago at this point, and since Toni was still dressed as if she'd just gotten out of bed, Margot wasn't sure what to make of her lifestyle.

"Toni, where were you early this morning, around two to six o'clock?"

"Workin'."

"Do you mind if I ask what you do for work?"

"I'm a nurse in a hospice clinic. Do the overnight shift most of the time. Sometimes I grab extra shifts from the other nurses if I can. It's hard to raise a kid in this city as a single woman, you know?" There was a conspiratorial edge to her words, like this was something Margot should understand completely.

While Margot *could* appreciate how hard it was to live on a single income in San Francisco, she was also blessed to live in a building where her landlord seemed more concerned with giving a home to people he liked than he was with gouging them for every dollar they made, so she got by OK.

She smiled to Toni and nodded. "I get it. So, you work overnight, and you got home when...?"

"Today? Eight or so, I think. Ewan was already gone, so

must have been after eight. School starts at eight forty, but he likes to get there early. He's a smart kid."

"Where does he go?"

"Lowell."

Margot was surprised. Lowell was one of the best schools in the city, probably in the state. As far as public school went it was one of the most academically rigorous. It also wasn't *close* to Chinatown, being practically on the other side of the city. He must have needed to leave an hour early to get there every day.

Margot said as much and Toni smiled, the kind of pleased parental smile that couldn't be faked. She was obviously very proud. "He's such a good kid—never gets in any trouble, works so hard." Her voice was strained, and she paused before speaking again. "It's been hard for him since my boyfriend left; the two of them got along pretty well, but he's so motivated."

"When did your boyfriend...?" Margot's voice drifted off, not sure how to politely ask what she wanted to know.

"Last year." She looked away from Margot, shifting uncomfortably. "I'd been seeing someone a long, long time before that, but when we moved here I thought it might be time for a fresh start. Turned out I wasn't over my ex." Toni shrugged but said little else.

Interesting. So the recent ex would have known Shuye. Would have known how to get into the building. Certainly worth looking into. Margot got his name and jotted it down, which didn't seem to concern Toni in the least. She was off on a tangent about how Ewan's deadbeat dad still owned her child support payments and men who were afraid of commitment when Wes returned to the living room. His expression gave nothing away, but he did catch Margot's eye.

Margot didn't ask Toni about Ewan's habits in the back alley. "This may be a strange question, but is your son a heavy sleeper?"

Toni laughed, which turned into a phlegmy cough, and

stabbed out her cigarette in a nearby ashtray. "Boy has been a light sleeper since the day he was born. A mouse fart could wake that kid up. Makes it impossible to sneak back in after a late shift—he's up instantly. But he's an early riser, too. We like to have breakfast together before he goes to school usually."

"Toni, would you mind if we talked to Ewan?"

"Well, it's what, Thursday? He has debate after school, so he won't be home until six at the earliest."

Margot gave the woman her card. "We can either come back when it's convenient, or he can come see us at the station. It's all routine, but he may have been at home during the time we think Mrs. Zhou died, and we'd like to know if he heard anything. You're welcome to come with him, of course."

"Sure. OK." She put the card down on the coffee table and Margot made a note to be sure they circled back to talk to the kid. Between time spent in the back alley, and him being such a light sleeper, he might be their best hope of narrowing down when Shuye had died, and he might even help provide a clue as to who had killed her.

"Thank you for your time, Toni. Please have Ewan call me and arrange a time to meet. Whenever suits him."

She and Wes headed into the hall together, where she managed to wait until they were down one floor before practically backing him into a wall. "I saw that look, Fox. Tell me what you found."

A smirk ticked up the corner of his mouth. "Impatient." He pulled out his phone and opened up the photo app, then handed it back to her. "Kid might be an A-plus student, but he's got some pretty interesting reading material in his room."

Wes had snapped a photo of a bookshelf in a bedroom that appeared just as messy as the rest of the house had been. Margot zoomed in. There, between the usual teen boy fare of fantasy novels and books clearly for school, was a book she recognized instantly from the red and yellow spine alone.

A shudder sent the hair on the back of Margot's neck up and she almost recoiled from the photo.

Killer in the Classifieds: How I Caught America's Deadliest Man

The quintessential book on Margot's father. By Special Agent Andrew Rhodes.

What was a high school kid doing with a serial killer's biography in his bedroom?

SEVEN

Oakland, CA

Eddie sat on the front steps of his row house, watching other children run up and down the street. Their laughter was loud, grating, he didn't like to listen to them enjoying themselves.

Next door, Dandelion the cat was basking in the glow of the mid-afternoon sun, his puffy white tail flick-flick-flicking back and forth like it was keeping time. Eddie stared at the cat for a long time, and the sound of the children playing grew quieter, further away.

A nameless thing stirred inside him, a dark urge he'd been feeling with more and more frequency lately. There was a voice deep inside his belly, whispering. And when it whispered, it told him to do things he had never imagined doing before.

Things that would make Mama mad.

Eddie clenched his fists as he watched the cat. It was big, as a cat went, but he was bigger. He wondered if he could catch it and get it alone. He didn't really know what he'd do, but he imagined the way the cat's bones would break under his hands. He thought about the way it would yowl and try to get away.

He thought about the cat's fear, and it delighted him.

Dandelion looked up from where he was lounging, his yellow eyes fixed on Eddie as if he could hear what the boy was thinking. Miss Shirley opened the door and Dandelion darted inside the house, forcing Eddie's attention back to the street.

"Hello, Eddie," Miss Shirley said. "Why don't you go play with the other kids? They look like they're having such a nice time."

He didn't look at her. "Because they're stupid."

"Edgar!" She closed her house door and sat down on her own stoop, looking over at him with concern. He thought of Miss Shirley as old, but realized she was probably the same age as his schoolteacher Miss Petty. He only knew Miss Petty was young because Mama complained that she was *a little tart* and *barely older than Sarah* after a parent–teacher meeting had gone poorly.

All adults seemed old to him, but he guessed Miss Shirley wasn't really that old.

He wondered why she didn't have kids instead of that stupid, ugly cat.

Mama had called her a bad word once; he thought it might have been *bike*, but Sarah had said it was a curse word for lesbians, whatever those were. Maybe that was why she didn't have kids, though. Maybe lesbians couldn't have children.

"You don't mean that, Eddie, do you?" Miss Shirley asked, hugging her knees to her chest.

"That they're stupid? Sure, I mean it. Ain't you never talked to any of them before?"

"*Haven't you ever*," Miss Shirley corrected. She did that sometimes, but for some reason in her nice lady voice it never made him mad like it did when Mama or Miss Petty did it.

"Haven't you ever?" Eddie repeated.

Miss Shirley looked back out to the street where the kids were playing tag. Sarah was skipping rope. One little girl was drawing out hopscotch squares on the cracked sidewalk, but she was doing it all wrong and by the end they were so small you couldn't jump in them.

Eddie couldn't imagine better proof of his assessment.

"I can't say that I spend a lot of time talking to any kids other than you and your sister, but I think they seem all right."

Probably it was a good thing she didn't have kids.

"I don't wanna..." He paused, seeing the look on her face. "I don't *want to* play with them."

"Well, that's OK, I suppose. I won't force you to play with anyone you don't want to, Buddy. But remember: if you sit on the sidelines your whole life, you're never going to have any fun." She reached across the short distance between their stoops and ruffled his hair.

Eddie watched her go back into her house, and for a brief moment he wondered what *her* face would look like screaming.

EIGHT

Margot left Wes at the end of her shift, but instead of going home—where she would much prefer to be headed—she drifted through the rush hour traffic until she reached FBI headquarters. She was actually early for her appointment to meet with the team to prepare for her next interview with Ed. Since it was later in the day, she was able to find parking right out front, which was a rare blessing.

Inside, she knew the routine; she had been here enough in the last few months that the woman at the front desk had actually started to smile at her and greet her by name.

"Evening, Kelly," Margot said, showing her identification. Recognition or not, this was the FBI, there were processes.

"Nice to see you again, detective. Special Agent Rhodes is in a meeting at the moment, so Special Agent Yarrow will be down shortly to escort you." Kelly, who must be in her early thirties but looked as if she had embraced a serious skincare routine right out of the womb, handed Margot a clip-on visitor badge.

Kelly had to know why Margot was here, but she never asked any questions about Ed, or what the task force was working on. Margot had to assume that a casual indifference was a major factor to success in Kelly's line of work.

The elevator doors swished open and Special Agent Alana Yarrow came out, her high cheekbones and perfectly tailored peacock blue pantsuit making her look like the head of a luxury fashion brand. Only the gun clipped to her hip gave her away as law enforcement.

Her signature red lip was back, and if Margot had been a makeup person, she might have asked what brand it was, because it never budged an inch.

"Margot, nice to see you." Alana didn't bother shaking her hand; they had seen enough of each other over the past few months that they had eschewed such formality. They weren't *friends*, but they got along. They took the thankfully modern elevator up to the office area dedicated to the Ed Finch task force, and the entire way managed to avoid any kind of small talk.

A blessing.

When Margot had first started meeting with the task force, she'd been separated from most of the FBI team investigating potential murders that could be tied to Ed Finch. She had met primarily with Andrew, along with his three team leads: Alana, Carter Holmes, and Greg Howell.

Greg, who sometimes got called Gory, was a delightful weirdo whom Margot had grown attached to over the past several months. He was, politely, obsessed with her father's cases, and because of that was willing to ask Margot any number of intrusive questions that normally would have bothered her.

Coming from Greg, though, she didn't mind so much. He had a kid-in-a-candy-store giddiness to him whenever she would offer some sliver of what childhood had looked like in the house of a serial killer.

Normal was the answer, but that never seemed to disappoint him.

Carter was more inscrutable than the others. He didn't tend to chitchat, but when he did talk with her directly, he was always polite and deferential. So it wasn't that she was a woman, or that she was a cop, that made him keep his distance. She found him to be an interesting person primarily because of how disinterested he was in her.

There were a dozen other agents working the unit, all of whom she now recognized by face if not by name. While Margot didn't love being a participant in any of this, it never ceased to amaze her how much manpower and dedication was being funneled into this investigation.

All of it hinged on her willingness to participate.

Since the first time she'd received a call from Ed's lawyer the previous summer, Margot had understood that personal choice was an illusion. If it weren't for her talking to Ed, this entire team would have little to go on beyond previously existing information.

Right now, since Ed was in one of his coy moods, they were trying to mine the phone call he'd made to her back before Christmas for any scant details they might have missed.

Do you remember the summer you were eight?

Margot had heard the message a hundred times by now. So often she wished she'd never recorded it. The experts wanted to hang on every single word, even the tone with which he *said* the words. Since they weren't able to record their meetings with Ed at San Quentin, this phone call was the closest thing they had to speaking with him themselves.

The current process was to compare the call to Ed's old letters sent to the *San Francisco Sentinel*, to see if any of the language was similar. They'd hauled in a forensic linguist for this, and he had been spending agonizing hours trying to compare Ed's little tics to the letters he'd written.

Margot could have told them this was wasted energy. The letters weren't in Ed's natural speaking cadence. He was trying to be bombastic, larger than life. The way he spoke on the phone call was a performance as well, but in this performance, he was playing to an audience of one: her.

Now, after months of passing along pointless messages through his lawyer, Ed was ready to talk to her directly again for the first time since that phone call, and the FBI wanted to prepare Margot to ask the right questions. Andrew's unit believed there was no such thing as wasted time, only more opportunity to prepare, so they'd been meeting with Margot weekly to review potential victim profiles and go over the best approaches to get information from Ed.

Margot wasn't sure any of it would make a difference in the moment, and every time they put a new woman's face on the board, she wondered if that was just one more life Ed had scrubbed from the world. One step further from Margot finding justice for these women.

Her stomach churned.

Alana guided her to a wide-open space that seemed more likely to house a group of Google techs pitching new ideas than a group of specialized serial killer hunters. Everything was glossy white and brightly lit; there were huge photos of San Francisco landmarks on the walls.

The big mural of redwood trees felt like it mocked Margot every time she came into the office. *Unsolved*, it screamed.

She turned her attention to the team in the room. Many of the agents on the task force were practically babies, as far as Margot was concerned. Sure, like Greg, they had specialized degrees and were incredibly intelligent, but there were at least six agents here who were under thirty. Margot felt ancient whenever they talked to her.

Greg was standing in front of a large whiteboard, affixing several photos to it while the others watched. It looked like the setup for a game of Pictionary, rather than preparation to visit a high-security prison. Greg's red curls looked brighter against the white backdrop, his freckles standing out on his pale cheeks.

He waved enthusiastically to Margot when she approached the group. She smiled and gave him a nod of acknowledgment. While Margot knew she stuck out like a sore thumb in this group, with or without her visitor badge, she still took a seat next to Alana in the front row and tried to pretend like she belonged.

After months of visits, no one looked at her like a sideshow freak anymore, and no one had accidentally called her *Megan* even once this year. They were getting used to her, even though she'd never get used to *this*.

"We're going to wait for Andrew to come back," Alana said, leaning close. She wore a perfume Margot thought was designed to only be smelled when Alana got a little too near to someone. It was a soft vanilla scent, with a hint of floral. It made Margot feel more at ease.

Soft chatter carried around the room as they waited. Casual discussion, what people were doing for the weekend, thoughts on a recent episode of a show that Margot hadn't even heard of before. She liked TV, but tended to stick with comfort shows where there were unlikely to be any plots of murder. She got enough of that at work.

It was nice to simply sit and listen to a normal discussion, despite the fact that Greg had pinned portraits of a dozen smiling dead girls onto the whiteboard. In his neat printing, he wrote each of their names underneath. By the time he was finished, Andrew Rhodes had appeared and patted the younger man on the back, taking over the show without saying a word.

Andrew had aged well in the years Margot had known him. He had been handsome when they'd first met, almost as fresh-faced as some of the kids sitting around her, and he had stayed handsome as he aged, taking on the look of a tenured college professor with his salt-and-pepper beard and tortoiseshell glasses. There was something about Andrew Rhodes that told you at a glance he was an authority figure.

"Thanks for waiting, everyone. Margot, thanks for joining us. I was finalizing our next visit with Finch, and we are all set to go for Saturday morning. In the meantime, we want to go in prepared. Finch has a habit of trying to control the narrative in these conversations, and while Detective Phalen has done a remarkable job of keeping him in check, we know he's liable to give us misdirection, or draw this out for attention. He likes to feel needed, and he likes to be in control. If we can go in and already have a good idea of what he's going to tell us, then Margot... Detective Phalen, can have the upper hand."

Margot gave a thin smile. That was cute. The idea that she could ever have the upper hand against Ed. The man would never concede that so long as he was drawing breath.

The best she could hope for was to go in and not be shocked by what he'd tell her.

The summer she turned eight.

This had caused some initial confusion for the FBI, something Margot assumed Ed had done intentionally.

Margot had a November birthday, meaning that even though she was born in 1980, they had originally thought Ed was referring to the summer of 1988, but Margot was sure he meant the summer of 1989, when she would have *been* eight. That had changed things drastically.

1989 was the summer *after* he'd stalked and eventually killed Marissa Loewen, a long-lingering missing persons case they had been able to close the previous winter. Based on what they'd learned from her previous visits to Ed, he had spent months hunting Marissa, going as far as to meet up with her before finishing her off.

But he'd gotten a liking for fun in the summer.

Margot wondered if he'd picked the year after Marissa

specifically to remind them how futile their efforts were. They had spent ages with him unraveling just one case, only for him to immediately start dropping hints that there were more. How endless was his list of kills?

Did he pick kills so close together as a way to smirk at them and say, *You'll never know the extent?*

Knowing Ed, that was probably precisely the level of malicious mental chess he was willing to play.

Andrew gestured to the board behind him where the photos of seven different women were displayed. "These are the cases we have narrowed down as being the most likely candidates for Finch to be responsible for. Obviously, following what we now know with the Theresa Milotti and Marissa Loewen cases, we've had to adapt our initial profile of Finch's MO slightly. We initially believed he killed all his victims in or near their homes —or sometimes near roads if they were hitchhikers—but it had previously been assumed that he did not hide his victims' bodies. As we now know, there have been changes to that pattern, so we've had to broaden our pool of potential victims to include missing persons that fit Finch's profile."

Andrew paused, looking around the assembled group to see if anyone was going to ask questions, but this was a team that did nothing but think about Ed Finch. They knew all this. The performance was purely for Margot's sake.

She sat back, letting Andrew explain it to her, but she had been here, too. She'd spent weeks reliving that summer with a team of fresh-faced kids who were probably raised in very nice, loving homes where neither parent was a serial killer. This might have been intended to be for her benefit, but in reality, she thought it was all for Andrew's.

"The women we have on the board represent our most likely candidates to be the victim Finch mentioned to Detective Phalen in the November phone call. He was very sparing in his details, but based on what he indicated we were able to narrow the time frame down. He used phrases like *when no one was watching*. We know from our previous meetings with Finch that he was discovered by his wife, Kim, returning from disposing of Marissa's body. We can presume—and this was confirmed by Detective Phalen's own recollections—that getting out to pursue the kill would have been a lot more difficult for Finch in the months following the Loewen death, simply because of the additional scrutiny from his wife, who believed he was being unfaithful."

One of the younger agents next to Margot scoffed.

She turned her gaze to him and watched until he looked at her. She didn't have to say a word, just stared. The way he crumpled in on himself like a wilting flower proved she didn't need words to make her point.

Her mother had been imperfect in many ways, but Margot wasn't going to let someone besmirch Kim's memory by adding posthumous guilt to her shoulders. Who would have believed their own spouse capable of murder? Infidelity was more logical, and Ed had copped to it almost instantly.

The agent didn't apologize, but Margot knew he'd never make a mistake like that in her presence again.

Andrew, if he'd noticed the interaction at all, hadn't missed a beat.

"We believe this murder had to take place sometime in the month of June 1989, as Finch's wife and children were across the country visiting family." He moved so everyone could see the cluster of photos Greg had hung. "We have three missing women who were all reported during that time, none of whom have ever been found, and four murder victims who fit Finch's profile and the general area in which he committed the crimes. These were never previously attached to Finch for a variety of reasons. Two of the victims were shot, and using a gun has never been in Finch's wheelhouse. It doesn't line up with his diagnosis as a sexual sadist, because he wouldn't have gotten the same amount of pleasure from a gun as he did from the knife." His tone was matter of fact, but there was a slight tic in his eyelid that betrayed the disgust he felt.

Margot's stomach churned and she shifted uncomfortably in her seat.

"One of the victims was strangled, and the other was drowned. We think based on that alone we can probably rule out Jane Doe '89, and Brenda Fargo, but we'll keep them in mind in case Finch lets it slip that he may have tried out gunplay at some point." Andrew moved the photos off the board, handing them to Greg who waited nearby. "That brings us to five likely candidates. Of those, we think twelve-year-old Jenny Roundtree is too young to fit the profile. Finch's youngest known victim at this time is Laura Welsh at fifteen. He has made repeated claims that he had no interest in children, but I think we can agree his definition of children tends to be how old the girls *looked* rather than their actual age. Welsh and Milotti both presented themselves as much more mature than they were."

Raising a brow at this description, Margot wondered if Andrew realized he was close to crossing the line into victim blaming. It didn't align with his character the way she knew it, so she let it slide, but in the back of her mind a tiny red flag was waving.

"Similarly, we also thing Mei-Ling Fan, one of the missing women, is an unlikely victim for Finch's preferences, as he has solely targeted young white women based on what we know."

One of the agents interjected here. "I think we shouldn't discount Fan. Finch is set in his ways but he's also an opportunist. We know from Fan's friends and family she was a bit of a party girl, and she went missing after a night of bar-hopping. I'm not sure her ethnicity would be enough of a factor to dissuade Finch if he saw what he perceived to be an easy target."

A few others in the group mumbled their own opinions on this. It was Alana, who was the de facto expert on Ed's victim profiles, who spoke up. "Normally I'd say that we should eliminate Fan, but I'm inclined to agree with Agent Rousseau on this. If we consider that Finch had been restricted from hunting his usual targets because of pressure at home, he might have let himself deviate from his normal profile if he saw a chance to get a kill he perceived as being easy."

Andrew nodded and there was a hint of a smile on his face. Margot wondered if perhaps this show and tell *was* for his agents after all. This was, she realized, a learning environment for them. Since Ed was off the streets, there was no fear of him killing anyone who wasn't already decades in the ground. The FBI had assigned all these younger agents to this team so they could get their feet wet on a project where their mistakes couldn't potentially result in someone dying.

Margot wasn't sure how she felt about being a part of an active classroom environment when her mental well-being was at stake every time she went to visit Ed in prison. This wasn't a fun learning experience for her.

She reminded herself that, in the core team of Rhodes, Yarrow, Holmes, and Howell there *were* established pros working this as well, people who had handled the scary active killers of the world. It helped Margot reason that the Bureau was taking this seriously, otherwise why would they devote so many resources to it?

Margot pointed to the photo of a middle-aged woman on the board. "Why is she up there?"

Andrew turned his whole body to look at the image Margot had pointed to. The woman was attractive, but her age showed very clearly in the creases around her eyes and mouth.

"That's Sandra Shupe. She disappeared in the early summer of 1989, not far from Petaluma."

"How old was she?"

"Forty-five. Single mother."

Margot was already shaking her head. "No, that's not Ed's type."

The room went silent when she called him *Ed*. She might as well have called him *Dad* with the reaction it got. But he wasn't *Finch* to her. She didn't want him to be anything to her, honestly, but *Ed* was where her mind had landed. *Ed* was distant enough from *Daddy*.

She grimaced.

"If we're willing to accept that Fan might have been a suitable victim before he got to Marissa, why not Shupe?"

Was Andrew *quizzing* her?

"I don't think it's her age, necessarily. I remember her file. She was a sex worker, at least part time. Ed might have overlooked her age in the right circumstances, but he had a *thing* about sex workers. I don't think any dry spell would be enough for him to change his opinion on that."

Someone behind her was rifling through notes, and she suspected they were looking over the report from one of her visits to Ed last year, where she had asked him specifically about his lack of interest in sex workers. Ed thought they were too easy, in terms of a victim profile. He had likened it to going hunting and having the deer walk up to the rifle.

Ed liked a good hunt.

Ideally, he liked a victim who didn't know that hunters existed.

Fear was the driving element for Ed's pleasure, and a world-weary sex worker who knew the risks of her trade wasn't going to be as fun for him as a drunk girl stumbling home from the bar, even if they were both *easy* targets.

Margot hated how much she knew about Ed now. She hated that she had begun to understand his thought process. It made her sick how much space he took up in her brain.

Andrew moved Shupe over to the unlikely side of the

board. That left them with three women. Three smiling faces staring directly at Margot.

"He wasn't specific about much in that call, and we know that was by design. He indicated the woman had brown hair, that she was pretty, but was careful not to mention any age or distinguishing characteristics. And he said he wasn't close to home. We know he liked to minimize the amount of time he killed in and close by to Petaluma, and all these kills took place within a sixty-mile radius, but none in Petaluma itself. If we can get him to confirm something about these women, we should know after this visit who it was. Two of them were found, so we know the cause of death. Fan's body was never located, so if we narrow it down to her being the victim, we'll need him to give us her location."

Margot stared at the picture of Mei-Ling Fan.

"I think I know exactly how to get him talking."

NINE

Margot sometimes wished she smoked.

It would give her an excuse to quietly disassociate outside, and no one would bother her. As it was, after the meeting she had ducked out with a cup of coffee and gone down to the main floor to stand in the cool February air.

She didn't want to talk to anyone.

Andrew either missed that memo or decided to ignore it, because he was soon standing next to her, a coffee of his own in hand, staring out into the same nothingness she was.

Margot knew him too well at this point to think he'd stay silent for long.

"Sorry about Jessup," he said finally.

It took Margot a moment to realize he was talking about the young agent who had been dismissive of her mother's naivety. Margot shrugged and sipped her coffee. It was miles better than the sludge they brewed at the station.

Margot had bought the detective break room a Keurig for the holidays, but the old guard seemed to like making their shitty coffee the old-fashioned way. It suited Margot fine; it meant she had the single-cup brewer all to herself. She'd been contemplating moving it into her and Wes's office until she'd seen the captain using it one day and knew she had to leave it.

"I don't care about Jessup," she said finally, because it seemed like Andrew needed her to say something. "He's got his opinions, and it's not the first time someone has questioned what my mother did and didn't know. But she *didn't* know."

Andrew squeezed her shoulder and nodded. "I know, Margot. I remember her, and I know what the whole ordeal did to her. I have never had a single doubt about your mother."

Margot stared out into the street; someone was getting a parking ticket nearby. Poor schmo. "Thank you." She wasn't sure why Andrew's opinion mattered when Jessup's hadn't, but maybe it was because Andrew *had* met Kim, and he'd been around for the trial and the fallout. It was important to Margot that her mother's name was clear in his mind.

Because although she didn't blame her for being naive, sometimes she did wonder about her mom, and she hated herself for that. Kim wasn't around to defend herself anymore, and for *that* Margot often blamed her mother.

Whatever she was paying her therapist, it probably wasn't enough.

"You ready to go back in and run some scenarios?"

It was Margot's turn to make a scoffing noise. "I'm not going to improv a meeting with Ed. It's not going to help anything. We've seen how he is. If I go in with a script, he'll know. He always knows when people are trying to fuck with him, and he doesn't like it. If we're going to get him to talk, we need to let it come naturally. Otherwise, it'll only end in misery." She paused. "More misery."

Andrew looked as if he might argue, but Margot just handed him her nearly empty coffee cup. It was one she had taken from the break room and clearly it belonged to someone, since the side was emblazoned with the pine tree logo for Stanford University.

"I'm going to go. I'll see you on Saturday?" she asked, her gaze locked on him, practically daring him to challenge her to stay. Sometimes she felt like it might be a relief to pick a fight with him, because at the end of the day they would still be the same people, and they'd still share the same history.

He accepted the cup, pouring the dregs into a nearby ashtray. If he had something to say, he kept it to himself. "I'll meet you there, same time as usual. You sure you're feeling prepared?"

Margot had to laugh at that.

"I'm not sure it's something you can ever really feel prepared for, Andrew."

Margot usually liked the quiet of her apartment at night. She had cultivated a space for herself that felt like home, with a hodgepodge of thrift store furniture and items other cops had posted on a bulletin board in their break room. None of it matched, yet it was somehow all cohesive, and she liked it that way. There was something almost organic about the space, like it had grown to fit her precise needs and wouldn't make sense for anyone else.

She liked the feeling it gave her, like a familiar old sweatshirt.

Tonight, though, it seemed that everywhere she looked there was something that bothered her. There was a stain on the couch she couldn't recall ever seeing before, and the old dining room table had begun to wobble, reminding her of the imbalanced chairs they kept in the interrogation rooms to quite literally keep their suspects off balance.

Her home wasn't her safe haven tonight, and she wanted to crawl out of her skin. It was the kind of night she would have loved to call someone up, take her mind off the million and one buzzing thoughts by having some meaningless but distracting sex, but right now she didn't *want* meaningless sex.

Instead, she was thinking about Ed, and the way she'd promised Andrew she could get him talking. She was already second-guessing herself, because it would mean using an angle she didn't like.

But in the past, she *had* been able to get Ed to open up when she told him about cases she was working on. She couldn't help but wonder if feeding him details on her current Chinese victim might get him to share details on *his* potential Chinese victim.

She poured herself a tumbler of gin, adding a splash of lime fizzy water to it, and paced around her apartment nursing the drink. Her TV was on, but she wasn't paying any attention to it. She went to the curtains, peering out into the San Francisco evening. People were out walking. She was so close to some of the most popular areas in town, there were always people around, and normally that made her feel more at ease. Tonight, she watched two girls giggling to one another as they walked, without noticing the way a man passing slowed down to watch them go.

Margot couldn't look away, she waited, breathless, willing him to keep going and leave them be. When he finally continued strolling in the opposite direction, she shut her curtain tight again and refilled her drink.

Her phone sat on the dining room table, and she picked it up, opening her message history with Wes—one of the only people she talked to regularly—and then set it back down again. Her drink was getting warm; she hadn't added more ice when she refilled it, and the juniper-heavy flavor of the gin was more assertive without the drink being cold.

She couldn't stop thinking about Shuye Zhou. Usually, she could leave the victims to their eternal rest and focus on the here and now of catching the person responsible for their murder, but Shuye wouldn't let her do things the way she normally did.

The old woman might as well have been sitting across the table from Margot in her bloodstained nightgown, watching her with the unseeing milk-white eyes of the dead.

The thing most people didn't understand about murder investigations was that *typically* there was a very short list of potential suspects, and usually it was the most obvious person who was responsible. It was the husband, the wife, the jealous ex, the rival gang member, the guy she had a restraining order against. The actual *mystery* element of a murder was largely atypical, and a good homicide detective was just very good at putting obvious puzzle pieces into a conclusive final answer.

In this instance, there wasn't an obvious killer. Shuye's husband was dead. Her children were grown and had no evident strife with their mother. She and Wes had spoken to them by phone and they were clearly devastated. They visited her regularly—but not as regularly as they would have liked—and she did not have a large fortune to leave them, so an insurance angle was quickly ruled out.

At her apartment building she had been either ignored or beloved by others in the building, and no one had an unkind word to say about her. Sometimes, when someone dies, there is a retroactive smoothing of their memory, where people will gloss over all the negative opinions they once had of the deceased, but Margot didn't get the sense that was what was happening here.

She thought of those little red envelopes. According to anyone who had lived in the building longer than a year, Shuye made sure to drop one of those envelopes with every single resident of the building on Lunar New Year, wanting to herald in tidings of prosperity for all her neighbors.

Maybe someone thought she was flush with cash? But Margot wasn't a stranger to Lunar New Year; usually those envelopes contained single dollar bills. It was more about the symbolism of sharing wealth than it was about flaunting money.

She picked up her phone again, and this time, emboldened by reaching the bottom of the glass, she did send out a text.

> The book bothers me

Wes replied within minutes. Either he was at home, or whatever date he was on wasn't holding his attention.

> Are we in a book club I didn't know about? What's this month's selection? If it's Infinite Jest I can fake my way through it.

Margot had to smile to herself.

> You've never read Infinite Jest, don't lie to me.

> I swear to you it's on my shelf. Come see for yourself if you don't believe me.

Margot stared at that last line.
Come see for yourself if you don't believe me.
She glanced at the clock on her microwave. It was after ten o'clock. She didn't think the line was *that* kind of invitation but, given how she was currently feeling in her own apartment, she didn't necessarily care, so long as it gave her something to do.

Margot put her empty glass in the sink, grateful she hadn't had a third. She'd been a cop and a drinker long enough to know where the line of impairment was, which was why she normally stopped herself at two. She would just need to decline anything Wes might offer if she wanted to drive herself home later.

She didn't trust cabs or Ubers. Certainly not if she was under the influence.

> Fine, but if it's being used as a door stop, it doesn't count.

TEN

In over two years of being partners, Margot had never seen inside Wes's apartment. She tried to recall, as she stood in his building's security vestibule, if she had ever been invited. To a party, perhaps, once upon a time? But Wes didn't really host events.

The only social gathering Margot was willing to put her comfort on the line for was Leon Telly's annual summer barbecue, and only then because it took place in the middle of the afternoon, and she was surrounded by other officers.

Plus, being outside made it easier for her to breathe.

She was *not* presently in her comfort zone.

He buzzed her up without confirming it was her, which made her sick to her stomach. She didn't want to play a parental role, but sweet Jesus, man, at least check. This was the exact reason she lived in a building with someone sitting at the front desk twenty-four-seven.

It was also why she never invited anyone over.

To date the only person aside from herself who had ever spent the night in her apartment was her brother.

When she got to Wes's front door he was standing there,

waiting. He leaned against the doorframe, casually cool in a navy-blue sweatshirt, jeans, and bare feet. "I made a bet with myself," he announced, distracting her attention from his damp blond hair. He had showered recently.

"You buzzed me up without checking who it was," she answered.

He glanced at his watch. "Under fifteen seconds. I won."

Ushering her into his apartment, he took her by the shoulders and turned her so she was facing the wall behind his front door. Her whole body went rigid from the unexpected physical touch and the moment he felt it, his hands dropped.

"Shit, sorry, Margot."

There was a small screen mounted above the intercom system. Margot could see a pizza delivery guy in the vestibule checking for the right apartment to buzz.

"Oh." Her cheeks felt hot. "Sorry."

"Well, we're both sorry and we're both forgiven, so why don't you come in and relax a little? I promise not to touch you again. Without asking."

Those two little words sent an unexpected shudder of excitement through her body that she tried to pretend she hadn't felt.

Taking in the view of the apartment, she was surprised by what she found. Wes was a career bachelor, and for some reason Margot had expected that to be reflected in his home. She'd imagined Spartan living quarters with a big leather sofa, an enormous TV, and everything in black leather and chrome. Aggressively masculine.

She couldn't have been more wrong.

Wes's apartment was a studio—not uncommon with rent being what it was and police wages being what they were—but it was spacious. The floors were hardwood, and the space was primarily lit by lamplight, making it feel warmer and softer.

He'd divided the room using bookshelves, establishing

distinct zones for the living room and bedroom. His furniture didn't look like it had been rescued off a street corner. The sofa *was* leather, but a soft brown leather that looked comfy rather than austere. The TV was a normal size, and was currently tuned in to an old black and white movie.

"This is... nice," Margot said finally, her gaze still scouring the room, drinking in every little detail like it might be another clue about who Wes was. The framed *Bullitt* movie poster hanging over his kitchen table was so unbelievably clichéd she couldn't help but tease him about it.

"What percentage of male San Francisco detectives have that exact same one, do you think? Sixty? Eighty?"

"Unfortunately, I think the *Bullitt* generation is aging out. Not sure who the fresh faces in the academy are glomming on to these days—I just hope it's not *21 Jump Street*." He locked the door and then gave her a look. "You want me to put the chain on or...?"

He was trying to gauge whether that would make her feel safer or more trapped, she realized.

Her heart filled.

"On. On is fine." She suspected he probably infrequently used the chain in his own day-to-day life, but he'd been to her place. He'd seen the multiple locks she used every evening. He hadn't said a word.

Margot wandered over to look at his bookshelves, which housed a more robust collection than she had imagined him owning. They weren't pretentious titles, either, for the most part. No crime fiction, but a good mix of popular spy novels, the *Jack Reacher* series—which he had argued to her at length once did not qualify as a crime book—and more biographies and non-fiction than she'd expected.

Overall, she felt a kinship to his shelf because it gave her the same vibes as the entertainment she sought out in her own life. Something to distract from the horrors of their reality. Leon

Telly listened to romance audiobooks his wife recommended to him. Margot found that incredibly sweet.

"So where is *Infinite Jest?*" she teased.

Wes had poured her a drink while she'd been looking and handed her a tumbler of whiskey on ice. She sniffed the glass, which smelled old and expensive.

He pointed her in the direction of the bookshelf that clearly divided his living space from his bedroom and Margot's cheeks flushed. She hadn't intended for this visit to take on any kind of a booty-call aura and considering she had just come off a rough meeting with the FBI, even badly needing distraction, she wasn't feeling particularly romantic.

She didn't know what she wanted from Wes, honestly, which bothered her. Usually, she knew if she wanted to sleep with someone, or if she wanted to be friends with someone, and she did both of those things so rarely she felt like she didn't know how to navigate his waters. Usually, she didn't *know* the person she was weighing up all that well. This was different.

While there was obviously a mutual attraction between them, Margot had never had a healthy adult relationship. She'd never had *any* adult relationship, because she found it easier to keep people assigned to tidy categories, and she also had no interest in sharing her past with anyone. And how do you build a healthy relationship when you can't tell someone who you really are?

Dr. Singh, her therapist, brought this up with her a lot, so she suspected it was one of her biggest shortcomings, but she was also inflexible about it.

But Wes didn't fit into neat, tidy boxes anymore. Once he was simply *partner*. Then he became *partner* and *secret keeper*. Now he was also *friend*. That was more boxes than she was accustomed to any one person fitting into. Adding *lover* felt like too much, too complicated, too messy.

She moved away from the bedroom and to his small kitchen,

where she sat on a barstool and propped her forearms on the bar.

Wes didn't say anything, merely worked off her cues. Instead of sitting next to her he put the kitchen peninsula between them and leaned against the far counter, sipping his drink casually.

"You said the book bothered you," he nudged.

Ah, familiar seas. Talking shop was safe, something she could chart a course through.

"Show me the picture again." She held out her hand and he passed her his phone without hesitation.

A tiny part of her wanted to look at his text messages. It was a jealous girlfriend pang, because she knew she'd find a long list of messages from other women. Wes made no secret of his personal life. While he saved the lurid details for himself, the older detectives seemed to enjoy living vicariously through Wes; with their own marriages getting long in the tooth, they yearned for the youthful dalliances of the past, something Wes hadn't yet given up. So, Wes would give them a little teaser of whatever girl he was dating that week, and the men in the office would joke about being jealous, and Margot felt safe and happy, because she knew that none of those women had staying power.

There was a certain appeal to being the only woman in his life he kept around longer than a week. For some reason Margot relished that.

She didn't read his texts but did switch over to the phone's photo album and was relieved to see no scandalous dick pics or photos of him and other women. The images were largely of crime scenes, though it did appear he had a penchant for photographing funny street signs.

Margot found what she was looking for and zoomed in on the bookshelf, this time leaving room on either side so she could see the other titles Ewan kept next to his bed. Aside from the book about Ed, there were a few beat-up paperbacks of typical high school classics like *The Catcher in the Rye* and *East of Eden*, some graphic novels in a pile represented some darker fare, like *Hellblazer, 100 Bullets,* and a series called *Crossed* that Margot recalled reading a pearl-clutching article about several years earlier thanks to the graphic violence depicted on the page.

Ewan's tastes were varied. While he did seem to enjoy dark themes, there was also a copy of *Charlotte's Web* on the shelf and a handful of *Star Wars* action figures. It spoke to a boy discovering himself and pushing boundaries, but not necessarily one who was screaming *at risk*.

Loads of teenagers went through a serial killer phase, she knew that. A new uptick in true crime podcasts recently had reminded Margot of how that interest in the dark and twisty never really went away.

She could do without twentysomething women sipping cocktails and making jokes about her father, though. Not that she felt any inherent need to defend Ed—fuck that guy—but it dredged up a lot of things about her past, none of which felt particularly funny to her.

Margot set the phone down on the counter and sipped her drink. "I don't know. Maybe it's not the smoking gun I thought it was. Did you ever have that phase as a kid? Reading about death?"

Wes considered this thoughtfully. "When I was about thirteen, I got—my mom would argue—obsessed with Jack the Ripper. I don't think I'd set foot in a library willingly before that, but I couldn't get enough. I decided I was going to solve it. Like some thirteen-year-old would be the one to crack one of the crime world's longest-standing cold cases." He smiled into his glass.

"Did you?" she asked, grinning.

"I have my theories. All I need is the time machine. But, honestly, it's probably what made me start to think about becoming a cop, a detective. I don't know that we can villainize this kid based solely on him owning that one book. We don't flag everyone who owns, like, *Green River, Running Red*, do we?"

"Ann Rule deep cut," Margot said.

Margot actually found Ann Rule to be a complex and fascinating person within the realms of true crime history. Unlike podcast hosts who opened up a Wikipedia article and started recording, Ann Rule had worked alongside the police. It was funny that writers like *The Wire*'s David Simon got championed for their immersive time within the police force, while Ann was frequently relegated to thrift store bargain bins.

Sometimes, Margot wondered what it would be like to have their own Ann Rule entrenched in the muck and mire of the precinct, but then reminded herself what an absolute shit show it would be to have to tiptoe around a journalism-minded writer all day.

She had a hard enough time with Sebastian Klein from the *Sentinel*, and he had figured out her secret almost immediately. Redheaded cop meets regularly with the FBI? The stretch would be mild for someone who was really looking.

"We'll meet with the kid once he calls us," Wes said. "You've got a good gut feeling for people, so let's wait and see if he raises any red flags in person. But Margot, be *nice*. He's only a teenager, and quite frankly, you scare the shit out of most grown men in an interrogation room."

That made Margot smile. "Good."

Wes laughed and set his empty glass on the counter as he removed the lid from the whiskey bottle and inclined it in her direction. "Want a top-up?"

Margot's immediate thought was to say no. She wouldn't be able to leave, since neither of them would be able to drive. The idea of being trapped somewhere unfamiliar made her skin crawl, and her anxiety made a valiant effort to overtake the happy buzz she had going, but the booze won out.

Plus, the idea of going back to her empty apartment sounded so much worse than taking this one little risk. She glanced at the couch. "How comfortable is that to sleep on?"

Wes seemed to be doing the mental math of this comment, and then he must have remembered her whole thing about taxis. "I'm going to say this, so don't take it the wrong way. I'm a gentleman." He grinned, mostly to himself. "You are welcome to stay, but I'll be damned if I make you sleep on the couch. Somehow my mother and sisters would sense a disruption in the chivalrous universe, and I'd never hear the end of it. You can have the bed."

It was on the tip of her tongue to suggest that two grown adults were perfectly capable of sleeping in the same bed together, but she didn't. Because she wasn't sure she *could* just sleep next to him.

She nudged the glass toward him.

"If I'm going to have to listen to you snore, you better make it a double."

ELEVEN

Margot had a panic attack in Wes's bed the following morning.

She woke up in an unfamiliar room, momentarily forgetting where she was, and the anxiety hit her like a ton of bricks. One moment she'd been in a deep, dreamless sleep—later she would need to ask Wes about his mattress—the next moment she was on the floor, her back against his nightstand, trying desperately to catch her breath.

Even when it clicked where she was and why, her animal brain wouldn't listen to reason.

She closed her eyes and counted to ten, and with each number she told herself something that was true. *One.* Breath. *I work for the San Francisco Police Department. Two.* Breath. *My favorite food is Thai.* She continued with this until the final thing. *Ten.* Breath. *I am safe.*

With that last one, she was able to open her eyes and untangle herself from the mess of sheets that had slid off the bed with her. Nice sheets, really nice. They were wasted on her, given that she had gone to bed fully clothed.

Wes's deep breaths filtered in from the living room, and she was grateful that she hadn't woken him. There was a fine line between knowing she had certain neuroses, and *seeing* what an absolute hot mess she could be. She didn't need him to wear kid gloves around her, thinking of her as something breakable.

Yes, she was a disaster in her personal life, but she didn't want him to bring that with them to work.

Looking out the window—this man just left his blinds open?—the early signs of dawn were turning the sky pink. She had plenty of time to get home and get ready in her own space. Grabbing her jacket from the back of one of the kitchen barstools, she glanced at Wes, his long limbs jutting off the too-small couch, and smiled to herself.

Panic attack aside, this was a small, positive step for her.

She'd stayed up late sharing stories and learning genuinely personal things about each other, and then she'd let herself fall asleep with someone else around. Whatever else it meant between her and Wes, it was a big step for her personally. She ducked out of the apartment, feeling guilty for leaving his door unlocked, but needing to be back in her own space.

As she drove home, she thought about what Wes had told her about his boyhood obsession with Jack the Ripper. Margot had never had a phase like that, but she would have been lying if she claimed her motivation to become a police officer wasn't a direct result of a serial killer.

Hers had just been a lot closer to home.

Perhaps her unease about Ewan was merely a case of imagining smoke where there was no fire. The boy next door being Shuye's killer wasn't a stretch of the imagination, and most murders were committed by someone who knew the victim.

She hoped they could talk to Ewan soon, to either clear or confirm her suspicions of the boy.

While a part of her wanted to close the case quickly, a much deeper part hoped the boy was innocent. He was so young.

But killers were all young once.

. . .

Wes was waiting for her outside the apartment on Washington, looking far too well rested for someone who had spent his night on a couch.

"Did you do a lot of camping as a kid?" Margot asked him.

Wes, who was holding out a coffee for her, wrinkled his nose. "What a strange question, Phalen."

She took the coffee gladly, having missed the opportunity to make one at home before she needed to head out again. They were alone on the street, or as alone as two people could be when bustling groups of tourists and locals were already milling up and down the sidewalk.

At least she wasn't worried about anyone they knew listening in.

"That couch was pretty small for you, made me wonder if you used to get crammed into a tiny bunk in an RV at some point in your life."

"Funny, that's why I bought myself such a nice bed. And to answer your question, *yes*, my parents were very big into camping, and it makes you a scary person to have figured that out."

"Well, I *am* a detective." She smirked and sipped her coffee, which was precisely the way she liked it and begged a chicken-vs-egg question of whether this was how she had always preferred her coffee, or if she had come to prefer her coffee the way Wes brought it to her.

The streets were getting busier by the minute; the Lunar New Year coming the next week and events leading up to the big day made Chinatown a bustling destination. Margot breathed in the scents filling the air, even this early in the morning, from the nearby fortune cookie factory, mingled with the Peking duck cooking in the restaurant next to the apartment building.

If Margot ever moved, she was going to find an apartment

over a restaurant and live fat and happy for the rest of her days.

They left the bustling streets behind and headed back into the apartment complex. Marie, the landlady, had given them a buzz code that would allow them access to the building at any time. Though Marie insisted this code was never provided to tenants, Margot did wonder at how frequently it was changed and how many people might have ended up with access to it over the years. If old construction workers or delivery drivers knew how to get access to the building, that expanded their suspect pool well beyond the confines of the building, or people Shuye might have buzzed in willingly.

Margot wanted to go through Shuye's apartment without the swarm of technicians from the medical examiner's office and the crime scene investigators combing the place for hair fibers. Quite often, the killers they were chasing weren't considerate enough to do their dirty deeds inside, meaning crime scenes were exposed to the elements.

Investigating a murder in a building with doors that locked was a gift, allowing them to slowly unfold the aspects of a crime scene rather than racing against the clock.

Of course, the scene had been trampled through, and almost every surface was covered in fingerprint dust, but there was still something to be said for taking your good luck where you could find it.

Margot thought of the bodies in Muir Woods, and how the elements and Mother Nature herself had stolen so much of what may have existed as evidence of those crimes. Crimes Margot was starting to wonder if she would ever solve.

Was there a killer out there, like Ed, reveling in the fact that the police were at a loss to find him? She hated there being an invisible monster somewhere, gaining more power every day she didn't name him and bring him into the light.

She hoped she could find that person for Shuye faster than she had for the women in the woods.

She and Wes drifted through the apartment in opposite directions, two moons circling the same planet on different orbits. Margot wasn't looking for anything in particular. If she tried to be too focused it was a surefire way to miss the detail. But going in with open eyes and an open mind meant things could find her.

Margot circled the living room. The little red envelopes and cash were gone, bagged up as potential evidence already. The space was tidy but had a certain charm to it that reminded her of visits to her maternal grandparents' home. She couldn't recall ever meeting Ed's family, though there was a photo of her as a baby with her father's sister at a wedding. She never saw her aunt Sarah again after that. Never met Ed's mother, Gloria, who had died when Ed was only ten years old.

But her mother's parents had been about as quintessentially *grandparent* as they could get. Grandma Teddy—Theodosia—had baked endlessly, even in the height of summer, and Grandpa Theo—Theodore—had tried to teach her and Justin about fishing and stamp collecting.

Shuye's apartment gave Margot the same feeling she'd gotten from Teddy and Theo's old mid-century rambler. Cozy, out of date, but welcoming. There was a basket of toys suitable for a toddler tucked under the TV cabinet, and a stack of well-loved children's books on the lowest shelf of a small bookcase, right where crawling hands could easily grab them.

Higher up were freshly dusted knickknacks like a pretty jade tree, some Chinese coins in a ceramic dish, and a half-dozen framed photos of the people who had been important to Shuye when she was alive. There was a painting over the couch of a Chinese landscape.

A basket of slippers sat next to the door, waiting for guests who might want to slip something on after they took off their outside shoes.

Margot looked down at her own boots and felt guilty for

wearing them.

She crouched in front of the basket and lifted a couple pairs of slippers up. Toward the bottom of the basket, something crinkled in her hand as she grabbed hold of the slipper. Her breath caught in her throat.

"Oh God. *Wes*." She was grateful she was wearing gloves.

Wes appeared from down the hall and came to stand behind her. Once he saw what she was looking at, he let out a curse of his own under his breath.

It was a page from a book, with bloody smudged finger marks on the edges.

Margot didn't need to see the book's title page to know what she was looking at.

The face of Laura Welsh stared up at her, a toothy teenage grin in the photo most people knew best of her.

Laura Welsh.

Ed Finch's first victim.

TWELVE

Oakland, CA

"You're *filthy*," Mama screamed, dragging Eddie through the living room. Her thick sausage fingers dug into the flesh of his arm so tightly he couldn't help but let out a little yowl of pain. "Oh, that *hurts*? It *hurts* the baby?" Her face was twisted into a mask of anger, and Eddie knew there was no getting out of her way tonight.

The hurricane had hit, and he was right in its path.

He was a little dirty. He'd been playing in the back alley, the space between his house and Miss Shirley's. Dandelion the cat had been outside, and Eddie had been able to grab its tail, pinning it down, but the cat had scratched his hand to hell and bitten him, getting away in the process. It had climbed underneath Miss Shirley's back stairs.

Eddie had spent a good ten minutes in the dirt and spiderwebs trying to coax the damn thing out. He just couldn't shake the thought of feeling those neck bones crunch under his hands. He was desperate for it, hungrier for it than he'd ever been for any kind of food.

Then Mama had found him, and since she couldn't be mad about the cat, she was pissed to high heaven about the dirt on his clothes.

In the bathroom, she began roughly undressing him, jerking his shirt over his head, and yanking off his pants even though he was trying to do it himself. "Mama, I don't need help." He was crying, and he hated himself for crying. He hated that cat for getting the best of him. He hated Sarah for being the better child all the time. Mostly, though, he hated Mama.

He hated her with a depth that rivaled what he'd felt in the back alley, trying to coax the cat out of hiding so he could catch it and feel the pop and grind of his own power as he choked the breath out of that useless animal.

Imagining the way Miss Shirley would cry made his stomach feel like it was full of butterflies.

Mama slapped him.

"You're disgusting. A disgusting little freak just like your useless father." She slapped him again, this time so hard pain blossomed like a firework across the side of his face, and his hearing in one ear sounded distant, like a bell ringing underwater.

Maybe it was for the best because it turned the volume down on Mama's shouting.

She shoved him roughly into the tub and turned on the water. It was ice cold, and he gasped, a full-body shudder chattering his teeth.

Why did she do this? Why did she need to humiliate him like this? He wondered, sometimes, if it wouldn't be easier for her to kill him. To sneak into his room while he was sleeping and put a pillow over his face. He'd seen someone do that in a movie once, and it hadn't seemed like a very efficient way to kill someone, as far as he was concerned.

It also hadn't seemed like much fun.

With a pillow over their face, how could you see the

moment the lights went out? The exact instant that whatever kept them animated and alive—Mama would have called it a soul, something she constantly told him he didn't have—snuffed out. That was the moment it was all for, wasn't it? Otherwise, what was the point?

Eddie curled himself into a ball as the water began to move from icy to blistering hot. There was no sense in fighting her, that would only make it last longer. Mama scrubbed him, every inch of his body, telling him over and over again how filthy and disgusting he was.

Perhaps she was right.

Maybe he had been born all wrong, and she was just trying to make him right again. A small part of him wished she *could* scrub away the thoughts he had, the things he never heard other kids talk about.

If she could, maybe then she wouldn't hate him so much.

But Mama scrubbed his skin so raw he thought it might bleed, and when she was done, he lay in his bed staring up at the ceiling.

And in the dark, he dreamed about holding Mama's head under that red-hot water, until her cheeks blistered, and her eyes bulged.

He fell asleep, listening to her scream for breath, and offering her none.

THIRTEEN

The crime scene techs were back, a buzzing hive of white-clad bees, scouring the apartment again to see if there was more that they had missed in Shuye's space. Margot wasn't holding her breath, but she hadn't anticipated finding such a glaring clue missed in the first place.

It was possible to overlook the obvious with so many people in one space and so much going on. The basket was so front and center it was likely that the technicians all assumed someone else had already checked it. It wasn't great, but stuff like that *did* happen.

Margot knew that it had been left intentionally, but it being hidden meant the killer hadn't wanted it found immediately. This brought up more questions than it answered.

Margot and Wes were standing outside Toni's apartment waiting for her. Based on what she'd said about her schedule, Ewan wouldn't be home at this point, but Toni should have arrived back from work an hour or so earlier, and Margot hoped the commotion would be enough to keep her from being asleep.

The door opened, the chain holding it ajar only a few inches once again. Toni appeared, somehow looking even more exhausted than she had the previous day, the dark circles under her eyes bruise-purple and sunken. Her skin was sallow, as if she hadn't been out in the sun in a very long time, which Margot thought was probably true.

Margot flashed her badge as a formality, but it was obvious even in her sleep-deprived stupor Toni recognized them.

She closed the door and reopened it a moment later, rubbing her face with her hands. She wore the same old robe and sweatpants combination as yesterday. Her hair was rumpled, like she *had* been in bed, and Margot felt bad for ruining the sleep of a hospice nurse, but not bad enough to not knock.

"Toni, do you mind if we come in again?"

"I suppose. But Ewan isn't here. I gave him your card, he said he'd call you."

Margot nodded. "This is actually about a book we saw in your son's room yesterday. Would you mind terribly if we went and had a second look?"

"In Ewan's room? When were you in Ewan's room?" Her brows pinched, and what had previously been a friendly, if confused, expression shifted into something harder.

"I happened to notice something on the shelf when I was looking for the bathroom yesterday," Wes said.

Toni wasn't buying it. "Do you have a warrant?"

"We can get one. Easily," Margot replied. "But that would waste a lot of our time and yours, when all we want to do right now is look at a book on his shelf. If you let us do that, we'll be out of your way." That last part really depended on what they saw in the book, but there was no point in splitting hairs until after the damage was done.

Toni's lips formed a thin line and she stared at them with plain suspicion. Margot felt certain she was about to tell them to fuck off and come back when they had a warrant, but after a moment of pause, Toni's shoulders sank.

"Is he in trouble?" she whispered. "He's a good boy, detectives. I wish I was home more for him. You don't think..." Her gaze drifted to the far wall of her living room. The wall that would have been shared with Shuye's bedroom. She didn't finish her question.

"We're simply trying to eliminate possibilities. We noticed a specific book in Ewan's room yesterday and right now that's the only thing we want to have a look at."

Toni wrung her hands together for a moment before shutting the front door behind them and leading them down the hall to Ewan's bedroom. The space looked unchanged from the photo Wes had taken the previous day, but it was dark with the lights off and curtains closed, giving the space a tomblike quality that made the hairs on the back of Margot's neck stand at attention.

The overhead light snapped on, and Toni stepped out of their way but remained hovering in the doorway. Margot wasn't sure if her goal was to keep them from poking around too much, or if she needed to see with her own eyes what they were trying to uncover.

Wes made a beeline for the bookshelf, while Margot's gaze scoured the room to see if there was anything else worth noticing. She couldn't rifle through the space, that would set Toni off and end this opportunity to look at the book without a warrant, but she was hoping there might be something else in here that would make it worth their while to *get* that warrant.

Wes had slipped on a new pair of latex gloves and delicately removed the Ed Finch book from the shelf, hesitating as if worried it might be booby-trapped. The book came out with only slight effort—it was wedged tightly between other titles—and he set it gently on the cluttered desk beside him.

On Margot's phone she toggled to a photo she'd taken of the bloody page. "It's page seventy-four," she said. Her eyes were locked on the book, trying to see if there were flecks of blood on any of the pages, something that might indicate they were one and the same. But as Wes opened the book to page seventy-four, Margot's heart sank.

Laura Welsh smiled back at her. The page intact, pristine.

Margot turned back to Toni and gave her a tight-lipped smile. "Thank you, Toni. We appreciate the time. Please have Ewan contact us as soon as he's able."

"Is he in trouble?" The woman's fingers were worrying at the collar of her robe, and she stared at the book like it was something she had never seen in her house before.

"No, it doesn't look like it." Margot tried to keep the disappointment out of her tone, but it was hard to have such a promising lead fall flat. "We'd still really like to talk to him, though."

Back at the station, Margot used the ancient printer under her desk to print off a copy of the photo she'd taken earlier of the page in the basket. They'd get a high-resolution version from the lab later, once the techs were done processing it, but for her immediate purposes, the old inkjet version would suffice.

She stuck it to a rolling whiteboard they kept in their office and stared at it for a few minutes. Wes came in with two paper bags and dropped one on her desk, along with a plastic bottle of Diet Coke. He flopped into his own desk chair and rolled it over, so he was sitting beside her, his head at her waist level.

"Are you hoping it's like one of those magic eye things, and if you stare at it long enough the name of the killer will appear?" He rifled noisily through his own paper bag and withdrew an Italian sub with so much shredded lettuce on it the janitorial staff would likely be finding the green ribbons for weeks to come.

Margot glanced at him as he prepared to take a bite. "How

is it that you *never* have stains on your shirt when you eat like such a slob?"

He raised a pinky at her as he took a mouthful of his sub, bits of lettuce and tomato tumbling into the bag on his lap. "Excuse you," he said, once he finished chewing. "I do *not* eat like a slob."

Margot raised an eyebrow, leaned over and wiped a smear of mayo off his cheek. "Mmhmm."

She wiped her fingers off on an old napkin sitting on her desk and opened the bottle of soda he'd brought her, sipping a mouthful of bubbles fizzy enough to make her nose wrinkle.

"I thought for sure it was the kid," she admitted.

"I know."

"Now we need to ask everyone in that building if they own a copy of the book, and our killer isn't just going to say, *Oh, you bet, officer, but mine is missing some bloodied pages.*" Margot rubbed the bridge of her nose.

"What do you think it means?" he asked.

Wes would certainly have his own theories, but he often deferred to her to let her give her opinions first.

"I'd like to wait to say anything concrete until we hear what Evelyn has from the autopsy. But I'd be willing to place a five-dollar bet that when we go to the morgue, Shuye will have twenty-two stab wounds." Margot walked over to the board and tapped the small paragraph visible underneath.

Laura Welsh, 15, was Finch's first known victim. She was picked up while hitchhiking and was taken to a remote location, where Finch ultimately stabbed her twenty-two times. Her body wasn't discovered for six days.

"Did he stab her in the head?" Wes asked, scratching his temple in a gesture that Margot didn't think was intentional.

"I don't know. The publicly available details of Ed's kills are pretty detailed, but when it comes to the actual murder part of things, they're surface-level. Number of stab wounds, any antemortem injuries, et cetera."

"It's too bad you don't have personal connections with a task force that would know those answers." Wes dumped his sandwich bag in the trash and pointed at Margot's desk, nudging her chair back to make room for her. "You can't be Sherlock Holmes on an empty stomach, kid. Eat and then detect."

"I can multitask." She sank into the chair and pulled out her own sandwich, noting the extra sweet pickles that had been loaded on to it. He was a clever guy.

"My question is, if even *you* don't know about a knife wound to the head, do you think our killer would?" It was Wes's turn to stare at the board like it might turn into an all-seeing oracle.

"I think we might be putting the cart before the horse. If—and it's a mighty big *if*—this guy is trying to copycat Ed, then look at all the inconsistencies. The victim was an elderly woman, not a teen girl. Killed in an apartment, not a remote road."

"Well, location and opportunity go hand in hand. Let's play Devil's advocate with our young Ewan as an example. Kid is seventeen, he doesn't have his own car. The teenage girls he knows are plentiful, but also people are going to notice if he's spending time with someone he goes to school with. Teenagers pay attention to that sort of thing, especially if Ewan isn't a typically social guy. A senior giving attention to a sophomore is going to stand out."

Margot had finished her last two years of high school via homeschooling, so she had no barometer for what the normal teen experience was like, but she tried to imagine how her freshman and sophomore friends would have reacted to a senior talking to her, and had to admit, it would have created a lasting impression.

"OK, point taken. And it's not as if, even if he had a car, we have a surfeit of young hitchhikers waiting on the side of the interstate. It's not 1980 anymore."

Wes touched a hand to his heart. "It will always be 1980 in my heart and on my stereo, but you're picking up what I'm putting down."

"Location and opportunity. You want to have a similar first kill, and you know about an old woman who lives alone. Maybe mirroring twenty-two stab wounds is enough to make you feel like you've lived up to your mentor?" Her stomach churned at the very idea of someone on the outside wanting to mimic Ed's crimes.

Someone tapped on the door of their office and Wes and Margot both turned simultaneously. Leon Telly was standing in the doorframe, his tweed suit looking ten years outdated but somehow perfectly at home on him.

"I don't want to interrupt whatever is going on here, but I thought you guys should know..."

Margot set her sandwich down, swallowing a lump in her throat. Whatever was coming next, it wasn't going to be good.

Leon was speaking to both of them, but his gaze was locked on hers.

"They just found a woman's body on a hiking trail less than a quarter mile from the Muir Woods main gate."

Margot raised a single brow at him, and he gave a subtle nod.

"It's early to say, but based on the photos they sent me... I think it's our guy."

FOURTEEN

Leon was in the driver's seat, and Margot had relinquished shotgun to Wes, knowing he'd never ask for it but that his longer legs would be more comfortable up there. She scrolled through the three photos Leon had received from a Marin County deputy who had been first on the scene.

It had been their old friend Ranger Abbott, who worked in Muir Woods proper, who had sent the deputy in their direction. Margot was grateful to Abbott for saving a lot of possible lost days of investigating by cutting through the confusing jurisdictional regulations and getting them brought in right away.

She did feel terrible that this was now the third body Abbott had been around to find, because he seemed like a good person, and that was a lot of peripheral trauma for a civilian.

Maybe she'd give him Dr. Singh's card.

Doc loved trauma.

The photos the deputy had passed along were inexpertly taken, but certainly gave them a sense of what they could expect. The victim was female, in her mid-to-late thirties Margot guesstimated from the photo, and bore a striking resemblance to Rebecca Watson, the first Muir Woods victim they'd found—though second to have died, chronologically. The woman was slim, dressed in athleisure wear, and while Margot was only a nose-job expert when it came to plastic surgery, she had her suspicions that the woman's appearance had been augmented in some fashion.

The woman was lying on her back, a wide-eyed expression on her face, though her pupils had already turned milky, giving her a haunted, eerie visage. She was, like the others, fully clothed, but her clothing seemed incongruous with her setting. Could someone go hiking in fancy yoga pants? Obviously yes. But would she go hiking in platform espadrille heels?

Margot was reminded, in a flash, of something retired park ranger Wally Albright had told her about a dead woman who had been found in the park about a decade earlier.

Her shoes seemed wrong.

Margot wasn't convinced the case Wally had mentioned could be connected to these murders, and shoes were certainly no smoking gun, but it did bear consideration.

It took about forty minutes for them to get to the bend in the road where the Marin County cruiser was parked, alongside an ambulance. The roads leading to the park were narrow and twisting, without much room for parking along the way, so cars were being forced to veer into the opposite lane to get around the scene, and Margot witnessed more than one rubbernecker among the drivers that passed them.

Whatever they were imagining, the truth was much worse.

Leon parked his car behind the deputy's cruiser, and before she was even out of the car Margot saw a familiar silver sedan pull up in front of them.

"Fucking hell," she groaned.

Leon glanced over his shoulder at her, then pivoted his attention to the car that was the obvious source of her ire. "Friend of yours?"

A handsome brunette man in sunglasses got out of the

driver's side of the car, slinging a messenger bag over his shoulder. When he spotted the detectives, his chin jutted up in acknowledgment.

"It's Sebastian Klein from the *Sentinel*," Margot explained.

How Sebastian had gotten here this quickly was a mystery to her, but he was an excellent journalist and had a nose for trouble. She wouldn't be surprised if he had alerts set up for major crimes in this area following the last two murders.

The reporter met them at the side of the road. "Afternoon, detectives."

While she *did* regularly feed Sebastian safe bits of information on cases, and even considered him something of a friend, his being here complicated things. Margot merely nodded a greeting at him. Other folks on the force—Leon included—didn't see the necessity of crime reporters, and wouldn't take kindly to her buddying up to one. Sebastian understood that. He wouldn't be offended by her aloofness.

He sidled up to the three of them, the bright yellow mimosa blossoms around them reflected in the lenses of his sunglasses. A quick smile was meant to disarm them, but the three detectives remained stoic.

Sebastian went on, undeterred. "Heard we might have another victim of the Redwood Killer."

Margot, despite her best intentions, groaned aloud. "You are *not* naming this guy, sweet Jesus."

Sebastian didn't miss a beat. "Did you guys want naming rights? That's fine. Maybe you know something we don't. Has he sent anything in BTK-style, laying claim to a name of his own?" He had a recorder in his hand, poised and ready to catch their every poorly planned quote.

Leon, an old hand at managing the media and his temper, approached Sebastian and shook his hand, a friendly gesture, but based on the way Leon's knuckles tightened, Margot could tell he was putting some *oomph* into that shake. Sebastian's smile never faltered. This wasn't his first rodeo.

"Mr. Klein, I know you're familiar with how the SFPD likes to issue statements. And while I'm keenly aware you have sources inside the department, please rest assured that there is nothing we are currently able to say on the record regarding this current case. And that includes your departmental sources."

Margot half expected either Leon or Sebastian to cast a meaningful look in her direction, but neither of them did. If Leon knew she was the one speaking to Sebastian, he wasn't going to call her out on it here. And for all she knew she probably wasn't Sebastian's *only* insider on the force, because he certainly got access to information that didn't come from her.

"Can you at least confirm if you believe this case is connected to the two previous Muir Woods deaths last year?" Sebastian asked, looking first to Leon and then to Margot and Wes.

"We have not yet even confirmed that the two deaths last year are related," Leon reminded him.

Sebastian gave the older detective an incredulous look, as if to say, *Come on, old man, I'm not stupid.* Leon simply smiled in return.

"Please don't start printing things about the *Redwood Killer*," Margot interjected. "You know better than that."

"Never hurts to have a good moniker at the ready, detective. We gotta call him something."

Super. If Sebastian went ahead with his reporting on this, making the very logical leap that the three cases had enough in common to scream *serial killer* to anyone with half a brain, the public were going to lose their minds.

Meanwhile, if Shuye's murder was what Margot believed it was, but prayed it wasn't—a copycat—then there was potential for more bodies in both cases.

Two serial killers active in the same area at the same time. It was going to be a shit show.

Right now, as far as anyone outside her and Wes's office knew, Shuye's murder was a one-off tragedy, and not an ode to the work of Margot's father. She wanted to keep it that way.

Sebastian made no move to return to his car, and Margot knew he'd seize on any opportunity to talk to possible nearby witnesses. They couldn't force him to leave as long as he stayed out of their way, and Sebastian knew that perfectly well.

As Margot, Leon, and Wes headed toward the trailhead, Margot took a look back at Sebastian, who gave her a cheeky wink. She flipped him off, which only made him smile more. He was both a giant pain in the ass and sometimes also a decent friend, so she knew what she could get away with. In her world, where friendship was a rare commodity, she wouldn't risk pushing him away, but she needed to show a united front with her colleagues.

It was all part of the game.

There wasn't anything for them to tell him yet anyway. This was a crime scene they'd only seen in photos, and while the old adage said a picture was worth a thousand words, a picture alone wasn't the same as an investigation. Did the photos immediately tell Margot these cases were connected? Yes. At least they loudly insinuated that. But she wasn't about to make giant leaps in logic based on photos alone, and Sebastian certainly shouldn't make them based on chatter he'd overheard on a police radio.

The walk back to the crime scene was over uneven terrain, with branches reaching across the narrow path to grasp at Margot's hair and face. She kept her eyes on Wes's back, letting him clear the way for her as he held the more aggressive foliage at bay. What a gentleman.

The three detectives soon found telltale caution tape greeting them on the path, and a collection of deputies along with two harried-looking EMTs clearly wondering why they were still here.

What, Margot wondered, was the group noun for a gathering of police officers? Squad was too obvious. A *worry* seemed much more accurate.

This assembled worry were all looking at the ground, as if the victim might suddenly rise from the dead and chase after them. Margot followed their gaze to an area a few feet off the trail where—at first glance—one might think a garbage bag was tangled in the young trees and tall grass.

It was amazing what the human brain would jump to before it finally accepted *body* as the only plausible answer. Mannequin was the most common, of course. But this looked nothing like a mannequin, at least from the path. And it had looked suspicious enough that the morning hikers had gone into the dense brush to get a better look.

Those hikers were nowhere in sight now, thankfully. They must either be back at the cruisers or at the Sherriff's Department already giving statements that Margot wished she was the one taking.

Margot took the initiative to head into the trees while Leon made a beeline for the deputies. He was the lead on the case, so it made sense for him to get chummy with the locals, grease some wheels politely to get access to whatever information had been missed in the initial reporting.

It paid to be friendly in situations like this.

The woman's body was about a hundred meters off the path. Close enough to be visible in the light of day if one was observant, but far enough that had she not been dressed in black spandex, she might have gone unnoticed for a long time.

Margot wondered about this, and her killer's logic. Did he *want* them to find the bodies? He certainly left them in visible locations, wearing often glaringly obvious clothing. She thought about Rebecca's pink tracksuit.

Had the women been nude, they would have blended right into the forest growth.

Rebecca, the second victim chronologically, had been sexually assaulted, her pants missing and underwear around her ankles. This victim, though, was still fully dressed, same as the first victim Leanne Wu had been. It was a not insignificant difference, and one Margot couldn't ignore if they were going to connect all three murders together.

Let the evidence define the conclusion, she reminded herself. *Don't let assumptions guide you.*

Margot swatted at a branch that had dug itself firmly into her ponytail, yanking her head back so aggressively that it gave her a momentary stab of panic directly to the guts.

Someone has you, her brain screamed.

"Hold tight," Wes said, freeing her from the clawing fingers of the tree.

Margot let out a little shuddering sigh, pretending she hadn't just had a fight-or-flight response from a stupid tree. "Thank you."

Wes gave a nod. If he'd noticed anything, he wasn't going to comment on it.

They reached the body and Margot squatted down to get a closer look. The body had been hastily covered by some leaves and branches, but not enough to actually obscure her. It was a half-assed effort at best, an afterthought. The woman's eyes were open, but unseeing, milky white. Her skin had a gray-tinged pallor to it, and while Margot was not as expert as Evelyn, she had enough experience to roughly guess at the woman's time of death.

The woman must have been dead a few days, but less than a week. Based on her condition—and the lack of visible violation from wildlife—Margot assumed she'd been in the woods less than twenty-four hours.

Flies buzzed lazily around her head, landing on the

woman's face. One brazenly waltzed across her exposed eyeball and Margot cringed. Blowflies were incredible. They could sense death with ease and wasted no time laying their eggs by the hundreds.

There were no maggots yet, further confirming Margot's suspicions it had not yet been a full twenty-four hours that the victim had been out here.

She'd been killed elsewhere and brought here.

Just like the other victims.

The cause of death seemed obvious enough. As with the other two, there were multiple stab wounds to the woman's torso, visible through the sliced fabric of her T-shirt.

Margot slipped on a pair of gloves and gently lifted one of the woman's hands. There was something under her broken fingernails. Dirt seemed the obvious answer, but Margot had a suspicion of her own.

"That looks like it might be blood," she said, leaning back so Wes could get a good look.

"Could be from breaking the nails. But could be she broke the nails defending herself. We'll get that checked for DNA."

Margot nodded, since Wes was mostly talking to himself. She got to her feet, her body protesting with the little creaks and pops that seemed to haunt her more frequently as she approached forty.

Looking around, she tried to see how their killer had gotten the woman's body here. It had only been a few days earlier that she had sat in Muir Woods trying to figure this out.

They were outside the bustle of the park itself, so it would be easy to pull over to the side of the road and carry the body to this point. But the stretch of highway leading up to the park was a surprisingly busy one, and a car on the side of the road might stand out more at night.

This killer's whole MO bothered her.

If he wanted the bodies to be found, why go to such exhaustive efforts to bring them to places where he might be caught? Was that part of the thrill, or did the location itself mean something?

Leon crunched his way into the wooded area, struggling to find a place to stand that wasn't overwhelmed by branches or skinny tree trunks crowded together vying for light. Saplings didn't usually fare well in old-growth forests, but this space had enough access to light that some of these trees might actually live to become their own forest.

"What do you think?" Leon asked, having finally found a convenient place to stand where nothing was trying to stab him in the eye.

"Cause of death appears to be multiple stab wounds to the abdomen, consistent with the previous cases. The general age and features of the victim are in line with the previous victims. No obvious signs of sexual assault, though I'll leave that to Evelyn to confirm." Margot shrugged one shoulder. "There's a chance he's learned that he doesn't need to sexually assault them to get the sexual gratification he wants."

Margot avoided making eye contact with Leon or Wes. What went unspoken here, but what she knew both men understood, was that this was how Ed Finch had evolved as a killer as well. Sexual sadists derived pleasure from the act of killing, rather than an actual sexual violation to the victim. Sometimes they did both, but if this killer was evolving, his patterns might change as he learned what did and didn't satisfy him.

"Or it could be that the cases aren't connected," Leon reminded her. "We can't discount the differences just because we *want* these to be connected."

Margot nodded, knowing this perfectly well herself. This case *wasn't* a perfect match to the previous two, but it was so damned close she didn't want to think it could be three different killers.

A serial killer was a terrifying thought, but three individual killers with scarily similar MOs working in the same area was much, much more frightening.

Leon looked down at the woman, absorbing the scene.

"Well, first things first. Let's find out who she is so we can tell her family."

FIFTEEN

The hard thing about February was the way the light never seemed to last long enough.

By the time Leon pulled up to the precinct, it was already dark outside, night having crept in as they drove back from Muir Woods. The medical examiner's van had pulled up as they were leaving the park, so Margot knew they weren't going to have anything firm from Evelyn until the next day at the earliest.

She would be at San Quentin tomorrow, she remembered with a sick feeling. She secretly hoped the results would be delayed until Monday. It was selfish, but she didn't want to miss any major breaks in the case.

Before Margot packed up her things to head home for the night, her phone buzzed in her back pocket. An unfamiliar number was on the screen when she pulled up the text.

> Hello, my name is Ewan, my mother said you wanted to speak to me.

Margot's heart was in her throat. While she knew they had

no tangible evidence pointing to Ewan as a suspect, something in Margot's gut told her she needed to talk to the kid.

Wes wasn't in the office, so she made an executive call.

> Hi, Ewan, I'm Detective Phalen. Would you be able to come in after school on Monday?

This would mean staying after their shift ended, but that was a worthwhile sacrifice if it meant finally pinning the kid down for an interview. She knew Wes wouldn't mind.

> OK. Is five OK? I have things after school.

Nothing about these texts screamed *killer* to Margot, but that didn't mean anything in the long run. She'd seen baby-faced killers before. The formality of his words seemed to suggest a polite—if likely a little weird—teenage boy. *Mother* and *Hello* rather than "Hey my mom told me to text you" certainly stood out, and Margot mentally cataloged them, but it wasn't enough to make her suspicious. Just wary.

The boy owning a book about Ed Finch when the killer had left a page of that book at the crime scene was what worried her more.

But that book *had* been a *New York Times* bestseller. Thousands of people owned it.

Margot let out a long sigh, because thinking of Ed again reminded her what awaited her the following morning. Could it be worth seeing if there was any record of Ewan ever reaching out to Ed in prison? Ed's mail was all pre-screened and cataloged. He was the kind of killer who got a lot of attention, and some of that attention could be fairly concerning.

Likewise, all of Ed's outbound mail was read and scanned to be sent to the FBI. That mail was now handled by Andrew's team. If anyone might know about a connection between Ewan and Ed, it would be Andrew and the FBI crew.

One more flimsy lead to pin her hopes on.

It was a long shot, but one worth taking. The only issue was she needed to clear the request through the captain before she went ahead with it. In the past she'd made arrangements with the FBI thanks to her personal connection to Andrew and, while it had been beneficial, it had definitely left a few people annoyed with her.

She didn't feel like dealing with that again.

There was still no sign of Wes. Margot wondered if he might have gone home without saying good night, which would be unusual but not the ultimate offense. It *had* been a long day, and it wasn't like Margot was hanging onto a hope that he might invite her over again. The thought had crossed her mind, perhaps, but she needed to be in her own space tonight.

Her anxiety was at its worst the days she went to visit Ed, and she didn't need to add waking up in a strange bed to that.

Margot headed to the captain's office, hoping he might still be around despite the hour, and was relieved to see the light on. She tapped lightly on the frosted glass until she heard his gruff, "Come in."

When she entered, she tried to gauge his mood, but his face was a blank canvas, giving her nothing. If she'd been hoping for a smile, she'd have to settle for the lack of a frown.

"Evening, captain."

"Margot, have a seat."

She obeyed, suddenly feeling like she was about to get in trouble, even though she'd been the one to seek him out.

"I was hoping to float an idea by you, sir."

"If the idea is unlimited overtime, try again next month, detective." There it was, a hint of a smirk. Margot's shoulders sagged slightly in relief.

"No, sir. I admittedly like regular time in my bed too much to hope for that."

He made a grunt of agreement, casting his eyes around the office as if to ask why they were both here and not at home.

"Sir, it's about the Shuye Zhou case. The elderly woman killed in Chinatown this week."

He gave her a gruff nod to urge her on.

"We found documents on site that indicate there might be a connection to Ed Finch." He would already know this if he'd read the day's briefings, but he might have been too busy for it if he was still hanging around into the evening. She also realized, belatedly, it might not be in her best interest to bring up the connection to Ed.

The captain had considered removing her from cases for much less.

She didn't want to give him an excuse to kick her off this one and didn't consider it to be a conflict of interest. Just an uncanny coincidence.

He didn't say anything immediately, but she could see the gears working.

She quickly explained the page of the book and spotting the same book in Ewan's room. "I'd really like to cross reference the FBI's database of Ed's... of Finch's fan mail. To see if there's any connection."

The captain remained quiet for a long moment, his expression thoughtful. There were a million things she imagined going through his mind as the silence drew out, and with each ticking millisecond she suspected more and more that this wouldn't go her way, and she might have actually gotten herself booted from the case.

This was why the whole *beg forgiveness rather than ask permission* route was so popular.

Captain Tate laced his fingers together and rested his hands on the desktop, leaning forward almost conspiratorially. "Margot, you're a damn fine detective, and you have proven to me time and time again that your... history does not color your ability to do your job. I had my doubts about hiring you, I think we both know that."

"Yes, sir." She felt certain this was a compliment, however oddly handled it was, so she decided to take it as one.

"So, I'm going to let you continue with this, but if we learn that your... that if Ed Finch does have some kind of direct involvement in this, then we will need to find a way to reassign you. Something that won't draw attention, of course. But it's important we keep things unimpeachable for when this goes to trial."

"Of course."

"With that in mind, I suppose I don't see the harm in you using your FBI connections to get us some insight into this. If there is a link to be found. From what you've told me, it sounds likely to be an overzealous fan, but you're right to think he might have been in contact with Finch in the past." The captain sighed and leaned back in his chair. "Fucking whackos."

It might have been the first time Margot had heard the captain share a moment of personal vulnerability. He rarely let his inner voice out, so she was surprised he was doing it in front of her. She said nothing.

"Sorry, detective. Sometimes the years weigh on you. I think you're almost at that point now, where you've seen so much of it that the depravity of it doesn't surprise you anymore."

"There are always surprises, sir. I think it would be more accurate to say that nothing feels out of the realm of possibility. Things surprise me, but nothing shocks me."

He nodded.

"Get out of here, detective. Your shift is over. Don't be like me, spending all your time in the muck and mire. You're still young, Margot, you should be out there, living life."

Margot gave him a soft smile, not sure what she could say that wouldn't immediately make him think she was off her rocker. "My idea of living the good life is pad Thai and animated sitcoms. I can't say I have the energy for much else."

"Well, *find* the energy. Get out and *do something* with your life. That's an order."

Margot pushed her chair back, fighting off the wave of panic that was building inside her chest like a tsunami ready to crash into shore.

"Of course, captain. Whatever you say."

SIXTEEN

Oakland, CA

Mama slept hardest on the nights she was angriest. It was like the fury drained her to the point she needed to recharge, her rage battery depleted. While Eddie feared those days, the nights made it almost worthwhile.

He had started to lay in bed on those nights, listening to the drawl of late-night television shows, until the tone of her snoring would drown out the laugh tracks, and he'd know he was safe.

What Sarah did with her time on those evenings, Eddie never asked. Maybe she stayed up with a flashlight under her covers, reading the dime-store romance novels her friends were always stealing. Mama would be furious. She'd called those things unholy abominations and told Sarah any girls who read them were vacuous sluts. Eddie didn't know what vacuous meant, but the word *slut* got stuck in his brain like a fishhook covered in barbs. Sometimes he'd whisper it to himself in the dark. *Slut*. It tasted good to say. He used it any chance he got.

So, Mama thought Sarah was a slut.

Sarah read the books anyway. Eddie had seen them stashed under her mattress. Women with thick windswept curls and heavy breasts, men with their shirts unbuttoned, all in lusty poses Eddie didn't really understand.

He didn't mind the breasts, though.

Tonight, as Mama's snores drifted through their little house, Eddie felt a need, a *hunger* to get out. He slid open the window over his bed, where he knew how to pull a little pin out of the bottom corner of the screen so he could squirm his way out.

His bedroom window faced the back lane, so there was less opportunity for a nosy neighbor to spot him leaving or returning. But he was still careful. He watched the back alley, looking for signs of movement, listening for the footsteps of anyone out taking their dog for a late walk, or a vagrant digging through the trash for bottles. The air was silent, muggy. Summer was coming in hot, but humid. Mama wouldn't let them go to the pool, she thought it was unseemly, people walking around in next to nothing where anyone could see.

With no lights on in the buildings across from him, and no sign of interlopers, Eddie popped open the pin in the corner of the screen, listening carefully in case Mama might have heard the sound. He could hear her snoring, and Johnny Carson's voice monologuing something Eddie didn't understand. The audience sure laughed, though.

Eddie slid his skinny body between the window and the screen, the metal corner of the screen scraping against his skin since he couldn't take it all the way off. He had to hope none of those scratches would show next bath time or he would need to figure out a good lie to tell Mama about how he got them. Once he was free of the screen he landed with a soft *thump* in the scraggly grass under his window.

Free.

The world felt different somehow, on this side of the windowpane. The night scents were richer, the sounds of bugs chirping and cars on the nearby highway were elevated. His skin tingled, excitement stirring inside him. Yes, he was often left alone during the day, but when the sun was out there was a cabal of mothers in front-room windows or sitting on stoops, all with a keen eye on what the neighborhood children were doing.

No one was watching him now. It gave him an exhilarating sense that anything was possible, even if that *anything* was confined to a few blocks around his house. He didn't dare risk going further afield, at least not yet.

He stuck to the back lane, snooping through people's backyards, seeing what other children had left out for the taking. Some errant jacks and army men were quickly pocketed, things he could easily hide without raising suspicion from Mama. Someone had left a baseball mitt on their back step and Eddie was aching to bring it home with him, but it would be sure to cause commotion at home and he knew the joy of owning it wasn't worth the hassle. Plus, someone was likely to know it wasn't his if he dared play with it out in the yard.

He felt grown up, being out at night on his own, with no one to tell him what to do, no one waiting for him to slip up so they could rat him out to Mama. He was well aware of the way the other mothers on the block watched him, their faces pinched in distaste, eyes sharp and wary.

Eddie didn't know why they didn't like him. He always assumed it was because of Mama, but he wasn't sure. The other mothers would still let him interact, let him play, but they were never far, always ready to call someone home for lunch, or say, *Eddie Finch, don't make me tell your mother what you're doing.*

Those words were usually enough to get him to give back a toy or stop pushing kids over. It wasn't his fault that the other children on the block were so pathetic. He was only trying to have a good time.

A lit window stopped him in his tracks.

His first response was to run. A lit window meant someone

was awake, someone who could spot him and ruin his whole night, and likely any future nights. Eddie stayed rooted on the spot, terrified, but also drawn to the light in equal measure.

He wanted to see inside.

Sometimes, sitting out on the front steps in the evening, he could see into the houses across the street so clearly. People settling down to watch television, or eat their dinner, their curtains open in an oblivious invitation to look into their homes.

Now someone new was inviting him in.

Eddie crept closer, ever aware of the sounds around him, any creaking storm door or rubber soles on concrete that might be a sign he needed to make a run for it. But the world around him slept, just one more sign that this was meant to be. It was a gift.

As he approached, a faint waft of steam emitted from the open window, giving him momentary pause. Was the house on fire? How would he handle that? Going back home to tell Mama would only raise questions about how he'd known. There was simply no way he could say anything if that was the case.

Still, the siren song of that window was too much to resist. He climbed up onto the rickety back step, which was little more than a platform for the clothesline but was built directly under that brightly lit rectangle. The window itself was open a crack, which was how the thin line of steam was escaping, and when Eddie peered in through the crack, he understood what was happening.

The layout of this house was very much like his, but it seemed to be reversed. Where this would be his bedroom a few houses down, it was a bathroom here. And in that bathroom a woman was showering.

Eddie froze in place. The quiet lull of late-night street noise disappeared in a haze, only his pulse hammered in his ears now.

The scent of soap and shampoo wafted out, powdery, delicate scents that were powerfully feminine.

The woman had a glass shower door, made of pebbled material, so he could not see her clearly, but the insinuation of her flesh thrilled him. The sliver of space the window was open was much too small, and the distorted glass turned her figure into a blur, but that blur had shades and curves. He *knew* this was something he shouldn't be looking at, and that made it all the more valuable to him. This was a currency far greater than the dimes and quarters Mama would sometimes give him if she was feeling beneficent. This was something all for him.

The faucet of the shower squeaked off, and a moment later the woman stepped out of the shower. Despite the ample steam that filled the room, he could see her perfectly. She wasn't a beautiful woman, wasn't slender like the girls in magazines. But Eddie was fascinated by her all the same. He'd never seen a naked woman before.

To him, that flesh, that bareness, was an exotic land he'd never visited.

But he knew he'd visit it again and again if he could.

Car tires crunched on gravel a few houses away and Eddie abandoned his perch, slipping soundlessly into the night and back to the confines of his bedroom, neither Mama nor Sarah any the wiser.

That night he slept better than he had in months.

In his dreams, it wasn't water that moved down the woman's bare body in rivulets and drops.

It was blood.

SEVENTEEN

Margot walked into the little diner shortly after eight in the morning. The sun outside was coming up warm yellow and the sky was clear. It was going to be a beautiful day in San Francisco.

But Margot felt like she had a belly full of rocks.

Andrew Rhodes waved to her from a booth near the back of the restaurant, tucked into a corner, with no one sitting on the other side.

Privacy.

She mustered her best approximation of a smile and made her way over to Andrew, who looked to be the perfect blend of casual and professional. Appropriate for visiting a prison.

"We look like we're getting ready for a shift at Radio Shack," Margot observed, indicating their matching khaki pants.

"Oh, we can be cooler than that, surely. The Gap, maybe?" Andrew pushed a coffee cup over to her, fresh steam still wafting out of it.

The whole diner smelled wonderful. She was surprised she'd never heard of the place. Margot didn't go out much—or at all—to eat, but she had a pretty good awareness of what restaurants were popular around the city, and this place had never come up.

It had a vintage diner atmosphere to it, but in a way that actually *felt* old, rather than approximating the nostalgia of a bygone era. The leatherette booths were cracked in places and fixed with semi-matching red duct tape. The Formica tabletops were chipped, and no effort had been made to repair those. The jukebox in one corner had a faded handwritten sign on it that said *Temporarily Out of Service*, but based on the paleness of the marker and the yellowness of the paper, Margot assumed the thing had been out of order for decades.

The place smelled good, like a diner ought to. Toasting bread, fresh coffee, and the ever-present grease fog of bacon and onions on a grill. It was enough to chase away the nausea that had been hounding her since she'd woken up that morning.

It had been a long time since visiting Ed had made her throw up.

Maybe she *could* indulge in some breakfast. Though she didn't think Andrew had asked her to meet here simply because of the food. The place was haunted by a few old-timers in booths on the other side of the room, and not a single person in here looked like they were toting a *Fromer's Guide to San Francisco*. The diner was in Russian Hill, which bordered plenty of touristy hot spots, yet this place seemed to come from a San Francisco of the past. Like it had a magical cloak over it that made it invisible to the eyes of anyone who hadn't been coming here for twenty years.

If Margot was the kind of person who went places, she'd want to go to places like this.

A waitress sporting a cute gingham uniform complete with a little apron came up to their table, smiling warmly. She was sixty if she was a day, her bleached-blond hair permed and teased into an updo that would make Dolly Parton proud, and she had a nametag on that read *Dot*, which was about as perfect as Margot could have imagined.

"Hey, there, darlin'," Dot greeted warmly. "I already know what this scoundrel wants, but I can't say he's ever brought company along with him. What a treat. You work at the Bureau with him?" Dot's blue eyes twinkled.

"Dot, it's eight in the morning on a Saturday. I'm scandalized that you didn't assume she was a date from the night before." Andrew sipped his coffee.

"Do I look stupid to you, Andy? Pretty girl like that knows better than to get involved with an old worn-out lawman like you." She returned her attention to Margot. "So, what'll it be, hon?"

Margot *loved* this woman. She'd never enjoyed nicknames like *darlin'* and *hon* because they normally came from men, and the last thing in the world Margot wanted was half-assed compliments from men. But from Dot, they were a jolt of pure dopamine to Margot's world-weary system.

A quick glance at the plastic-coated menu in front of her told Margot that this was classic diner food through and through, which made it easy. "I'll take the number two special. White toast, eggs over-medium, bacon, and a little hot sauce if you have it."

"You want those hashbrowns cubed or shredded, hon?"

"Shredded, please."

"With grilled onion?"

"Oh man, yes, please."

Dot winked. "That's his exact order, just so's thatcha know."

Margot watched the older woman walk off, not a single note taken, and had no doubt whatsoever that her order would be delivered to perfection. "Your exact order, is it?" She picked up her coffee and sipped it, impressed that it was still hot.

"She's kidding. I take my eggs scrambled and my toast rye, but it's pretty darned close, I gotta say."

"Good taste, I guess."

"I guess so."

They stared at each other across the table, in a pointless contest of wills to see who would break first.

Andrew finally broke the silence. "I got your email last night. About the fan mail."

"You need to compartmentalize your work–life balance if you were checking your email that late."

Andrew snorted at this but thankfully didn't point out the obvious irony of her statement. She appreciated his restraint. Wes wouldn't have hesitated to roast her.

"I obviously can't send you all the letters. For one, it's decades' worth of data, and we can't share links to our storage externally. But we can arrange some time this week for you to come by if you want to go through it, that's not an issue." Andrew inched forward in his chair. "This does bring up something I feel like I need to tell you, though. Something that wasn't relevant to share earlier, but you're going to figure it out as you go through his mail, and I think it's better I tell you than he does."

Any good mood Margot had built up since her arrival vanished. The gut full of rocks was back, as heavy and uncomfortable as ever. She stared at Andrew, trying to guess from his expression alone what was so important he had to share it with her in person.

Dot returned with their meals before Andrew could continue, placing bottles of Cholula and Tabasco on the table between them. "Anything else for right now? Top-up on your coffee?" she offered.

"No, thanks, Dot," Andrew answered. "We'll wave you down if we need anything."

Dot nodded and headed off to check the other tables. Meanwhile Margot's gaze hadn't moved from Andrew's face.

"What do you need to tell me, Andrew?" she said, picking every word carefully, because she wasn't sure she was breathing.

"We managed to keep it out of the media, had to get a few NDAs signed, but back in 1999, Ed started getting letters from a woman named Rhonda. At first it was the usual fan-letter garbage you'd imagine. How she didn't believe he'd done what they said, that he was a media scapegoat, that he wasn't responsible and she wanted to help get him free. You know the nonsense I'm talking about."

Margot *did* know. She had dozens of letters that had been forwarded to her from her lawyer over the years, largely so she would have evidence on hand if any of them ever escalated to a stalking situation. Some of them were deeply unhinged, blaming Margot—or Megan, as they knew her—for Ed's incarceration, because she wouldn't speak up for him at the trial, and for dozens of other perceived failings on her part.

There was even a subset of Ed's fans who believed an absolutely demented theory that Margot, as a baby, had directed Ed to kill his first victim. That she was the mastermind behind the whole thing, much like David Berkowitz and his neighbor's dog.

Of course, even Berkowitz admitted he'd lied about Sam the dog compelling him to do the Son of Sam murders, but people out there were willing to believe any wild theory so long as it made for a good story.

"You wouldn't be telling me this if Rhonda was only some random fangirl. Ed has had hundreds of those over the years."

"Can't get anything past a detective," Andrew said with a smile.

Margot wasn't sure if this was a compliment or an insult.

"In late 2002, their communications became more frequent. This was when he was in New York, of course. She met with him, at least a dozen times. She put money in his commissary accounts, wrote him a letter every other day, spoke to him frequently on the phone. It wasn't a passing interest for her. She had convinced herself she was in love with him. And because he continued to reply, she believed he loved her, too."

The feeling in Margot's gut intensified. She could see where this was going now, and she didn't like it. Not one bit.

"As you know, your mother was granted a divorce shortly after the trial, and in May 2003, Ed married Rhonda in a ceremony at the prison." Andrew reached into his pocket and pulled out a photo; it was blurry and painfully out of focus, making it impossible to really *see* what Rhonda looked like, aside from a smudge of dark hair. But the two colored blobs in the picture both appeared to be smiling broadly, white teeth flashing. Rhonda wore a simple white dress. Ed was in his Clinton Correctional best. There were armed guards on either side of them.

Margot held the photo in her hand, like it was an object from another planet. It made that little sense to her.

"What the hell are you saying?"

"Margot, Ed is married."

EIGHTEEN

As she drove to San Quentin, Margot existed only in a fog. She had eaten her breakfast because she couldn't stand the idea of offending Dot, but now there was a leaden ball of eggs and bacon in the pit of her stomach threatening to come back up at any moment.

Ed was married.

Ed had a wife.

It had been almost fourteen years since Ed and Rhonda had wed back in New York. Who was this woman, where was she now? A thousand questions pinged back and forth in Margot's brain. The biggest one was *why*. Why had Ed married this woman? It wasn't love, that much was for certain. And it couldn't be sexual, because Ed had never, and would never, be granted conjugal visits.

So how did either of them benefit from this union?

Why?

The question was gnawing at her even as she pulled into the visitor parking lot at San Quentin, next to Andrew's familiar sedan, and they walked together to the visitor's center to go through screening.

She went through the motions of handing over her keys—everything else she had left in the car out of habit—and waiting for Andrew to do the same. She knew people were speaking to her, but the voices seemed to be coming at her as if she was under water. Answers fell from her mouth, but she didn't know what she was saying.

They were taken from the visitor center to the prison, marching along familiar paths, through the nauseating disinfectant stink that never managed to hide the smell of the men living there and of the creeping water outside which coated everything in salt and sea air.

Margot wondered if those who could see it liked the view. Only miles away in Sausalito, people paid millions for it.

These men paid with their freedom.

Ford Rosenthal, Ed's lawyer, was sitting in his usual spot at one of the empty tables, and Andrew joined him. The two men exchanged polite greetings, neither including Margot in their conversation.

She settled in at the same table she'd sat at every time she'd been here, her gaze raking the scene, and still the question dogged her heels at every turn.

Ed didn't do anything without a reason. He hadn't married that woman for love, hadn't married her to get to Margot somehow —at least Margot assumed, since it had never happened—but there was this extension of him out there, walking free, and Margot hated that. Based on what Andrew had said, the pair were still legally married. There wasn't much else he could tell her. The FBI had kept tabs on Rhonda for several years before deeming the ongoing monitoring unnecessary. Since Ed's mail and phone conversations were all meticulously cataloged, they figured if Rhonda ever became a concern, they would be alerted to it that way.

As far as they knew, she never had.

She continued to communicate with Ed regularly, though

over the years this had diminished to a monthly letter. Andrew said they knew she was still giving him money for the phone system and the commissary, but there had been no records of visits since he'd moved to San Francisco.

Margot didn't, couldn't, understand. She had accepted a long time ago that Ed's marriage to her mother had been a convenient cover for him. A way to keep prying eyes away from what he did at night. There may have, at some point, been a part of him that thought he loved Kim, but Margot knew there was no part of Ed that could feel romantic or even familial love. His brain just didn't work like that.

Playing a loving husband and father was merely a role that suited him at the time.

So why step into those husband shoes again? Had he been hoping for a big media sensation? When Charles Manson had gotten a marriage license a few years earlier, the media had gone ballistic over it, so perhaps he'd been onto something. But obviously that plan had been dead in the water. So why stay married?

How did it benefit him?

The swirling thoughts had her so unsettled she didn't even notice Ed's arrival until his jangling restraints scraped against the tabletop, snapping her out of her distraction and forcing her to focus on the man in front of her.

She took a quick glance at Andrew to see if he had noticed her distracted state, but he merely gave her a nod of approval. It unsettled her, slightly, knowing she'd become so skilled at keeping her feelings locked away that no one could tell when she was out of sorts.

On her previous visits, Ed had looked ill, his cheeks hollowed, his skin waxy. Today he looked downright robust. He'd put on weight, enough to give his face a gentle roundness that reminded her of the way he'd looked when she'd been younger. His skin wasn't exactly glowing, but it no longer looked as if he had one foot in the grave.

The small, unkillable part of her that recognized this man as her father felt the slightest shift of relief to know that he seemed better.

The logical adult part of her brain that hated him with such a profound depth that it frightened her sometimes, was disappointed he wasn't already dead.

"Megan," Ed said.

Margot bristled, wanting to correct him, but knowing she couldn't, not without giving up that one small part of herself that he couldn't touch. "Ed," she greeted in return.

"You know, when you were little, you called me *Daddy*. When you outgrew that and got too cool for your old man, it was Dad. Or when you wanted something your mother had said no to, it was *Daaaad*." He affected a high-pitched whine, one that Margot was loath to admit probably *did* sound like her teenage dramatics.

She stared across the table at him, her mind running a mile a minute.

They'd come here for a reason, to put a name to one of his victims, and to find that woman's body and bring her home. It was a dance she and Ed had done several times now. One she knew the steps to. She understood the give and take, the highwire act of restraining her fury and learning how to tease his out to a point.

She'd had a plan to bait him with information about Shuye in the hope of getting him to confess, but now all of that was out the window. Weeks of careful planning, obliterated in a single breakfast.

Because sitting here right now, across from him, she only had one question.

"Who is Rhonda?" she asked.

Before the question was across her lips, she practically *felt*

Andrew cringe from the other side of the room. But it was partially his fault; he'd told her this information at the worst possible time, and because of that, he'd need to deal with the consequences.

Ed looked startled.

That alone made her think the question had been worth asking, because it was such a rarity to throw Ed off balance; seeing him at a loss for words was an elixir she hadn't known she'd been craving. His confidence was shaken, and while it took him only a few seconds to come back to his cool, calm state, hands folded neatly on the dining table, she'd seen the other Ed.

The nervous one.

"How do you know about Rhonda?" Ed's steely gaze moved from her and over to where Rosenthal and Andrew were seated, holding both of them in a contemptuous glare at the same time, as if he wasn't sure which secret-holder had given up the goods.

Rosenthal visibly squirmed, while Andrew's expression didn't change a lick.

When Ed finally looked back at Margot, she was waiting for him. She'd schooled her own expression, gathered her wits. She had fucked up by going off script, but it could help them in the long run, because it might remind Ed that there were other ways to learn his dirty little secrets.

He tapped out a staccato rhythm on the table with his fingers—Margot noticed his nails were chewed ragged and slid her own hands off the table to hide her similarly tragic thumbnails—while he watched her like a hawk, trying to find a spot of weakness.

"I know a lot of things, Ed," she started. "But not as many as you." A little ego stroke, something to dampen the blow she'd just dealt him, to ensure he would keep talking.

This was why only Margot was able to get him to talk.

Because she'd been playing this game with him since she was a child. Even before she knew who and what Ed really was, she'd known his dark moods, his sullen unapproachability, the way he would withdraw or lash out in equal measure. He'd been an angry man as often as he'd doted on her, and Margot's greatest skill in her youth had been learning to pry a good mood out of her father.

Daddy's little girl, then and now.

Only now the stakes were so much higher.

"Do you really want to know about Rhonda?" Ed asked, quirking his head to the side.

The gesture reminded Margot of the velociraptors in *Jurassic Park* sizing up their next meal.

"Who would you rather talk to me about today, Rhonda or Mei-Ling Fan?"

The silence that settled between them was thick enough to chew on, and Margot tilted her head back at him, mirroring his expression so exactly that she saw a little shiver run through his body before he sat back on his seat and smiled. Like his dead eyes, he had the smile of a shark. There was nothing warm about it, nothing that invited friendliness. If anything, Ed looked a hundred times creepier when he smiled.

Margot hadn't always thought that, but once she'd learned that every smile was a calculated lie, she'd stopped believing the gestures entirely.

"Clever girl, Megan. Clever girl. A little this or that game, is that what we're playing at today?"

"You seemed to be getting cold feet about our conversations recently, so I thought I'd come with a few prepared topics to break the ice. How am I doing so far?"

"Consider the ice broken, Buddy."

"So, who is it going to be?"

"Well, I've got to say, as much as I'm curious how and what you think you know about Rhonda, I reckon that's going to be a conversation for a later date. Maybe a little daddy-daughter bonding conversation without all these prying ears."

Margot felt a chill, and for a split second pictured Ed Finch standing in the door of her apartment. She couldn't linger there, couldn't give that vision any more of her time, because otherwise it would never escape her.

"Mei-Ling Fan, then," she said, nodding tersely. "I think she's a good choice."

"I thought so, too."

Margot didn't look at Andrew, but she felt him shift in his seat. So, Agent Scoffs-a-Lot had been right on this one. While Fan hadn't been Ed's typical victim profile, she *had* been an easy target for him. This also meant something new for the hive mind back at the FBI headquarters to chew on.

It had long been believed that Ed was a planner. Aside from victims of pure happenstance—hitchhikers—as Ed grew in confidence, he liked to pick his victims out in advance, learn their habits, follow them for weeks or more. It was how he'd become known as the Classified Killer, because the majority of his known victims were women he'd selected out of personal ads, their information stolen from his newspaper job.

But Mei-Ling had never placed a personal ad, at least based on her known profile. She'd been out drinking at a bar on the cusp of Chinatown and North Beach. She had just been a drunk girl walking alone, presumably while Ed was out hunting someone else.

"Tell me about her," Margot said, then, seeing the way Ed's brows pinched, she added with a mock saccharine sweetness, "Please."

"I prefer the days where I see myself in you, rather than the days I see your mother," Ed said casually, as if it didn't shred Margot up inside. How could he see *any* of himself in her? She had spent her whole life trying to be anything other than her father's daughter.

Margot clenched her jaw and felt her fingernails biting into her palms, but she tried to maintain a cool exterior. Now was not the time to lose it.

"You're never going to find that girl," Ed said, shrugging as if this was incontrovertible fact. "I mean, I suppose there's a chance you've *already* found parts of her but might not know it. But she belongs to the ocean now."

She belongs to the ocean now.

As badly as she wanted to reach across the table and throttle him—and she wondered if anyone would stop her—she had to keep her head on straight. Her question about Rhonda had already been one misstep too many, even if it had gone relatively well for them.

There was no doubt she'd get an earful from Andrew about that as soon as she left here. She could practically hear his *I'm not mad, I'm just disappointed* tone. She wasn't sure which version of a paternal lecture she enjoyed less.

"Are you willing to admit that you killed Mei-Ling?" she asked.

Ford Rosenthal made a harsh throat-clearing noise, marking one of the only times in her months of making these visits that he'd announced his presence in any capacity. He typically acted like he was at Ed's disposal, rather than working as his lawyer.

Margot shot Rosenthal a quick look, her expression certainly sharp, perhaps even mean. When she turned her attention back to Ed, she felt the blood drain from her face, seeing the same expression etched across his features. She had thought, over time, that she'd divorced herself from the idea of him as her father. She'd done her best to sever that tie when she was fifteen and watched the police and FBI drag him away for life.

But sometimes, no matter how hard she wanted to believe her father had died that day, there was no way to deny that she was related to the man sitting across the table from her.

And she wondered how she'd sat across the dinner table from him for fifteen years and never seen the monster before.

"What are they going to do, Rosenthal? Add another life sentence?" Ed scoffed. "I don't fucking care, man. That's why they're here, we might as well give them something."

Rosenthal hadn't needed to speak a word. Ed had been able to decimate him without one. The lawyer shrank in on himself, and despite his thinning hair and the dark bags under his eyes, Margot was reminded that he was actually a young man. Probably younger than her.

How he'd gotten saddled with Ed, she had never cared to ask.

"Yeah, Buddy," Ed said smoothly. "I'll give you this one for free."

"How generous."

NINETEEN

Sometimes, when Margot was young and her mother was busy trying to get baby Justin to go to sleep, it would fall to Ed to read her bedtime stories. Even as a child, Margot knew he didn't like doing it. He didn't make up voices the way her mother did, didn't craft funny faces to exaggerate the story. He simply read her the words on the page.

Margot was thinking about those bedtime stories as Ed recounted the night he killed Mei-Ling.

He was so much more animated now than he'd ever been when telling her about Prince Charming and happily ever afters.

"You and your mom had gone to New York for a month that summer, but I couldn't take the time off work. At least that's what I told her. I probably could have, but honestly, I never liked Kim's parents and the feeling was decidedly mutual. Me staying behind was a gift to everyone."

Margot couldn't help but notice the way Ed skipped over the existence of her brother. It wasn't the first time he'd done this, and she couldn't tell if it was an intentional slight—like he was waiting to see if she might bring him up, or slip up and use his new name—or if he simply didn't care enough to mention him. It made her heartsick to believe it was most likely the latter.

Ed had never warmed to Justin the way he had to her. Even when they'd been children, there seemed to be an unspoken awareness that Margot had been the favorite as far as Ed was concerned. Justin had spent *years* hungry for his father's validation, and now that was catching up to him in unexpected ways.

Margot always had Ed's validation, and she'd have given anything not to have it.

"You were gone almost six weeks that summer. It might have been the best six weeks of my life. You know about a few from that time, but you never did figure them all out. So, Mei-Ling, that's her name? Yeah, I'll give you that one."

Margot didn't turn her head, but she did dart a glance over to Andrew. They weren't allowed pens or pencils, but she knew he was taking the exact same mental notes she was.

Margot didn't believe for a second he didn't know the woman's name. He remembered them all, probably followed stories of their disappearances in the newspaper—he did *work* at the newspaper after all.

Yes, he was a cold, calculated killer who didn't care one bit about these women beyond the pleasure he'd derived from killing them, *but* he was a hunter, and hunters remembered their kills. Collected them like trophies.

He knew them all.

"Tell me what happened," Margot urged, repulsed, but needing the details if they were going to be able to close the case.

"Tell me what you're working on now," he replied.

This bullshit again.

Margot wasn't sure what he got out of her discussing her cases. Did he want the vicarious thrill of learning what other killers were doing, or did he hope to glean insight into who she was now? So far, they'd been doing this for months and he didn't know her new name or anything about her life, beyond her work as a homicide detective. And Margot went to great lengths to keep her name out of print, so she hoped no matter how diligently he prodded and poked she wouldn't give him what he wanted most.

Access.

But it still felt wrong to be telling him what she was working on. It made those women his, in a way, and she didn't want to give him the pleasure of it.

So, this time, she lied.

Margot hefted a sigh, affecting the demeanor of someone being forced to share something she didn't want to. "You don't get to have this every time," she said coldly.

"Funny, because you don't get to have answers every time either, now, do you?" He leaned back slightly, though the stools attached to the table had no backs. "I've got nothing but time here, Buddy, and plenty of secrets I can take to the grave."

Buddy again. He was using it more and more frequently, perhaps because he knew her previous name made her angry. But she suspected it was more likely his way of saying he could call her whatever he wanted and he would still own her name in some capacity.

Margot ignored that sick feeling in her gut. She knew she was making gains, as much as he tried to convince her he was the one with all the power.

"My most recent case is a domestic homicide." She was abandoning her original plan completely now, because she had a different idea of how to twist the information out of him.

Ed's expression shifted with such obvious disappointment it almost made her smile. This was what she wanted, something that wouldn't titillate him the way he hoped.

"Unusual case, because normally we see women being the victims in those scenarios, but in this case the husband was the one who ended up dead. But once we reviewed the history of calls to that address it was pretty clear that one or the other of them was going to go eventually, it was just a matter of time."

His mouth formed a thin line. If this had been a violent crime against a woman he'd be asking her for details, he'd want to know more. But violence against a man didn't interest him.

It was all Margot could do to keep her satisfaction hidden.

She was about to make it even worse. "Gunshot." She pressed her finger between her eyes. "While he was sleeping. Sonofabitch never saw it coming."

No knives.

No female pain.

None of this would do anything for him.

"I heard they found another body in the woods," he replied after a beat.

Margot shrugged. "There are a lot of bodies out there, Ed. Unless the body in the woods was Mei-Ling Fan, I'm not particularly interested in them."

He watched her, appraisingly, his eyes moving over her face. "At least I know who taught you how to lie."

While Margot digested that horrific sentence, Ed folded his hands neatly on the tabletop. "There were a lot of things about the eighties people want to forget, but what no one talks about is how much people fucking *loved* cocaine. I don't think you can appreciate it, Margot—that shit was everywhere. And cocaine does something to people's brains." He tapped his temple. "It convinces them they're larger than life. Indestructible. Better still if you mix cocaine and alcohol; people get almost ruinously reckless with their own well-being."

Margot waited to see where this was going, rather than interrupting his flow.

"You could drive by almost any bar in the city and see girls stumbling out, high as a kite, on a different goddamn planet. They'd walk home alone. They paid *no* attention to the world around them. If you want to know why there were so many serial killers in the seventies and eighties, it's because people just didn't know to be afraid yet. They didn't know what could happen to them." A thin smile crossed his lips. "I showed them what could happen to them, though, didn't I?"

Her stomach churned at his self-satisfied grin. And the problem was, she couldn't even correct him. He *had* taught a whole generation of women what it meant to feel real fear. He was *still* teaching women that danger lurked around every corner. There were monsters in the world worse than any in bedtime stories, and she was sitting across from one of them.

"Most of the time, I like to get to know my girls first. But, kid... sometimes an opportunity lands right in your lap and you can't turn it down. That was her. Walking home, barely standing right on her heels, I pulled up and offered her a ride. She didn't even think twice, she was so grateful to get off her feet. I don't even think she knew we were going the wrong way until a few blocks later. If you want to find her, though, you won't. Unless parts of her showed up in Sausalito." He glanced down at his ragged nails. "I didn't get as long with her as I'd have liked. But she wasn't exactly my taste either."

They stared at each other across the table, each willing the other to break first in some way.

It was Ed who spoke first, but he wouldn't have considered it losing.

He wanted to get the last word.

"If you thought the China doll was interesting, you'd *love* to hear about the girl I got the next night. Now *her*, her I played with for a good long time." His eyes gleamed with unrestrained delight, as if he could sense Margot's revulsion. "But that's a story for next time."

TWENTY

"I'd be royally pissed at you, except it seemed to work," Andrew said as they walked back through the parking lot. He'd at least waited until they were out of security and alone together before ripping into her.

And it was a much gentler ripping than she had anticipated.

"I don't want to point fingers here, Andrew, but I'm not sure what you thought would happen when you drop a bombshell like a secret wife on me an hour before I go in to see him. You *know* how he gets under my skin, and it was just sitting there, this little festering thing right at the top of my brain. You had to know that telling me beforehand was going to lead to a potential issue."

Andrew frowned. He didn't like having the blame shifted to him, but he knew she was right.

Either that, or he simply didn't want to die on this stupid hill, and that was enough for her to count it as a victory.

She felt like she needed a win. Whenever she left Ed, a part of her shrank inside, something imperceptible to the naked eye. She wasn't sure if it was her humanity, her grip on her sanity, but she lost more of it whenever she left the prison.

She didn't know if it was something she could ever get back.

So whatever wins she could come away with at least balanced the scales somewhat. Even if she *did* need to take those victories from Andrew instead of Ed.

"You're right," he acquiesced. "It was the wrong time to tell you, and I'm sorry. I'm not sure what the *right* time would be to break news like that, but I obviously picked the wrong one." When Margot opened her door, he held it for her as she got in. "You did good in there today. The story about the husband getting shot, you made that up on the spot, didn't you?"

Margot nodded. "I was sick of giving him my real victims. He doesn't deserve them."

"We might need to be careful going forward. He knew you did that intentionally, so if we don't play along with him next time, he might start feeding us lies of his own."

She stared out the front window of the car. A woman with two children no older than ten was walking through the parking lot toward the visitor check-in. Margot had never once gone to visit Ed when he'd gone to prison, not before these requested meetings.

None of them had.

What did it say about them, as his family, that they'd so readily believed him capable of the crimes he had been accused of, even before he was convicted? Did it make them bad children, a bad wife? Or was it simply that somewhere deep down they knew in their bones that he was every ounce the villain the world believed him to be?

She sometimes thought about the people who stood by the men and women she arrested. The wives, the girlfriends, all so willing to trust that their beloved couldn't be capable of such horrors.

Margot wondered if she would ever again be able to believe in someone with such blind faith.

"Look, I'm going back to HQ, write up my report. Do you want to come with me? We can brief the team on what we've learned and then I can give you some time with the correspondence database, see if you spot anything. I'm willing to bet good money Greg would offer to help you. He has spent a lot of time reading Ed's outbound mail."

Greg Howell's obsession with her father should have put Margot off the kid, but for some reason she liked him. There was an earnestness, a youthful lack of awareness, that made her appreciate him in a way she didn't the others who were bogged down in the lore of Ed Finch.

"Sure."

The last thing in the world she wanted to do right then was to go over the conversation a second time, but she had to. Memory was fickle, and the sooner they could discuss this as a team, the better. "I want to make a stop on the way back, though."

Andrew looked as if he wanted to ask her for details, but he didn't. Margot knew it had to kill him to relinquish control to someone he had known since they were a teenager, but she found that with each passing day the respect came in new ways. She wasn't that chubby-cheeked kid crying in a car anymore.

Though the crying in a car part hadn't gone away.

She was a colleague now. Someone he *needed* if he was going to continue dealing with Ed. Margot could see the gradual shift in the way Andrew treated her each time they were together. There were still elements of the paternal there, something she didn't think was ever going to go away entirely. But each time he watched her sit across the table from Ed, he came away looking at her a little different than he had before.

"All right. I'll see you back there. I'll ask Greg to get a meeting room set up for both of you for after our debrief." He looked at her intently and she held his gaze. There was more he wanted to say—a warning, or maybe a compliment about how she'd handled herself—but after a long pause he just nodded once and headed back to his own car.

Margot closed the door behind him and waited, watching his sedan drive off before pulling out of the parking lot herself. She drove without music or the radio, the buzz of her own thoughts too loud to allow for anything else.

She thought about Mei-Ling, about Rhonda, about Shuye. Three women whose lives had been touched by Ed in some way, most certainly for the worse. She thought about all the letters in a box in her own home. Letters from Ed, letters from those who wanted to believe Ed was innocent.

It occurred to her now that Rhonda might have written one of them. Her lawyer only passed on to her those he felt might be worth her while to read. She hadn't read any of them.

Perhaps there were things there she had been wrong to overlook. The FBI would have copies of those Ed had written her, but not those from his harem of worshippers.

But the letters would need to wait.

Right now, she had another trio of women she wanted to think about.

She forced Ed from her mind and focused on the Muir Woods case. Their Jane Doe—who was too nicely dressed, too polished a woman to stay anonymous for long—Rebecca Watson, and Leanne Wu. Three women who seemed to have very little in common with one another on the surface, but whose bodies had all been discovered in a tidy little area. Too close to be coincidence.

Leon could hedge his bets all he wanted. Nobody *hoped* for a serial killer, but the evidence was too overwhelming to be ignored. The possibility of three different killers dumping bodies in such a remote area was vastly more unlikely than it being one man.

Margot followed the same winding mountain path she had

before. She rolled her window down, breathing deeply the scent of rosemary and California eucalyptus, with its distinctive peeled trunks that lined the side of the road. The air out here was almost miraculously clean, smelling so different than it did just across the bridge.

A single marked car was parked on the side of the road by the hiking trailhead that led to the crime scene, and Margot pulled in behind it, gravel crunching under her tires and a sole motorcyclist whizzing by as soon as she was out of the way.

Before Margot was even out of her car a uniformed Marin County deputy got out of the SUV, sidling over to her with the affected swagger of a cowboy. He was maybe twenty-five years old, but he definitely had the makings of a man who would call her *little lady*.

She had her badge in hand as she got out of her Honda.

"Sorry, ma'am, but this trail is closed for hiking." He was sizing her up with a too-lingering gaze that made her feel a little queasy. She flashed her ID at him and saw the way his smarmy expression changed almost immediately. "I'm Detective Margot Phalen with the SFPD, I'm part of the team investigating this case. I need a few minutes, if you don't mind."

This last part was pure politeness on her part. It was *her* crime scene, and she could attend it if she liked, but she also wanted to keep the peace when it came to a multi-jurisdiction case like this. Pissing off the locals didn't do anyone any good. Even if this guy radiated frat-boy energy.

Guys like this were sometimes looking for a fight, and she wouldn't be the one to give it to him.

He looked like he was going to argue for the sake of arguing, but instead clicked the radio at his collar. "Dispatch, I've got a Detective Phalen here, is she cleared to go through?"

A moment later, a staticky voice on the radio came through and said, "Detective Phalen is all clear."

The deputy gave Margot a gruff jerk of the chin but didn't

offer to accompany her or suggest he'd be present if she needed help; he simply watched her walk down the trail. She could feel his gaze on her back as she disappeared into the trees, and despite him being an officer of the law, she was keenly aware that he knew she was alone out here.

And no one else did.

Idiot, she chided herself. She took a look at her phone, but of course there was no signal. For now, she'd need to be satisfied knowing that at least the dispatcher at the sheriff's office was aware of her presence, and that alone would have to serve as a minimal comfort.

Once she was out from under the weight of his gaze, she felt lighter, easier. She knew there were risks everywhere in life, knew someone on this very trail was dead because of those risks. But she also knew that living in fear was no life at all, and there were things she couldn't hide from.

Violence was not so much a threat as it was an eventuality.

All Margot could do was be prepared for it.

She made her way down the brush-strewn path, listening to birds singing in the distance, the pervasive chirrup of the Pacific wren and the eerie croak of the raven being the only ones she knew off hand. For some reason their fearless noises made her relax. Birds knew. They recognized danger. So, their songs were a signpost she could hang her worries on for now.

It didn't take long to find the place on the trail that had been battered down by footsteps, an inevitable side effect of several dozen people moving in and out of the area. No one was here at the moment. They'd spent hours collecting debris from the forest floor. Any candy wrapper or cigarette butt within sight of the trail had been photographed and bagged up. There had been three different condoms found—two had been in such decrepit condition Margot had no false hope they would be of any use—but the third was new and not far from the body.

Their killer had been careful to this point, but he also had the earmarks of someone who really wanted attention. A man who knew his DNA wasn't in a database might not be as fearful of leaving it behind.

It seemed unlikely to belong to him, but they weren't going to let any possibilities get ignored.

Margot stood on the main hiking path. The trees here were leaner, shorter. This wasn't part of the majestic redwood growth that people came to Muir Woods to marvel at, but it was still pretty, the mountains in the background, sun overhead. If she was the kind of person who hiked, she could see why people would come on this trail. Wildflowers dappled the undergrowth with purple and yellow, and bushy rosemary made the air smell nearly edible.

She rubbed her fingers on a nearby rosemary bush, remembering how her mom used to caution her against doing that as a child because wasps and bees loved the flowers.

Nothing stung her.

Looking up and down the path, it was incredible how remote the place felt, even though she knew the highway was close. She couldn't even hear cars passing, but they must be.

The vegetation off the beaten path was thick. If the killer had taken Jane Doe only a few hundred feet further, Margot sincerely doubted anyone would have ever seen her, especially if he'd covered her properly with leaves and branches. It would have been someone's adventurous dog who found her months or even years from now, bringing a jawbone or femur back to their owner as a grisly surprise.

But no, he'd left her where someone was sure to spot her, sooner rather than later. The same way he'd left Rebecca's bright pink tracksuit on and dumped her on one of the most heavily traveled walking paths in the state.

Hidden in plain sight.

His first victim, Leanne, she'd been the one who had taken the longest to find, but even then, she was just off the trail. Waiting.

What was he trying to say?

Rebecca bothered her the most. The ballsy nature of where her body was disposed, and how risky that would have been for him to pull off. Had he gone in when the park was open and waited for the right time to leave her?

In all three instances the women were left behind like garbage, tossed by the side of the road, as if burying them or even hiding them wasn't worth the effort. With Jane Doe there had been the haphazard effort to throw a branch or two on her, but even that felt more performative than anything.

He wanted his work found.

But did he want to get caught? Or was this all part of the thrill for him?

It made her think about Shuye's case, still so fresh in her mind. The knife in the dumpster and the page of the book left hidden but not destroyed. The killer *wanted* those things found, or he would have done a better job getting rid of them.

She could never tell if taunting police was part of the thrill —a killer's way of proving how smart they were, to leave clues and not get caught—or because maybe in some sick, twisted way they *wanted* to get caught.

Margot stepped off the path, moving through the branches of new-growth trees, until she was standing where Jane Doe had been spotted. Looking back to the path, she was obscured but not hidden. Someone passing by might not notice her right away, but if they looked into the trees, they'd be able to see her.

Had he stood here after dropping the body, sweaty from the effort of hauling her, and looked back to the trail, hoping someone might pass by and catch him out?

Or did he sit in the dark alongside his kill and watch dusk or dawn hikers go down the trail, relishing their lack of awareness?

Ed had loved to watch his victims. He'd sit right outside their apartments, sometimes for days at a time, learning their habits and routines. What brought this killer that same rush? Was it the risk? The closeness? Did he crave an audience?

Margot had an idea of how to find out.

TWENTY-ONE

Oakland, CA

Eddie became obsessed with windows.

Whenever he would play in the street, he'd crane his neck to see who had flimsy curtains. At night, he'd stare out of his own front window, looking hungrily from house to house to see which of his neighbors left their homes open to prying eyes deep into the darkest hours of the night.

He learned quickly that people were more inclined to close their front curtains than those in the back windows. This served him well as he began to sneak out nightly, whenever Mama was snoring loudly, and he was sure Sarah was asleep, too.

Not that Sarah would be a rat, but he didn't want her to know.

He didn't want anyone to know what he did with his nighttime hours.

Summer was at its peak, and even well after sunset the air retained a sticky, oppressive heat to it. For over a week they hadn't had an ounce of rain, and people were starting to leave their windows open as soon as the sun went down, hoping and praying for even the slightest breeze to ease their fitful slumber.

Over the weeks of nighttime exploration, Eddie had developed a routine. The woman at the end of the block must have had a job that brought her home late, because she seemed to shower between ten and eleven almost every evening. Except weekends. If it was Saturday or Sunday, her bathroom window lay dark and dormant through the night; a disappointing realization to him when he'd sat waiting for almost an hour, finally giving up when another car pulled down the back lane.

A couple across the street left their bedroom curtain up, and one night Eddie had watched as the man rolled onto his wife and thrust into her repeatedly. His aggressive grunts meant nothing to Eddie but occasionally the woman would shriek—a sound he could not identify as pain or pleasure; perhaps it was both—and it thrilled him. He visited their window several more times during his explorations but had yet to see them at it again. He didn't know much about sex, only what Mama had told him, which was that it was sinful and disgusting, but the sounds he'd heard coming from that woman echoed in his ears as he lay in bed at night.

Sometimes he found the windows of his own schoolmates, and a satisfying sense of power overtook him as he watched them sleep. Their mouths hung open, legs kicked free of overly hot sheets, and it occurred to him that everyone was vulnerable as they slept.

No one noticed him.

Everyone up and down his block had the most certain belief that they were safe and protected inside their own homes. He believed it himself, that his small bedroom was a sanctuary from the outside world. But what he'd learned as he craned his neck and stretched his legs to get glances into his neighbors' most sanctified spaces, was that *he* had been granted a unique gift.

Eddie could slip inside the safety zone people had built for themselves.

On some level, perhaps they wanted him to see them. Otherwise, why leave the curtain open? Why follow the same routine, day in and day out? Why make it so easy for him to witness their most private moments?

They must have wanted it, because otherwise they would have been more careful.

Over time he learned about the people in his neighborhood who wanted to be seen. Those who dozed with windows open, sheer curtains billowing in the lightest of breezes. He memorized which wives were alone at night, which women had no sons or husbands sleeping next to them. He liked them best of all.

Those were the windows he came back to again and again.

Those were the women he thought about when he went home at night and drifted off, his own window closed and locked, curtains tightly drawn.

Eddie was building his collection one night at a time.

TWENTY-TWO

The main team of Andrew, Alana, Carter, and Greg were assembled in the meeting room for the debrief when Margot arrived. They must have already been in the thick of it, because they'd sent a young agent down to get her from the front desk. The woman's name was Sydney Onyema, and while she and Margot had met on previous occasions, Margot got the sense Sydney had not warmed to her.

That was likely Margot's fault, as she rarely gave anyone a reason to warm to her.

Sydney stayed on her side of the elevator, as if ignoring Margot's presence, and by the time they reached the team's floor, Margot was wishing for Greg's overly enthusiastic energy instead.

"They're in there," Sydney said, gesturing to the familiar office, before heading back into the main work area.

Margot briefly wondered if she'd ever said or done anything to offend the woman, but she suspected the prickly demeanor was more about being sent on such a menial errand, as opposed to the issue being Margot herself.

At least, that's what she was going to go with.

She joined the team, who had already activated the fogging feature on the glass, and when Margot came in, they were in the midst of reviewing a slide deck on the large monitor.

Margot nodded in greeting to the four agents around the table, keenly aware that the sticker on her lapel marked her as an obvious outsider among them. Alana was the first to offer a smile, her bold red lipstick accentuating the gesture. Margot had no idea how a woman who looked like the love child of Cate Blanchett and Michelle Pfeiffer had ended up as an FBI agent instead of a model, but her striking presence always threw Margot off balance.

Alana was seated next to Carter as usual, and while the linebacker-sized agent had acknowledged Margot with a quick look, he kept his focus largely on the monitor.

Andrew sat at the head of the table and gestured unnecessarily to the empty seat next to Greg, where Margot almost always sat in these meetings. Greg, for his part, was too busy presenting the material to greet her. While he had paused at her entry, he continued so as not to lose his place.

"We know we need to home in on missing persons and unsolved homicides from the summer of 1989. Now, we had previously been aware of two murders that Finch was responsible for during this window, those of Stacey Birch and Whitney Allory. This was well into Finch's tenure, and he was getting a lot bolder with his kills. Adding Mei-Ling Fan, as well as his reference to this being a *busy summer*, we will have to do some additional cross-referencing in the towns between Petaluma and San Francisco."

"You'll want to check around Dillon Beach, too," Margot said.

The four of them turned to her in unison, and she wasn't sure if it was because this suggestion was obvious or because they had no idea what she was talking about.

"Ed..." She paused, as they all seemed to flinch at his common name. "From when I was about seven until I was maybe eleven or twelve, Ed used to spend a lot of time with a guy he met at work. We called him Uncle Jim. I remember being jealous that he got to spend time with Uncle Jim whenever we went to visit my mom's family, because Jim had a boat. He took us out on it a few times in the fall. He had a slip in Marshall, I think."

They continued to stare at her, then at each other. Margot felt guilty of something, though she didn't think she'd done anything wrong aside from interjecting her opinion.

Carter and Alana were both on their computers in an instant, and Greg was looking at Andrew waiting for... something.

"Sorry, Margot, can you clarify what you're talking about?"

"Uncle Jim?"

"Your father only has a sister. Sarah Hubert. Her husband's name is..." Andrew looked over to Greg, who supplied the answer.

"Phillip."

"Yes, I know who my Uncle Phil is, thank you." Margot frowned. While her father wasn't close to her Aunt Sarah, they had received the occasional parcel at Christmas, signed *Much love, Auntie Sarah and Uncle Phil.*

"Who is Jim?" Andrew asked.

Margot couldn't believe that in twenty-two years since Ed's capture no one knew about Uncle Jim. That seemed impossible, surely. This room was filled with the people who knew Ed's case like the back of their hands. How could they not know about one of his only friends?

"Ed had a friend he would sometimes grab beers with or go on weekend outings with. Jim lived in Petaluma, I assumed, but we never saw his house, so I can't say."

"And you met this person?" Andrew saw the shift in her

expression, as if she'd just been accused of making up a Santa Claus-like apparition who might not exist.

"Yes. He came for dinner a lot. I don't think my mom liked him very much, she'd always put us to bed early on nights Jim came by. I know he wasn't married, or he had been married but wasn't anymore. No kids. I was always disappointed he didn't have kids."

"You say he had access to a boat."

"Yes. I think he owned it. We went out on it a few times. It had one of those stupid names that men pick for their boats. *Wet Dream.* I remember because I didn't get why it was a bad name, but Mom was grossed out by it."

"Do you remember Jim's last name?" Greg asked.

Margot frowned and leaned forward. "I'm sorry, I don't mean this in a rude way, but are you guys telling me you've never heard of this man before?"

The four of them did not look at each other again.

"We spoke to all of Finch's known workplace colleagues, but going over the records there was no Jim, James, or Jimmy that we spoke with. No record of one during Finch's time at the paper. When we asked about acquaintances, there was no mention of a Jim," Andrew said. "I don't pretend to remember every single person we spoke to back then, but a boating friend feels like something we would have followed up on."

For a few years he'd been such a staple in their lives that Margot found it impossible to think no one had spoken to him. But then again, he had vanished from their circle *years* before Ed was arrested. He never told them why, just that he and Uncle Jim weren't friends anymore. No further discussion.

It was possible in the trauma at the time none of them had even thought about Jim.

Margot hadn't thought about him for decades, not until this moment.

She held her hands out, empty, showing she had nothing

else to offer them. "All I remember is that when we would call to check in while we were out in New York those summers, Ed would often say he was planning to spend time with Uncle Jim. I can see, now, how that looks like an excuse he'd tell us, and maybe it was, but we all met Jim, we knew him. I'm sure if any of our photo albums were still in evidence there'd be photos in there."

Kim had only wanted the photos of her children back when the FBI were done scouring through their family albums to see what counted as evidence and what was just lies. Many *many* childhood memories that involved Ed had been abandoned or destroyed. Margot had no idea if the FBI had kept what was left, but she only had what her mom had in her possession when she died.

"Do *you* have any photos of Jim?" Andrew asked.

She mentally indexed the few items in her possession. "I don't think so, but I need to go through some things when I get home anyway. I can have a look. Not sure how much good a photo will do. Wish I could remember his last name. I think it might have started with a Mc or a Mac, maybe?"

"That's a place to start."

Margot glanced back at the screen, where the PowerPoint remained paused, the faces of several women and girls smiling back at them, oblivious to the fate that awaited them. Margot wanted to apologize to them for stealing the spotlight, but she found she couldn't look at them for too long. Their stolen smiles fed the pit of guilt that swelled deep in her belly.

There was a strange feeling in her, aside from the grief and guilt, that Margot could only think of as... pride? She had given the agents information they hadn't known before. The foremost experts on Ed Finch, and there were still things they could never know, would never know. But Uncle Jim was certainly a thing they *should have* known.

Margot thought of her own life, of the scant few people in it who she might call friends, and wondered who might slip by forgotten if anyone had to look at the totality of her life in terms of all those she had touched.

She thought, too, about how empty her life felt sometimes. It was by design, and by necessity. At least, she had always told herself that. But spending more time with Wes, even connecting with Leon, it made her wonder if she *could* make room in her life to let someone else in.

Even a little bit.

Greg, with a nod from Andrew, returned to the presentation at hand, and they reviewed the most likely candidates of missing women or unsolved homicides from the summer of 1989. There were seven women in total who fit Ed's profile and the timeline, with ten more who fit the timeline but not necessarily Ed's MO or victim profile.

With Mei-Ling being confirmed as one of Ed's victims, they had to reassess a lot of what they thought they previously knew. The summers his family were away, Ed may have been less controlled, less careful. He had no one to get home to on time, no one to answer to. There was a chance he was simply killing whenever the opportunity arose, and that was a chilling thought to accept.

As the meeting wrapped up, Alana and Carter drifted out with a nod and whispered goodbye, and Andrew reminded Margot to have a look through her things when she got home, as if she might have forgotten the request over the course of a twenty-minute slideshow.

That left her and Greg alone, awkwardly side by side, in the large conference room. Greg, for his part, was completely oblivious to any awkwardness. His boundless puppy-dog enthusiasm seemed to only increase in her presence, and he spun his chair in her direction, beaming.

"What amazing work, detective, truly. The things you can get Finch to say. I keep asking Special Agent Rhodes to let me attend with you, but he insists it would throw off the existing setup too much."

"I do think Ed might find you a little distracting," Margot said with a polite smile, trying to imagine how Ed would respond to the gangly redhead who probably knew more about her father than anyone else on the planet.

"Ed. Yeah." He nodded, as if fascinated that she could so casually refer to him by his first name. That wasn't her fault, though, really. She couldn't call him *Finch* the way they did. That had been her name once, too, and while she no longer claimed it, she couldn't use it casually. It had been hers, her brother's, her mother's.

She certainly couldn't and wouldn't call him *Dad*, or *my father*, two titles which he no longer had any right to, no matter how hard he seemed to want to try to cling to them.

The Classified Killer, or his pre-letters moniker of *The Bay Area Killer* or *Bay Area Butcher* were too flashy, and he'd enjoy her using them far too much.

Ed was the only thing that felt right.

It was bland, it was brief, it denied him any menace or power.

"You told Andrew you wanted to look through some of Finch's correspondence?" Greg said.

"Yeah, not related to this case, but something else on my plate." She briefly walked Greg through Shuye's murder and the page they'd found from Andrew's book. "We think there's a possibility it's a would-be copycat. I'm waiting on the final autopsy results to learn how close the crimes really were. But we think this might have been our killer's homage to Laura Welsh's killing. So, I thought there might be a chance this person reached out to Ed, to get advice or to brag about what he was planning to do."

"Well, we have all of Finch's incoming and outgoing mail scanned and digitized, it makes it easier to flag certain phrases that we would consider to be high risk and keep those messages from either coming in or going out. He's learned over the years to be careful with what he says, he rarely has his mail blocked. But we have *plenty* of incoming mail that gets scanned, flagged, and destroyed before he ever has a chance to read it."

Greg typed a few things into the database and a list of ten thousand results came up.

"Wow," Margot said, largely to herself.

Greg gave a little half-shrug. "He's a popular guy. He got more in the years closer to his arrest, and we usually see an uptick on anniversary dates, things like his birthday, his arrest date, so on. But all this, that's only the incoming. He's pretty prolific with his outgoing correspondence as well, we have a different search for that. I think, if there's anything to be found for your killer, the best place to start looking is inbound, because the mail might not have even reached Finch, but could still be useful to you."

He sat expectantly, staring at her.

She looked at the computer. "I think I can handle this on my own."

Margot didn't think there was anything especially cruel in her phrasing, but Greg still looked like the proverbial puppy who'd been swatted with a paper.

The fact was, Margot didn't work well with someone looming over her shoulder. Even though she and Wes worked in close quarters, they were never checking in on each other's work. She liked the closeness they shared, it was its own kind of intimacy, in a way, to be able to be near someone but not need anything from them except that nearness. At the moment, she wasn't feeling that kind of ease, and she didn't want to sit here and guess at search phrases that might trigger something in the database and share them with Greg to type in.

She was certain he wouldn't mind doing it, but she'd find it pointless and frustrating.

Greg looked regretful as he said, "I'm not really supposed to leave my computer with you." He caught his phrasing even before she could raise an eyebrow. "Not just with you," he quickly amended. "But, like, with anyone. Anyone who isn't me."

He struck her as a guy who was going to be a stickler for the rules, and she didn't want to waste time arguing with him. She wanted to look through some of the letters herself, then pass this off to some FBI lackey to keep poking around with.

She had a feeling that after she left here, Greg would volunteer to be that lackey.

Maybe, then, rather than getting rid of him, she could bend him to her will slightly. "Do you mind if I just check a few things? You can stay in here with me, make sure I don't do anything nefarious with company property, but I need to be able to do my own search. At least at first. Then maybe you could help me out? You know Ed and the letters in this database probably better than anyone. If I can't find what I'm looking for, I'm betting you can."

It was such a cheap, manipulative ploy she thought for sure Greg would see through it immediately. But he didn't. The sad expression shifted into one of excitement, and Margot felt so bad for a moment that she almost took it all back.

"Yeah, absolutely. I mean, you're a detective, obviously, I know you know how to work a database. But if you don't find anything right away, you could always send me your case notes and I can have a look in my downtime."

He pushed the laptop over to her and Margot decided that being a bad person might have been the right move. Just this once.

Greg pulled out his phone, busying himself with emails as she started in on the letter database. She did some base searches. The name of Andrew's book yielded hundreds and hundreds of results, too broad a field to be of any use to her. She tried Shuye, then getting no results switched over to her victim's nickname among the white residents of her building, Susie. Five results. Of those, three were from a woman named Susie, who had sent the letters in 2001, and a quick scan of them told Margot she was only another crackpot fan who believed in Ed's innocence. She stopped replying when he seemed to have declined her offer to introduce him to Jesus. In her last letter she told Ed it wasn't too late to turn his back on the Devil.

Margot was pretty sure Susie had that one wrong.

In another letter a male correspondent complained of a wife or girlfriend named Susie—he referred to her as *his woman* rather than by an official title—and wondered how it was that Ed hadn't succumbed to the urges to murder his own wife. This letter had a red bar across the top marking it as *Flagged—Undelivered*. Probably for the best.

The fifth one was a different Susie as the sender, and it had just one line.

You can be my Daddy.

Margot felt a wash of nausea flood her stomach, threatening to push bile up. This one had likewise been marked as *Flagged—Undelivered* and there was a scanned photo attached that showed a grown woman in pigtails sucking her thumb, wearing little more than underwear.

It had been sent only the previous year, and the girl in the photo looked like she was in her early twenties at best.

The girl probably hadn't even been alive when Ed was arrested and sent to prison.

What was wrong with these people that they craved the attention of literal killers? What was it about Ed's legacy that had prompted this girl to write the letter, to send the photo? These were people who kept a whole industry of serial killer playing cards and iconography in business.

What could possess someone to make them worship a killer like they were a rock star?

And why would anyone take it as far as to marry one?

Margot's fingers hovered over the keyboard. The FBI would track the searches she made. She had no doubt Greg or Andrew would review all the things she looked at. But Andrew had been the one to tell her about Ed's second wife, he had to know that planting that seed would push her to want to know more.

Ultimately the curiosity of it was more than she could bear. She would take a quick little peek to see what was there. She didn't have the time—or truly the inclination—to read the letters too closely. Love letters.

Margot typed in *Rhonda* to the search bar.

Hundreds of results. She noted that the vast majority of these results were flagged with a note that simply read *R*. They were cataloging which letters belonged specifically to Ed's Rhonda, and which were from others, or unrelated. They dated back *years*, and there were still ones coming in as recently as the previous month.

Margot selected the first one, going back to the very beginning.

Ed,

Can I call you Ed? That seems so casual, as if you and I are already friends. Yet I feel I know you already, and in that, I don't feel right just calling you Mr. Finch. That name is much too formal, I fear, for the man I think you are. Ed, you don't know me, we've never met, but your story has haunted me for many years now, and I couldn't resist reaching out any longer.

I know what they say about you, but I also know what I see in your eyes whenever I look at you. I'm not talking about that dreadful mugshot they've plastered everywhere—who could look themselves at a time like that?—but the other photos, private ones I've seen shared in papers and news stories. I see the man you are in those photos.

I'm sure many women have written to you, telling you they don't believe you are guilty. They may believe that. I believe that your body did commit these crimes, but for reasons your innocent mind may not want to believe. Ed, do you believe in demons?

Margot stared at the screen.

Perhaps she had had a stroke in the last five minutes and that was what was causing her to read what she thought she was reading.

Do you believe in demons?

Sweet, merciful Christ on a cracker. This woman was just as unhinged as the rest of them, which certainly went a long way toward explaining why she'd be willing to marry Ed, but Margot had a whole new question now.

Why had Ed wanted to marry her?

Margot couldn't pretend to know what demented thoughts swirled around inside the mind of Ed Finch at any given time, but she *did* know a thing or two about the man who raised her, and more than she would like to about the killer he'd become.

Factoring in all of that, she couldn't begin to fathom what it was about Rhonda—at least from this first letter—that would have compelled him to not only reply, but to keep replying.

Boredom? Wanting someone to send him money for the commissary? Just something to do with his time?

Certainly, there was more to glean about this woman in the rest of her letters, but right now it didn't make any sense, and Margot was too repulsed by what she'd read to give it more time and thought.

She backed out of the Rhonda letters and did some more

general searches to try to find Ed's fan—and with him Shuye's killer—but her mind and focus weren't in it.

Do you believe in demons?

Margot did.

But she believed they were men, not biblical scapegoats.

She'd met enough of them to know the difference.

TWENTY-THREE

When Margot left FBI headquarters and headed to her car, she didn't feel any better about her ongoing case, and felt significantly worse about her recent interactions with Ed and everything she'd learned about him.

They'd solved the murder of a woman who had gone without justice for decades. Tonight, Mei-Ling Fan's family would finally know what had happened to her. That was the sort of thing that should make Margot feel good about what she was doing here.

She felt nothing.

Yes, she was grateful that her presence in that room had helped solve a murder. But Ed wouldn't suffer for what he'd done. He wouldn't even go to trial for it, there would be no point. And Mei-Ling's family still had no body to bury, and likely never would.

These so-called victories didn't feel very victorious.

Margot had become a cop because she had believed—perhaps naively—that it was up to her to put some good back into the world. To bring justice to victims like those her father had killed.

Now she was bringing justice to his *actual* victims, and she didn't feel *anything*.

She sat in her car and stared out the window, looking at the bland grayness of the buildings around her. That was how she felt inside.

"Dammit, Margot, get your shit together." She slammed her palms against her Honda's steering wheel and accidentally bumped the horn. A group of pigeons flew off, clearly incensed, and two men walking by gave her a stern look.

She didn't even bother waving to apologize.

Her options for the rest of the day—somehow it was only two in the afternoon—were to go home and feel sorry for herself or go somewhere else and feel sorry for herself. Since Margot didn't really *go* places, she was at a loss. Home didn't feel that comforting at the moment, especially with the task of going through old photos on her to-do list.

She picked up her phone and stared at it, hoping there might be a text or missed call waiting that would give her guidance.

Finally, she called Wes.

He answered after only two rings. "You get precisely two days a week to yourself, and you can't bear to be without me even that long?"

Margot knew he was teasing, but she didn't have any other friends. And he was right, in a way.

"Well, damn. I was in the area and thought you might want lunch, but I take back my offer."

She was not in the area.

"Hey now. I'm a simple man. If this lunch offer involves any kind of deep-fried starch or abundance of meat, you have my attention."

"Maybe Wise Sons?" she offered. "I could meet you there in twenty in case you have a lingering overnight guest you need to rid yourself of."

Wes scoffed. "As if they would put up with me all morning. Twenty sounds good though, I'll meet you there. Or *meat* you there." He emphasized his homophonic pun, so she'd know how clever he was.

"Gross."

She hung up but was smiling by the time she pulled out from the curb. Wise Sons was somewhere they would order from while working, but she'd never eaten there before. It was a spur-of-the-moment decision to suggest meeting there instead of getting takeout, and Margot felt almost excited by the prospect of doing something against the norm. She couldn't eat Thai delivery every day of her life.

Wes lived near the Castro, something his male colleagues never tired of teasing him about, since it was the preeminent gay neighborhood in the city. Wes couldn't have cared less if he tried about the teasing. His apartment complex was beautiful and well-maintained, and his only complaint about his neighborhood was how loud it was through most of the month of June as Pride overtook the surrounding streets and bars pumped out upbeat dance music well into the night.

Wise Sons sat on a corner, its distinct white-and-black exterior easy to spot, and Margot headed in, hoping the later afternoon hour would mean an open table might be available in the small interior.

There was a table for two in the front window, a position which made her feel brutally ill at ease, but she knew deep down it didn't put her at any more or less risk than anywhere else in the restaurant.

Margot had not long before been witness to the horrific work of a sniper outside a coffee shop, and sitting near the window brought back instant memories of watching people fall dead in the street, their early Christmas shopping littered around them alongside so much broken glass.

She swallowed, shaking off the memory, and set her jacket

on the back of one of the chairs. The restaurant was counter-service only, so she got in line to order just as Wes came through the door.

He was in casual-Wes mode: jeans, a threadbare Giants T-shirt, and a lightweight windbreaker over it all. He looked like a weekend dad, something that appealed to Margot in a way she didn't feel like bringing up with her therapist.

Seeing her jacket at the open table, he left his as well and joined her in line. While he was all smiles, when he spoke there was a softness in his tone. "Hey, how was this morning?"

Ah, so he *did* know why she had called him. Of course, she'd told him about going to visit Ed again, but it never occurred to her that other people paid attention when she told them personal things.

It was unusual, the idea that someone cared enough about her emotional well-being to ask the question.

"We closed a pretty old cold case today." They moved up in line.

Wes nodded, but Margot was grateful to him for not offering congratulations or telling her what a good job she'd done. He seemed to understand without her saying it that she didn't feel *good* about the win they'd had today. They were between two other couples in line, so Margot didn't want to get into the nitty-gritty of her discussion with Ed until they were seated and could pretend at privacy.

Margot ordered the veggie deluxe bagel to Wes's meat-loving horror, and he ordered a Ruben to restore balance in the universe. Wes got his potatoes in fry form, Margot opted for hers as a potato salad. It felt nice, being somewhere and having to make choices from the board, rather than knowing the menu like the back of her hand.

They took their table number card to the front corner and settled in. Wes looked good, different somehow, even though she'd only seen him the day before. Perhaps it was just being out of context. It suited him.

Maybe everyone looked better when they weren't standing next to a dead body.

Wes smiled, and it was the kind of smile that toed a very fine line between friendly concern and pity. She couldn't handle Wes feeling sorry for her. Not after the day she'd had.

"Ed is married," she said, choosing the first topic that came to mind.

Wes stared at her for a moment, then sat back in his chair with a low whistle. "And here I can't even get a second date."

Margot let out an unexpected snort of laughter, before she could stop herself. "Like you *want* a second date."

"No, no, good point. But married. Ed Finch. That's the wildest shit I've heard in a good long time. Wonder how we missed that little tidbit."

"Can't say I was scouring the paper looking for an announcement," Margot said. She looked down at her hands; the napkin in front of her was in thin shreds and she hadn't even realized she was touching it. She set the debris down and folded her hands neatly together, hoping they wouldn't start shaking.

"Do you know anything about her?" Wes asked.

She shook her head. "All I know so far is from one letter she sent him. I don't think she's a very well woman. Mentally."

"And I thought only very sane people married imprisoned serial killers."

"You're hilarious."

They paused as a young woman brought over their lunch plates. Her gaze and smile lingered on Wes a little before she moved on with a quick, "If you guys need anything at all, my name is Gilda."

Gilda seemed like an unusual name for someone in her early twenties, but perhaps her parents were big enthusiasts of top-tier *Saturday Night Live*.

Margot chewed uneasily on her pickle spear, her hunger waning despite how delicious the meal looked. Wes dived into his Ruben like it had been months since his last meal.

"Why would *anyone* want to marry Ed?" she asked, though asking this question of herself on a loop had yet to yield any tangible answers. She didn't expect Wes to know, either, but it felt good letting the question out of her head and into the real world.

Wes shrugged. "It happens more often than we like to think. Sometimes these women believe that the prisoners are innocent, and they are the only ones to see the truth, so if they can show the world how wrong they've been, then they will be the ones to have saved him. Some of them have a twisted spin on the *I can change him* philosophy. Maybe it's the idea that he killed a lot of women, but he would never kill *her*. Maybe it's because they know it's safe. The same way people line up at the zoo to look at a lion. There's only a few bars between you and something that can kill you, and there's a thrill in that. Getting close to danger in the safest way possible." He picked up a fallen bit of sauerkraut and popped it into his mouth while Margot nudged a single caper around her plate.

"You know, Ed was interviewed in the past, right after he was sentenced. And he told them that the reason he killed all those women was because he really wanted to kill my mother, but it would be too obvious it had been him."

A tense silence descended on the table.

She hadn't meant to be such a buzzkill.

"God, this is why I don't tell anyone about this. It's so miserable."

"Margot, shut up. You didn't want to tell me, but you did. You didn't want to let me in, but you did. Now I'm here and you're going to have to deal with the fact that I know, and I care, and your past being a fucked-up little horror show doesn't make *you* an unlovable person unworthy of having friends, OK?"

Margot stared at him across the table, utterly gobsmacked. "Do you have a secret therapy degree I don't know about?"

"No, but I do have a very healthy relationship with my own therapist, thank you. She thinks I have commitment issues."

At this, Margot had to snort. "Mine too."

"No offense, Margot, but fucking *duh*."

She tossed half her pickle at him, watching it bounce off the front of his shirt and onto the diner plate, where she then snatched it back before he could eat it. At least now her appetite was solid enough that she could enjoy the bagel she'd ordered, and she let their conversation lapse into a companionable silence while they ate.

Margot admitted to herself that calling Wes hadn't been a wholly spontaneous instinct. She had brought Wes here for a specific reason, but she didn't feel in any rush to bring it up yet. The truth was, the idea that had been forming since her last visit to Muir Woods was a little risky. Before she brought it up, she wanted to feel normal for a few minutes.

Her version of normal, at least.

When she was finished eating and had licked the veggie cream cheese from her fingers, she skipped past further discussion of Ed and broached the subject.

"I want to release a false lead to the press about the Muir Woods case."

"What was it they were calling him?"

"The Redwood Killer." She grimaced.

"That's actually pretty catchy." He shrugged.

She rolled her eyes at him. "We don't *want* it to be catchy, Wes."

"Paper will do what they're going to do, and you know they *love* giving these guys names."

"Let's reel it back in to my plan, please."

"Sure, you're going to use your little buddy-buddy relationship with Sebastian Klein to plant something in his next article."

When Margot didn't react right away, Wes smirked at her. "What, you thought I didn't know that you've been quietly slipping that guy info for years? Please. He's a good-looking guy, Phalen, he making it worth your while?" A cheeky brow waggle emphasized his already clear meaning.

"Let's just say Sebastian would be much more at home in your neighborhood than mine."

This time only a single brow rose as Wes contemplated this new information. "Interesting."

"But yes, I would be using my connections with Sebastian to put something in the paper. I was at this guy's last kill site and the way he's been dumping them is driving me crazy. He *wants* them found, but not right away. I don't think it's laziness. If he was lazy, he wouldn't have gone to all the trouble of bringing bodies into a protected park. He'd dump them in the Bay."

"Hell, most of our perps just leave them in the street," Wes sighed.

"Exactly. The location matters. Them being found the way they are matters. So, I want to draw this guy out by making him think he left something behind. DNA. I want him to panic, to do something stupid. If we have him on edge, he's more likely to slip up."

Wes chased some ketchup around his plate with an errant fry. "You think the guy will try to give a plausible reason for us having that DNA, and he'll insert himself somehow?"

She was glad he understood her motivation. "Yes. He already wants the attention. I think a little nudge and he'd come right to us. We open a tip line, he'll call it."

Wes wiped his fingers clean. "It's not the worst idea you've ever had."

"I guess I'll take that as a compliment," she said, leaning back and crossing her arms.

"Margot," he said, without breaking eye contact. "When I give you a compliment, you'll know."

TWENTY-FOUR

On Sunday, still off work, Margot made her move with Sebastian. He answered almost too quickly when she called, and while he played it cool as only Sebastian could, he was also clearly glad to hear from her.

"I wasn't expecting to see you bend on this one," he admitted when they were seated across the table from each other at a coffee place Margot had never heard of before. It had been Sebastian's suggestion, and it was just pretentious enough to be right for him.

Margot realized she knew very little about who Sebastian really was, and wondered if she should try harder to be a real friend to him. The connection they had was comfortable and she enjoyed spending time with him.

Sebastian was one of the few people in her life who knew about her history. Well, he was one of the few people in her life, period. It would have been nice to be able to call him a friend, but Margot wasn't sure she'd ever be able to trust him one hundred percent.

What she *could* trust, though, was his commitment to a plan. She'd been feeding him press-safe tidbits for years, and she knew she could rely on him to follow through with this idea of hers.

He wouldn't do it without expecting something in return, though.

"I'm hoping if I give you some information it will help us draw this guy out."

Sebastian had no tape recorder, but he did pull out a small notebook. There was something charmingly old-fashioned about seeing a reporter with a pencil and paper at the ready. "Are you confirming these women were killed by the same person?"

Margot clucked her tongue at him. "I would never say that. What I *can* say is that three women have been found in a localized area outside the city showing similar signs of trauma. The SFPD is *not* considering this a serial predator at this time, but is exploring all avenues of investigation."

"You sound like Yvonne—did she give you that quote?" he asked, referring to the police department's media liaison.

"No, but I've heard her quotes often enough to know how to do her justice."

"The Queen of No Comment."

"She makes us proud."

Sebastian gave a thin-lipped smile and set his notepad down on the table, pausing to take a sip of his coffee. Margot sat back in her chair, holding an iced coffee despite it being February. While she wasn't sure how well she embodied the stereotypes of being bisexual, she could certainly admit to a deep-rooted love for drinking iced coffee even when it was inappropriate for the weather.

"Margot, I think we can agree that our arrangement has worked pretty well for us over the years, wouldn't you say?"

"I think so."

"So, you know I'm not going to say no to this plan. I understand what you're trying to do, and I don't mind playing my part in that. But if you want this guy to believe what I'm writing, you need to give me enough to make it feel real. You can dance around the idea of a serial killer all you want, but we need to be able to put in enough detail that whoever did this reads it and knows you mean business."

"I also need to keep what I know quiet."

"To a degree. Look, I'm not here to get you in trouble. Just give me enough that he knows *you* know something, and we'll see if he takes the bait."

Margot's phone buzzed before she could answer, a text from an unfamiliar number. She looked at the preview. *Hello, Detective Phalen, this is Ewan Willingham...* She held her breath. They were supposed to be meeting tomorrow. Was this little shit going to try to back out of it?

It didn't matter to Margot that his copy of the book had been pristine. Something about the kid put her hair on end, and she hadn't even met him yet.

"Just one second, sorry," she said to Sebastian as she opened the text message.

> Hello Detective Phalen, this is Ewan Willingham. I know we were supposed to meet at the police station tomorrow, but I have to be at activities all evening. Is it possible you could come to the school?

At first Margot was stunned by the kid's audacity. The police wanted to see him to discuss a murder investigation—something his mother had certainly told him—yet he was making them do all the work to come to him. It raised red flags.

But all the same, Margot did know how far the kid had to bus to school each day, and how seriously he took his education. Perhaps she was just looking for a reason to find him guilty before ever actually meeting him, and that was piss-poor police work.

Sure, she had to trust her gut, but even she could admit she had an unfair predisposition toward this kid because he owned Andrew's book.

Hell, maybe the kid wanted to be an FBI agent. The book was as much about Andrew's path to finding Ed as it was about Ed and his crimes. Margot hated to think it, but maybe there was a good reason people didn't work cases that were connected to their family and friends.

She needed to prove to both herself and the captain that she was capable of divorcing herself from her father's legacy and solving this case without blinders on. As hard as that was to do when the murder was so clearly connected to Ed.

But that didn't mean Ewan was guilty.

She texted him back.

> That's fine, would 4 o'clock be OK?

A moment later came the response, as if he'd been waiting.

> Yes, I'll be in the robotics lab, it's in the science building.

He sent a photo with a map of the school, the science building circled in red.

When Margot had gone to high school it had been in a single building—one held together largely by duct tape and the desperate hopes of a broke school board—and she'd thought it was impressive they had a pool. Based on the map Ewan had sent, this high school was basically a mini university campus. No wonder he was willing to make such efforts to do well there.

She set her phone face down on the table and found that Sebastian was watching her carefully.

"You do this thing, and I think you don't know you do it, where your brows get really pinched when you're annoyed about something," he observed.

"Are they doing it now?" she asked pointedly.

Sebastian flipped her the bird and picked up his notebook again. "All right, detective, give me something good."

So, Margot told him the details she and Wes had agreed on the previous day. It was enough to argue plausible deniability with the captain—these were tidbits that Sebastian might be able to glean from interviewing witnesses or others connected to the killings—but the lie buried in with the truth was this:

"We found foreign material under two of the victim's fingernails. Once we have a DNA profile, we feel very confident this will point us in the direction of our killer. Or at least a person of interest who might be able to help the investigation." This, she would need to allow him to quote, though not using her name.

Leon would be furious, but she hoped he would come around the way Wes had. Their killer was the kind of person who would be paying attention to this reporting, and if he could think of a way to insert himself, to explain why his skin might be under the women's fingernails—skin that might not exist—she was hoping he would pop up.

"Then add that anyone with information about these events should contact our precinct. You know the number."

Sebastian finished scribbling his notes. "Yeah, that'll do for a good read. But you're going to owe me something the next time a big case hits, Margot, I hope you realize that."

Margot said nothing, simply took a long drink from her coffee.

As Sebastian rose to leave, she stopped him. "One more thing."

He raised an eyebrow at her.

"Don't you *dare* call this guy the fucking Redwood Killer."

TWENTY-FIVE

Evelyn Yao was looking far too upbeat for someone in her line of work when Margot and Wes arrived at the San Francisco Medical Examiner's office on Monday morning. Wes had, as was his usual routine, brought Margot a coffee, and the fresh brew was still warm in Margot's belly as Evelyn led them to the morgue.

Two women were laid out on metal worktables, and Leon was waiting for them in the room when they arrived.

Margot noted the *Sentinel* tucked under his arm with a wash of uneasy guilt. He didn't catch her eye, but his expression told her he wasn't happy.

Coffee had been a mistake.

Wes, somehow, was still drinking his without a care in the world as Evelyn waved her arms over the two corpses before her.

"You've certainly presented me with an interesting week of work, kids." She looked directly at Leon when saying *kids*, and Margot wasn't sure if this was her way of flirting with the eldest detective in the room, or just taking a jab at his age. With Evelyn it could have been either.

She guided them first to the Muir Woods Jane Doe—likely so Leon wouldn't have to stay for Shuye's report if he didn't want to—and picked up a metal clipboard from the base of the table.

Their victim was nude and exceptionally pale. Her chest cavity had been closed back up after Evelyn's autopsy, but the garish red lines forming a large Y across her upper body were still present. With her body cleaned, Margot could make out all the individual stab wounds that decorated the woman's upper body, and a few in her groin area.

Margot made a mental note because their killer hadn't done that with the previous two victims, and it was a significant change of his MO. She wanted to ask Evelyn to start there but wouldn't dare tell the chief medical examiner how to run her autopsy review.

"We got lucky with an ID on this one, dental records were a hit, they came through about an hour ago." She flipped through the chart looking for something, and her face flashed with obvious annoyance when she couldn't find it. She strode purposefully to an intercom located next to the double doors and soon a staticky "What can I get you, Ev?" came through the speaker.

"I need the forms we just got submitted for our Jane Doe."

A minute later a tall woman with white-blond hair pushed back behind her ears came into the room and handed Evelyn a folder. The woman was familiar to Margot, someone she had seen at crime scenes from time to time, who Margot thought had worked with CSI but evidently was on Evelyn's team now. That wasn't surprising—people who worked in one field often had the existing education and skillset to change positions.

"Thank you, Roxy," Evelyn said, barely glancing at the woman as she opened the folder.

Roxy looked over at the detectives and gave them a warm smile and nodded goodbye before leaving the room. Margot felt as if the smile had lingered on her slightly, but perhaps that was wishful thinking, considering she was standing beside Wes.

Evelyn continued, oblivious. "Her name is Frederica Mercado. Date of birth was September 15, 1986. Her dentist, at least, is from Palm Springs."

"Three for three on them not being local," Wes said.

"Not *born* local," Margot corrected. "Rebecca Watson lived in Sausalito. Leanne had an apartment locally. So, they're not from here *originally*. We'll have to see if she had a local address." There was only so much the ME could do for them, the rest was going to be good old-fashioned police work.

Leon was already on his phone, texting furiously. Margot assumed he was getting someone back at the station to start pulling as much information on Frederica as possible before they got back, giving them at least a slight head start on the waiting process.

Evelyn stood at the head of the table and tucked the clipboard under her arm like she no longer needed it. "Our victim was assaulted prior to her murder. She had signs of initial bruising on her hands and forearms, as well as defensive wounds that show she attempted to block a knife attack by covering her face and head with her arms. There were signs of trauma to her shins and knees." Evelyn indicated dark patches on the victim's lower legs. They looked more red than purple, but considering the woman had died before the bruises could properly form, Margot supposed that wasn't unexpected.

Evelyn pointed out that on one of her shins was a deep-set bump that looked unnatural. "We can't be certain, but this was caused either by the victim running or tripping into a hard object, perhaps while running away, or she was hit by a blunt object. Based on the size and shape of the fracture of her bone, if it was a trip, she might have hit something like a trailer hitch, and if it was blunt force, a metal baseball bat would be most likely. Either way, this would have severely incapacitated her. She sustained eighteen stab wounds to her chest and breasts, and another six to her pubis and the area immediately surrounding her genitals. There were signs consistent with assault, and while we did collect a rape kit, I didn't see any foreign material." She shook her head. "Based on what we can see, the wounds to her chest were received when she was fully clothed, but the wounds to her genitalia were done while she was unclothed, and her assailant re-dressed her afterwards."

"What about the material under her fingernails?" Margot asked hopefully. She'd lied to the press about it being DNA, but she desperately wanted it to be true.

Evelyn gave her a pitying smile. "Mostly dirt. A few of her nails were broken so we think there might be some of her own blood in there as well. She was probably trying to crawl away on the ground at some point. We've sent that all off for testing, but it will be a while before we get anything valuable."

"We'll have the CSI team see if they can lift any prints off her clothes, since he re-dressed her, but I'm not holding my breath," Leon said, continuing to type into his phone.

"What's that?" Margot asked, moving toward the body, and leaning in close to the woman's shoulder. On the side of the woman's upper torso, below the curve of her breast, there was a small mark that was almost too minuscule to be considered a tattoo.

Margot got out her phone and looked at Evelyn. "Do you mind?"

Evelyn shook her head. "Go for it. We noted it as a tattoo, but it might also be a discolored birthmark."

Margot took a quick photo of the marking, then opened the photos so she could zoom in on it. She came back to Leon and Wes and showed it to them. "I think it's a small bird, maybe?" she said.

The marking nagged at her. It felt like a symbol she should be aware of, a band's logo, or a well-known brand perhaps. It wasn't ringing any bells, though, which frustrated her.

"Did any of the other victims have tattoos?" she asked, trying to remember if this had come up.

"Rebecca had one on her ankle that had been laser-removed. But I don't recall any others. Leanne had none, if I'm remembering correctly," Leon answered. "We can dig through the old autopsy photos, maybe see if we missed something similar on anyone else."

Margot doubted there was anything to the marking. Probably a lost bet, or someone wanting to try getting a tattoo and chickening out on something bigger. Most tattoos were meaningless unless they proved the victim was involved in the drug trade in some capacity.

Or helped identify bodies when there was nothing else to go on.

"Wonder if any local tattoo shops would remember giving the smallest tattoo in the world," Wes pondered.

"We can keep that wild goose chase on the backburner for now," Margot said, slipping her phone back into her pocket.

"Are we ready to finish?" Evelyn asked.

The three detectives fell into a hush, chastised for interrupting.

"Cause of death was exsanguination due to multiple stab wounds. I think it goes without saying that this is officially classified as a homicide."

They all knew that already, but official was official.

"Any questions about Frederica before we move on?"

While all three of them were working the case, it was Leon who shook his head in response. "No. I'll let you know if I have any follow-ups after I read the full report. Thanks, Evelyn."

Leon gave Wes and Margot a quick nod, but where Margot

was uncertain about Roxy's lingering gaze, she was *not* confused about the long stare Leon gave her before leaving.

It wasn't anger, exactly, but he was not pleased. She knew she'd need to do some serious groveling before this day was done in order to get back in Leon's good graces.

But before she could do that, Shuye Zhou was waiting for them.

TWENTY-SIX

Oakland, CA

Fall was usually one of Eddie's favorite times of year. He liked going back to school, not because he got any enjoyment out of his classes, except perhaps gym, but because it meant full days away from Mama.

Sarah used to go to the same school as him, giving him one reliable face in the crowd, but she was in high school now, meaning he was by himself at a school where no one seemed interested in becoming his friend.

That didn't bother Eddie too much. But it did mean he spent an awful lot of time alone with his thoughts at school. Teachers rarely called on him, and when they did, he got the feeling they weren't expecting much from him. Eddie didn't excel at school. He was smart enough to do well, he *knew* the answers they were looking for, but for some reason he could never bring himself to give them what they were after.

It felt too much like letting them win.

So, he'd tell them the wrong answers. Or say he didn't know. And he'd do just well enough on his tests to get by. He remembered more than once on a report card that a teacher would bemoan Eddie's ability to do well on all his tests but poorly in his classwork. Another had suggested, less politely, that Eddie might be special needs and Mama should take him to a shrink.

She had been so mad at the teacher that she'd slapped Eddie around for a good ten minutes straight that night since she couldn't put her anger where she really wanted to.

This year, though, Eddie wasn't happy for the return of fall. Fall meant escape, certainly, but it also meant cooler weather, even in California. Windows were closed at night, curtains drawn earlier as the light faded in the early hours of the evening.

Eddie was miserable.

He kicked a pebble down the street, taking his time, moving so slow he was practically standing still. A piece of paper skittered by his feet, a sun-faded flyer that had been all over the neighborhoods that summer. *Missing Cat—Dandelion* with his neighbor's phone number on it.

He picked up the paper, a little pit of something unnamable forming in his stomach, then crumpled it up and threw it away. Stupid cat.

Wasn't *his* fault the thing got left out at night.

Bad things happen sometimes.

He stuffed his hands in his pockets and shuffled along. The chilly September air was warring with his desire to take as long as possible getting home. Tonight was a bath night, and Eddie really didn't want to deal with Mama, especially if she was in one of her moods.

Rain started to fall, slowly at first, fat drops landing here and there on the sidewalk. But soon they fell in a steady rhythm, turning the concrete a darker shade, and making the dead leaves underfoot slippery to walk on. Eddie tightened his jacket around him and hunched in on himself as he finally relented to the weather and started to make haste.

When he approached his house, there was a moving truck out front.

For one solitary, beautiful moment he wondered if someone was coming to collect him and Sarah. Loading up all their furniture and toys and taking them to start a new life, perhaps with their dad. He knew deep down that this couldn't be true, because Mama had told them time and time again how useless their father was, and how he wanted nothing to do with them.

But Eddie couldn't help it. He jogged down the sidewalk the rest of the way, wondering what his long-forgotten father might look like. Would they have the same color hair? Would he stoop down and call Eddie *son*?

As soon as he was within a few feet of their doorstep, the sick realization sank in. Movers were taking all of Miss Shirley's things out and loading them into the back of the truck. Miss Shirley herself lingered nearby, watching them, a cigarette tracing a constant path to and from her mouth as she dusted ash mindlessly onto the sidewalk.

There was something hollow about her, a deep sadness visible just by looking at her face, that hadn't been there when Eddie had first met her. He paused on the front step of his own house, watching her as she seemed to watch nothing at all.

Finally, he said, "Miss Shirley, you're getting all wet."

She didn't look at him, but down at her own shirt, which was sticking to her skin, wet through from the rain. "Yes, I suppose I am." She puffed her cigarette again, making no move to go into the house where she would be dry. Her gaze never moved in his direction.

A pair of men came out carrying an old dresser, the mirror on the back wrapped carefully in a blanket. They loaded it into the truck and returned to the house. The whole time Eddie wasn't sure Miss Shirley had even seen them.

"Are you moving?" he asked, which was as stupid a question

as he could have come up with, and he felt immediately foolish for having said it.

"Yeah, Eddie. I'm moving." She flicked the spent cigarette onto the sidewalk, grinding it under the toe of her shoe.

Now it seemed as if she actually might go inside, and Eddie's pulse kicked up with the unexpected need to stop her.

"I'm sorry you lost your cat, Miss Shirley."

Now she looked at him.

And when she did, her gaze cut through him like a knife, with the ferocity of its loathing. There was no mistaking that the only thing she felt looking at him was hatred.

"Are you, Eddie?" she asked, her voice hitching as she said his name. "I really don't think you are."

And with that, she went into the house.

TWENTY-SEVEN

Evelyn waited until Leon was gone before she picked up a clipboard identical to the one from Frederica's gurney, gave it a quick once-over, and then began her well-practiced routine.

"Here we have Mrs. Shuye Zhou, age eighty-five. Mrs. Zhou was, it's worth mentioning, battling stage four breast cancer, and had she not been so brutally murdered, she likely would have died within the year."

Margot wasn't sure if this made her feel better or worse. She already felt awful about what had happened to this woman, but somehow knowing she was *still* going to die was just a bonus bit of universal unfairness.

"Mrs. Zhou actually died when her trachea got nicked; one of her stab wounds. She suffocated. Which may have been a small mercy, as it means many of the wounds likely happened after she was already unconscious or dead. She was stabbed twenty-two times, primarily to the chest and head, including a wound over her ear that penetrated her skull. There were a few attempts to get that one right, based on superficial cuts to her scalp."

Margot barely heard what Evelyn said after she announced

the number of stab wounds. She'd been right. This *was* someone's homage to Ed Finch's first kill. No, they hadn't gone out to pick up a teenage hitchhiker, but all signs were pointing to a copycat, nevertheless.

Evelyn was still talking when Margot's focus came back to the present moment. Wes was standing between them, focusing hard on something Evelyn was pointing to. "Based on the bruising and the angles of the cuts we believe she received before she was pushed onto the bed, I think you're looking at a killer who is on the smaller side. Medium build, medium height. They had to stab her several times before she went down, and this laceration on her hand suggests that at one point she might have actually grabbed the killer's knife." She lifted Shuye's right hand to show an ugly-looking cut, so deep it had almost severed her thumb.

"In your opinion, was this done by someone who knew what they were doing?" Margot asked.

Evelyn shook her head. "Sloppy attack. Lots of the stab wounds were glancing, some even showed signs of hesitation. Others were a lot more intense, confident. I imagine once he got going, he got more involved in what he was doing. But no, those initial, uncertain wounds tell me this was someone who had probably never killed anyone before. Unlike her." Evelyn glanced over to Frederica. "Whoever killed her knew exactly what they were doing."

When Margot and Wes got back to street level, the weather had shifted to match their moods. It was overcast, and rain was starting to patter down on the sidewalk. A few people hustled by, obviously in a hurry to get to whatever their next destination was, and oblivious to Margot and Wes as anything other than obstacles on the sidewalk.

They got into Wes's car, where Margot had left her half-finished coffee, and she picked it up, to give herself something to do with her hands.

"It's a copycat," she said finally. "Like I thought."

Wes sat in the driver's seat, watching her. "I am willing to go with that theory, but I guess my question is, are you going to be OK continuing with this?" He picked his words carefully, but all the same, Margot felt them like a slap.

She gave him a quick, unfriendly look, even though she knew he was coming from a place of concern and not judgment. He raised his hands in mock surrender. "Hey, I was only asking."

Her coffee had gone cold while they were inside, but it was criminal to waste a half cup of Philtered Soul from Philz, so she sipped it anyway. "I know. I'm sorry, but it's a sensitive spot with me. And I think I can manage to separate the two."

She could understand his hesitancy though, because even she didn't fully believe the words she was saying. How could she really shut off the part of her brain that knew this was connected to her own father? It didn't matter how she felt about Ed himself, it was what he'd *done* that she could never escape.

The man himself was almost irrelevant.

This wouldn't even be the first instance of someone following Ed's playbook. He'd had a handful of would-be copycats over the years. This was one more unhinged superfan trying to live up to the legend of the worst hero imaginable.

"I'll be fine," she said, this time more firmly, making herself believe it as much as Wes. "This guy isn't smart. Even Ed wasn't that smart. We need to figure out where he slipped up. Leaving the page behind was intentional, but he's new to this, I'm sure it was his first kill, and he doesn't have Mother Nature working on his side like Ed did with Laura Welsh. He left us something, we just need to find out what it is." There had to be physical evidence somewhere. A fingerprint, a bit of the killer's blood, something to pin him to the place.

Wes pulled out of the parking spot and into light afternoon traffic, his windshield wipers working methodically in a rhythmic *swoop-swoop*. "If this was his first and he was trying to mimic Ed, I wonder if we ought to look into classified ads."

"See if Shuye placed a personal ad, you mean?" Margot gave him a look that said she wasn't buying it.

Wes shook his head. "No, not that. But maybe she placed an ad for in-home assistance. If she had stage four cancer, I bet she needed help with things like taking out the garbage or hauling groceries up the stairs. Things she might have been willing to pay someone to do. Or there's a chance the killer was the one to place the ad, maybe offering services to seniors."

"That would be very Ed," Margot mused, without realizing she'd said it out loud.

Wes paused, his expression unreadable, but if he was judging her for saying it, he didn't tell her so. "If this was a planned kill, which I think we can agree it was, he was looking for an easy first victim."

"Have we heard anything new from her family yet?" They had asked Shuye's children if there had been anyone new in her life, but they hadn't been mentally in a position to answer their questions at the time.

Wes let out a sigh, scratching at the faint stubble on his cheek. "Not since we initially spoke with them. I know some local officers had been over to break the news in person before we talked to them. They live in Colorado and I imagine they'll be coming here soon, but they haven't called me back yet."

Margot nodded. Often in cases of homicide the family went into a state of shock before they switched modes to the rally-for-justice drive that most people expected immediately. A period of quiet was not unusual.

She had seen instances where loved ones continued to work and attend to their regular affairs for days after a murder because they simply couldn't allow themselves to believe what had happened. Eventually Shuye's family would switch gears, and then they'd be a constant nuisance, as they rightly should be.

"Well, we can ask them if they know anything about a classified ad. Meanwhile, we can go back through issues of the local papers online, see if anything stands out. Check her bank records to see if she paid for something like that."

"We can ask Marie at the apartment if they had a community board, or maybe an apartment Facebook group."

They parked near the police station and got out in the rain, jogging the short distance back to the front door.

Margot had been so caught up in discussing Shuye's murder that she'd all but forgotten the look Leon had given her before he left the morgue.

She didn't forget for long, because when they went inside she found him standing in her and Wes's office, still holding the morning's edition of the *Sentinel*.

Leon didn't even wait for her to set down her bag before he launched into a speech he had very likely been practicing in his head all morning.

"*A source within the department has confirmed that while they are not willing to classify these as connected cases yet, two of the victims had foreign DNA on them that the police are hoping will point to a killer or killers. Anyone with information,* blah blah blah. I'm sure you know what the rest says, considering it came from you." Leon tossed the paper on her desk, looking as mad as she'd ever seen him.

It wasn't a brimming, explosive rage. It was quieter, which made it all the more menacing. She'd known she would be stepping on some toes by going to Sebastian, but she had hoped Leon of all people might look past the words on the page to see what her intentions had been.

"Leon, if you'll just let me explain—"

"Explain that you did this without asking? That you put our entire case in jeopardy?"

"Hey, that's not what she was doing," Wes interjected. "She discussed this idea with me ahead of time and I agreed."

"Oh, isn't that lovely? That the two of you idiots put your heads together hoping it would form a single brain." Leon was pacing the small space between their desks. Margot hazarded a quick glance at Wes, who looked about as guilty as she felt. "Neither of you thought at any time it might be a good idea to loop in the lead fucking detective on the case?"

"Well, you would have said no," Margot grumbled, feeling like an insolent child who refused to believe she'd done anything wrong, but knowing deep down she had.

"Obviously I would have said *no*," Leon said. He scrubbed his hands over his face, his usually tidy beard looking as if it hadn't been trimmed in several days, and deep bags until his eyes suggesting it had been some time since he had slept. He picked up a folder he must have placed down earlier and thrust it at her. "You're just lucky this stupid fucking idea might be working."

Margot opened the folder and there were several printed reports from the precinct's main hotline. About ten papers filled the folder, which wasn't many by hotline standards, but as she paged through them, one in particular caught her eye.

My ex-girlfriend, Freddie, and I got into a little bit of an argument last week and I'm concerned that you might have my DNA mixed in with the killer's…

Margot stared at the page, then looked up at Leon.

"Leon, we never released Federica's name. We didn't even know it until an hour ago."

He still looked pissed, but there was something else there, too. A little glimmer of victory.

"Why do you think I'm still standing here, kid?"

TWENTY-EIGHT

The phone number connected to the message belonged to a thirty-eight-year-old firefighter named Langston White, which was just about the most pretentious name Margot had heard in a good long while. That was a name destined for membership at a racist country club.

Wes had stayed back at the station, promising to get a head start on their classified research before meeting her at Ewan's school that afternoon.

Margot and Leon endured a painfully quiet drive together to the fire hall where Langston worked. Usually, Leon would be listening to a historical romance audiobook. He was on a Julia Quinn kick and had been going through a lengthy series about the romantic lives of one upper-crust family with a billion siblings. Not today. Margot supposed it was his way of punishing her, to not give her any kind of distraction from the awkward silence.

It was working.

"I'm sorry," she said finally, when it felt as if her skin might crawl off her body from the unbearable tension between them. "I thought I was doing the right thing."

He remained quiet for a moment, but when he spoke the former anger was gone. He was back to being Leon again, steady and warm. "You need to remember one thing, Margot. I'm not your enemy here. I know you've spent a lot of your life resisting help, and I understand that. But I'm not here to present more problems for you to solve. I know why you did what you did. I just don't like *how* you did it. I think we could have found a different way—maybe a more official way—to do this."

Margot sank low in her seat, staring out the window. He was being incredibly fair, but she also felt her guard go up every time someone who felt like a substitute father figure in her life was mad at her. She should probably unpack that with Dr. Singh one of these days.

"I'm sorry," she said again, because excuses or *but* replies would be useless to her here. Leon had said his piece, and having the final word would only make her look ridiculous.

"I know, kid. And I'm sorry I was an asshole about it. I haven't been home in two days, I'm a grouchy prick right now. I'm not saying it excuses what you did, but it also doesn't excuse how I acted. Sometimes I get pissed about things and it just simmers, but ultimately goes away. Today we weren't so lucky."

Margot wanted to ask him why he hadn't been home, but she assumed it had to do with the case and not any issues he was having with his wife. She also didn't want to overstep by dipping her toe into a potentially personal conversation.

They parked in front of the fire hall, and she was saved from having to navigate the conversation any further. She felt better —or at least as better as she could feel—and she needed to leave her own bullshit in Leon's car and not take it into their questioning. Langston White was the closest thing they'd had to a good lead on the case, and she wouldn't disrupt that because she felt guilty.

It was still raining, worse than before, as they made their

way inside. The fire hall smelled of cleaning solution and what Margot assumed must be a chili lunch. The main doors led into a small alcove, where there was a staircase going up—presumably to where the firefighters ate and slept—and another door entered into the main garage area where the trucks were located.

Margot pushed open the door to the garage. The space was quiet, making her boots echo as she crossed the concrete floor. There were three trucks total, and she'd noticed a pickup parked out front that had lights and logos on it, a supervisor vehicle.

As she approached the first truck a large man appeared from behind it, wiping his hands on a towel. He didn't look upset to see them in his space so much as he was clearly confused by their presence.

"Can I help you folks with something?" He was in his station wear, a navy-blue set with a short-sleeved button-down shirt. There was a badge over one breast pocket and a nametag over the other.

White.

"Are you Langston White?" Margot asked as she pushed open her jacket to reveal the badge clipped to her belt.

Langston's eyes followed the gesture and he looked at her carefully, then over to Leon, who was lingering a few steps behind.

Langston White was a massive man, someone Margot never would have let herself be alone with in a dark alley. He was pushing six-foot-six, and his muscular frame put him at about two-seventy, she'd bet.

He was handsome, in a too-conventional way that did nothing for her. His features were symmetrical, dark hair and eyes, probably used to being able to pick up any woman he was interested in.

As he tossed the towel over his shoulder, Margot noticed

angry red scratch marks on his forearm. He quickly crossed his arms over his chest to hide them.

"You guys are from the police, then. That was fast."

"Do you have somewhere we can talk, or would you like to come back to the station with us?" Margot asked.

"Are you arresting me?" Langston asked.

"Is there a reason I should?" She narrowed her eyes at him, waiting to see how he'd respond. He scratched the back of his neck, looking down at the floor.

"Guess you guys have some stuff you want to know about Freddie."

She had a *lot* of things she wanted to know.

"Are you comfortable talking here?" Leon asked.

"Yeah, yeah. Everyone's upstairs having lunch, it's fine."

"Why aren't you with them?" Margot asked.

Langston shrugged. "I'm vegan. They forget that all the time. I brought a sandwich, already ate it."

For some reason this sentiment made Margot hate the man. It wasn't the vegan thing, it was the weird way he victimized himself.

That and the strong likelihood he might be a serial killer.

"Mr. White—" Leon began, but was cut off.

"Oh, you can call me Lang, that's cool." He guided them over to a small card table surrounded by folding chairs. There was a copy of the day's *Sentinel* and some magazines on top, plus the crumpled wax paper that must have once been wrapped around Langston's sandwich.

Margot and Leon took the offered chairs, which weren't nearly as uncomfortable as they appeared at first glance. Langston sat across from them, his bulky frame looking utterly absurd in the small chair.

"I know this has got to look sus as hell to you guys." He leaned back, and while Margot was inclined to bring out her biggest question—how he'd known their Jane Doe was Frederica—she decided to see how deep he would dig his own grave first.

"You're the one who called us, Lang. Why don't you start with that?"

"I saw in the paper—that whole thing with the murders up at the park, and how you guys had DNA profiles for the killer, or you know, for someone—and I thought, well damn, that would suck to get arrested for murder just because you might have had a little scrap with someone and then they died? Y'know?"

"A tragedy," Margot said, her tone deadpan.

"And Freddie and I, we got into a really ugly fight before she left me." This time he held up his forearm, showing the scratches. "And I know, guys, I know that looks bad, but I promise it was just one of those things."

"One of those things?" Leon asked.

"Well, sure, you know. Your girl gets all wound up, throwing stuff around, calling you all sorts of names. And then she tried to leave, but, guys, she'd been drinking, and it didn't feel right letting her go off like that, right? So, I grabbed her. I admit that. I was just trying to make sure she didn't get herself into any trouble. And she started screaming at me, telling me I couldn't keep her against her will. Scratched the shit out of me. Maybe it makes me a bad person, but I let her go after that."

"Mr. White, when did you learn Frederica Mercado was dead?" Leon asked, watching the man carefully.

"I mean, this morning? In the paper." He tapped the paper, proving its existence to them.

"And your first thought, upon learning your girlfriend was dead, was to call the police to establish an alibi for yourself?" Margot asked.

Langston shifted in his seat and the metal chair groaned in protest. "It's not like that."

"What is it like?"

"Well, for starters, Freddie was my ex, y'know? I mean, we'd still fool around sometimes, but we just weren't good together as a couple. Personality wise. Sex was great, though." He seemed to realize then who he was speaking to and had the common decency to blush.

"When was the last time you and Frederica were intimate?" Leon opened his notebook.

"That night, the night she scratched me. We got in a fight after because she found out I'd been seeing some other girls, and she was pissed."

"That sounds like girlfriend behavior," said Margot. "Not *ex*-girlfriend behavior."

"What can I say? Bitches be crazy sometimes." His gaze cut to Margot. "Sorry."

"I'm not dating you," she replied coldly.

"Anyway, she was pissed, said she was done with me. Scratched me and left. I didn't hear from her again after that, and assumed she was ghosting me. But then I got the paper today and it was like *oh shit*."

Oh shit, but not tears, no emotion, just looking for a way to evade blame.

"What was Frederica wearing when she left your house that night?"

"Uh, yoga pants, ones with the elastic on the back. Guess a sweatshirt or something? Red underwear. That I remember." He tapped the side of his head as if to boast about it being a steel trap where underwear color was concerned.

Every time this man spoke, Margot felt her attraction toward men in general dull slightly.

The problem was, the more he talked the less she believed that Langston was some kind of criminal mastermind capable of committing three murders without getting caught. Of course, the dumb jock thing could be an act to throw them off, but as they sat across the table from him, Margot's confidence in a pending arrest faded, and the disappointing knowledge that this case would continue to plague them sank in.

"When did you and Frederica break up?" she asked. "Officially."

"Like from dating? I guess about four months ago."

"And how long were you together?"

"Maybe six months?"

Leon was scribbling this down, but Margot could sense his attitude flagging as well.

It was time to see what Langston did with their ace, then.

"Langston, you said that you discovered Frederica's death this morning in the paper, is that correct?"

"Mmhmm." He nodded, not missing a beat. Maybe he had convinced himself so thoroughly of his lie that he believed it to be true.

Margot pulled the *Sentinel* off the table and opened it to the inner second page, where the story had been relegated. Sebastian was likely pissed about being bumped from the front pages, but unfortunately a fresh presidential scandal was taking up space on the first two pages, so a would-be serial killer didn't quite make the cut.

Laying the article flat in front of him, she said, "Show me where."

Langston's jaw ticked, and suddenly the jovial, inviting expression on his face shifted into something cold and stony. He didn't even bother looking at the paper, just stared across the table right at Margot. She met his gaze unflinchingly, and he was ultimately the one who looked away first.

"I think I'd like to call my lawyer."

"Yeah, you do that, kid," Leon said, snapping his notebook shut. "And why don't you go ahead and tell him to meet us down at the station while you're at it?"

TWENTY-NINE

Margot had to make a choice.

She could either stay at the station with Leon and wait for Langston White's lawyer to arrive, or she could head over to Lowell High to meet Wes and do their long-awaited chat with Ewan Willingham.

Considering they had no idea how long it would take for the lawyer to arrive, and whether he would give them a chance to speak to Langston at all, Margot opted for the latter. After Leon had returned them to the station—with Langston promising to appear shortly, on threat of being physically detained—Margot grabbed her own car and headed to the school to meet Wes.

The afternoon traffic was thick and annoyingly slow, making her grateful she had some extra time to get there. Margot hated being late, it made her feel unreliable.

She found parking in a visitor section of the school's parking lot that was unfortunately about as far from the science building as was humanly possible to be. The school was massive. She'd driven by it in the past, but never bothered to pay much attention to it. Now that she was looking, it felt astonishing that this was a public high school.

There had to be thousands of students in attendance with a school that big. Would people even know everyone else in their graduating class? To Margot, it was imposing, and impractically large. Did teachers even remember all of their students' names in a place like this?

Margot had her doubts.

It was certainly a place where one troubled student might escape notice.

She walked briskly across the campus, with plenty of teens still milling about and a group of runners gathered on the nearby track laughing boisterously and doing some kind of made-up dance routine while other members of the group completed their laps.

The rain from earlier that day had broken, and while the sky was still a moody shade of gray, threatening more rain soon, several kids were parked on a big green lawn, sitting on their jackets, and reading or doing homework. Margot was surprised to see so many of them lingering after school, but she also understood the desire to be anywhere but at home.

Even before she knew who her father really was, there were days she'd stay at the library near their house until it closed rather than going home.

She stopped a passing boy wearing a Lowell High School Math Club T-shirt, and asked him which way to the science building. He pointed over his shoulder to a squat brick building not far away. "Are you Benny's mom?" he asked, giving her a careful once-over.

Margot stared at him, wondering how it was possible that she could be mistaken for the mother of a teen, before remembering that at almost forty she *could* be the mother of a teen. She was too horrified to process that information.

"No," she said, since he seemed to require some kind of feedback.

"Heard Benny's mom was hot, that's all. Same hair." He

pointed to his own head. "I mean as Benny. Cause he's a little ginger fuck." The kid shrugged, apparently not afraid to badmouth his classmate now that he knew Margot wasn't a relative.

"Um, thanks."

"Yeah, no problem." He walked away and his too-long arms and legs seemed to work against him as he moved. Maybe someday he'd turn into a real person whose body fit them, but today was not his day.

The science building was eerily quiet compared to the shouting and music that filled the air outside. Wes was leaning against a wall inside the door, looking at his phone. When she entered, he looked up and smiled, making her knees go a little rubbery before she told them to smarten up.

"I have been asked *three times* whose 'hot dad' I am, Margot."

"That's gross, Wesley."

"I don't disagree, but it's nice to know I'm DILF material."

"Gotta be a dad to be a DILF."

"Well, you never know, I guess. Could be a little Wes Jr or Weslina out there."

"Perish the thought that your gene pool was ever accidentally expanded."

"Bet if you stick around long enough someone will call you a hot mom, if you're jealous."

"I am not jealous, and someone already did. We need to get out of this place as soon as humanly possible." They climbed up a short set of stairs. "Also, why on earth did you come up with *Weslina* when *Wesleyan* is right there?"

"You think my daughter could be a baby ivy? That's very sweet of you."

The sound of voices from down one of the halls—enthusiastic shouts and whoops—drew their attention. Following the sounds, they made their way to a large classroom, where the wheeled worktables had been pushed against the walls, creating an open area in the center where two robots were currently in the process of beating the bejesus out of each other.

A group of six boys and one lone girl were surrounding the robots in a circle and eagerly shouting things at each other, and inexplicably also at the robots. Margot and Wes watched as one of the bots who seemed to have a hammer attached to its arm began to repeatedly wallop the one that looked like an augmented Roomba. It was fascinating in a sort of barbaric way.

Margot knocked on the open door just as the Roomba took Hammer Arm out at the legs, knocking the larger robot over.

"Aw, I *told* you the arm made him too top heavy. Now we need to reconfigure his legs again," said a boy with bright red hair that Margot assumed might be her so-called son Benny.

The crew of teens all looked to the door, finally taking in the presence of Margot and Wes, but none of them looked the least bit interested, aside from the annoyance of the interruption.

"We have the room booked until five," the girl said, an air of command in her tone that would have been impressive in someone so young if Margot wasn't presently irritated by it.

"We're looking for Ewan Willingham," Margot said. She didn't *want* to flash her badge and create unnecessary speculation around the kid unless she absolutely had to. She remembered the brutality of her high school life right after Ed was arrested and before they changed their names and moved across the country. Rumors frothed up hot and heavy and kids were so cruel to her she had to leave school and take her classes and exams remotely simply to finish the year.

She'd never gone back to school after that.

She wasn't going to put a target on Ewan until she knew with absolute certainty that he was involved in this. Teenagers were too nasty to give them ammunition.

"That's me." A boy had just come in through the second door at the far end of the room. He was well dressed, a nice polo shirt tucked into clean jeans, a pair of leather sneakers that were likely off-brand ones he found in Chinatown but looked convincing enough. His blond hair was gelled back off his face and Margot could see a striking resemblance to his mother in his eyes and mouth. He was a decent-looking kid, probably able to navigate high school without all the miseries faced by his robot club colleagues, who looked like they might be planning to mount a 2018 revival of *Weird Science*.

"Is there somewhere we could have a quick word?" Wes asked, pretending the other kids didn't exist.

The kids, however, were *not* interested in letting Ewan wander off with the detectives. "Ewan, do you know these people?" the girl asked, evidently their spokesperson.

"Yeah, it's cool, Nora, I'll be right back."

Ewan waved them back out into the hall where he walked in the direction of a small open sitting area that was likely a popular place to eat lunch or spend time between classes. Right now, it was empty, so Ewan took a seat on one of the low pleather chairs and Margot and Wes uncomfortably shared an ottoman across from him.

"I know you searched my room," Ewan said to them. "Thought you guys needed a warrant or something for that."

"Not if we've been given permission by a homeowner," Wes replied. "And we didn't search your room. We looked at one bookshelf."

Margot didn't think Wes needed to defend their actions to a teenager, but she let him have his say.

"Hey, man, chill. I was just saying it, I don't really care." There was something about how he spoke and carried himself that made Margot certain he cared very much. He was a meticulous person, and she was willing to bet the idea of having strangers in his space bothered him a great deal.

"Ewan, how well did you know your neighbor, Shuye Zhou?"

"Susie? I dunno, I guess I knew her to say hi to her. Sometimes I'd help her bring her groceries upstairs, or her laundry down to the machines in the basement. Stuff like that. Sometimes if she wasn't feeling well, she would ask me to go grab her something at the market."

"Sounds like you were a good neighbor," Margot said, shifting her tone and approach to something warmer. She realized she was taking skills she'd learned from sitting across the table from Ed and applying them to the kid. If he *was* their killer, she'd treat him like her hero and manipulate the shit out of him to get what she wanted.

"Yeah, I was." He seemed to catch his own hubris. "But I mean, anyone would have done it, she was a nice old lady. She brought us food she made a lot. I think she was really used to cooking for her family, always made too much for one person. And she was a *really* good cook."

"So, in helping her with chores and getting groceries, you had been inside her apartment, right?"

He shrugged. "A few times."

"And do you remember hearing anything the morning she died?"

Ewan stared at them, scratching non-existent stubble on his chin. "What time did she die?" he asked.

Smart kid. Smarter than the last suspect she'd spoken to, that was for damn sure.

"Estimates suggest probably between two and six in the morning."

"I'm a pretty heavy sleeper. I didn't hear anything until my alarm went off."

This was the opposite of what his mother had told them. An interesting lie. "You didn't hear your mom come in?"

"I almost never hear her come in unless I'm already awake."

"When was the last time you helped Mrs. Zhou in her apartment?"

Ewan raised an eyebrow at them. "Did you guys find my fingerprints in there, or something, is that why you're asking?"

"Well, we *will* want to get a copy of your prints. Just to rule them out against any others we've found, because it's likely they're all over the place in there." Margot watched him for any kind of response to this.

"In the kitchen and bathroom maybe." Again, he shrugged like none of this mattered. "I guess I've helped with her laundry and stuff, too."

"So, it wouldn't be out of the question for us to have found your prints in her bedroom, perhaps?" Wes asked.

"Maybe. I guess."

"Back to my question, though," Margot redirected. "When was the last time you were in her apartment?"

"She asked me to run down to one of the Chinese souvenir shops on Grant the day before she died. She wanted some of those red envelopes for Lunar New Year, but she wasn't feeling well."

"Were you aware that Mrs. Zhou was ill?" Wes asked.

Ewan nodded. "Yeah, she told me and Mom about it one day in the hallway. I think she did because she knows Mom is a hospice nurse and would probably keep an eye out for her, just in case something went wrong. And maybe to explain why she needed so much help lately."

"Did she pay you to help her?" Margot asked.

Ewan shook his head and glanced down at his wrist, where he wore an unexpectedly nice watch for a kid with no money to speak of. "She would try to, and I wouldn't take it. So, then she'd insist I keep the change from whatever errand she sent me on. I was keeping it all in a jar to buy her something, but..." He drifted off.

Margot got the sense that Ewan was very gifted at convincing adults around him what a great kid he was. She could see the way he was playing with them, being careful of what he said and how he said it. While he might not end up being their killer, something about him was setting off alarm bells left, right, and center. He was too perfect, too poised. He was the model ideal of a teenage boy and he knew it.

Just like any good psychopath would.

"You have a copy of Andrew Rhodes' book on the serial killer Ed Finch," Margot observed.

Ewan smoothed his already smooth jeans. Toni must have told him what book they looked at, because he didn't even hesitate before answering. "A lot of people have that book, detective. It was a bestseller."

Margot's hand tensed and her lizard brain said *slap him*, but she forced a smile instead. "Yes, but a lot of people don't live next to murder victims, Ewan."

His gaze lingered on her, and while he was smiling, there was no warmth in his eyes whatsoever. "I'm not really sure I see the connection. I have *In Cold Blood* as well, but I doubt you're grilling every Capote fan in Chinatown."

"We're not talking about other books, though. We're talking about *Killer in the Classifieds*." Margot met his gaze, her hands folded neatly in her lap. While he was just a boy, and she had all the power here, this interview reminded her chillingly of her meetings with Ed. All that was missing was an explosion of rage where he demanded her respect.

"I saw this *Dateline* episode a couple years ago about Finch and they interviewed Special Agent Rhodes. The way he talked about his work and how he'd figured out who Finch was, it was like, *oh shit, that's just a logic puzzle, I could do that*, and it made me interested in that field. I bought the book and read it, but that was it. If you think I used it as, like, a how-to guide for killing my neighbor, I think you guys are probably up shit creek without a paddle right now."

Margot felt Wes stiffen beside her. This kid really was a little prick, and he was seeing how far he could push them.

The problem, for him, was that his confidence was making him cocky. Margot hadn't failed to notice that neither she nor Wes had mentioned anything about the crime scene or murder being related to Ed Finch. Ewan was the one who had done that all on his own. And while he, and any lawyer worth his salt, would say that he'd made an inference from their questioning, Margot wasn't stupid. She was sealing that faux pas up in her memory.

"So just to confirm, the morning Shuye Zhou was killed, you were asleep in your apartment, is that correct?" Margot asked.

"Yes."

She didn't bother to ask him if he had anyone who could verify his alibi. She knew his mother hadn't been home.

The only thing bothering her was that Ewan's copy of the book was untouched. That obviously didn't rule him out, but it meant they had no smoking gun to pin the crime on him. "When does your robot fight club finish?" Margot asked.

"Five. Why?"

"So I know how long we have to wait before we bring you down and get those fingerprints done." She stared right at him as his gaze flickered from confidence to confusion and then to anger. "You know. Just to rule them out."

She waited to see if he would flinch, or try to come up with another excuse, instead he merely nodded. "Yeah. Sure. Whatever."

THIRTY

Margot half expected to see Ewan's mother waiting for them at the station, ready to read them the riot act for bringing her son in, but the chairs in the waiting area were empty, and Ewan gave them no indication he was expecting anyone.

"Does this, like, go on my permanent record?" he asked as they guided him to the processing area.

"Your prints will remain in the system." Judah Miller, the processing clerk, was being almost too kind to the kid, but he did that with anyone who wasn't arrested and was giving their prints willingly. He tried his best to make it not scary. Margot wished he'd be meaner. "But if you're worried about it flagging you for your future, don't fret, kid. Tons of people get printed for background checks. Nurses, teachers, even cops. If anything, you're a step ahead of the game if you ever go into a profession that requires it."

"So, this isn't going to give me a criminal record."

Margot looked at him like he was stupid, because she knew he was smarter than that.

Judah was about to reply, when Margot interjected, "*This* won't give you a criminal record, no." Heavy emphasis on the *this*. Ewan seemed to realize in that moment he was toeing a very fine line, and his usual charms weren't working here, because he nodded and held his hands out for Judah to take the prints.

Once he was done, Margot and Wes led him to an interrogation room. Wes offered to grab him a canned drink—Wes often played the *nice cop* role between the two of them—and when he left the room to collect a Coke, Margot and Ewan were alone together.

"You're a pretty smart kid, aren't you, Ewan?" she asked, her tone light and casual. "Your mom bragged about you a bit, and that high school is pretty well regarded. Kids there get into good universities."

Ewan sat back in his chair, the uneven legs wobbling slightly. "Yeah, I work hard."

"You want to go to university?"

"Of course."

"What do you want to major in?"

He looked around the room, gaze wandering lazily like he didn't know what he was trying to find. "Is that really relevant here?"

Margot shrugged. "Call me curious. You mentioned finding Andrew Rhodes interesting." She came within inches of mentioning she knew him, then pulled back. That detail was a little too close to revealing deeper truths about her, truths that very few people, and especially not this shitty kid, deserved to know.

"I guess I haven't made up my mind yet."

Margot didn't believe that for a second. This kid had every second of his future planned out. He was that kind of person.

"Where do you want to go to school?"

"Caltech."

She whistled. "That's a hard school to get into."

"I'm aware."

"Bet a school like that would think twice about enrolling someone who had been arrested on suspicion of homicide."

Wes—whether intentionally or not—picked the perfect time to re-enter the room, setting a sweaty can of Coke in front of Ewan, whose own forehead was now as dewy as the can. His jaw ticced.

There it is, Margot thought. The rage she was so good at getting out of Ed. It was simmering just below the surface with Ewan, and she was on the cusp of pushing him over that line. A high-wire tension simmered in the room as Wes took a seat next to Margot and the two waited together to see what Ewan would do next.

He leaned forward in his chair, methodically opening the can with a crisp *crack* sound, and taking a long, slow drink before setting it back down and smiling.

"Then I guess it's a good thing I didn't kill anyone." He smoothed the front of his shirt, plucked off non-existent lint, and nodded almost entirely to himself. "Well, detectives, this has been fun, but unless you have any other questions for me, I have an awful lot of homework to do. If I want to get into that good school."

When neither of them stopped him, Ewan pushed back his chair and left the room, wearing the same self-satisfied smile. Once the door clicked shut behind him, Margot unclenched her fisted hands.

"What a little fucking psycho," Wes said, nudging the drink can with his finger, the way a cat might prod at something it was thinking of knocking off a shelf.

Margot let out a long breath. "Thank you, I was worried I was reading him all wrong."

Wes shook his head, pulling his hands back to stop fidgeting with the can. "No, he was a weird one. Didn't like those vibes one bit."

"Doesn't make him a killer, though."

"No. But it certainly doesn't do him any favors as a suspect."

Margot nodded. "I want to talk to other people in the building about him. See if he really is a beloved Beaver Cleaver or if anyone else got a bad feeling from him. And I *really* want us to double-check that knife for DNA."

Wes was about to say something when Margot pushed the can of Coke toward him. "Since we *have* his DNA now."

A big grin spread across Wes's face. "I did that intentionally. Very much planned, not at all pure dumb luck." He got up, presumably to get an evidence bag for the can, but paused to look back at her.

"Wally," he said.

"The post-apocalyptic Pixar robot?" Margot raised a brow, questioning his sanity.

He shook his head. "No, you said he was Beaver Cleaver, but Beaver was always getting into trouble. Ewan wants people to think he's Wally Cleaver."

Margot sighed. "I think it's safe to say he's not the sweet boy next door, no matter which way we spin it."

Wes disappeared with the can, not bothering to wear gloves since his fingerprints were already on it.

Margot sat back in her chair and stretched. It was amazing how comfortably she and Wes could fall into their usual routine. She'd worried that by spending the night—even as a friend—it might shift their dynamic somehow, but her concerns had proven to be unfounded.

A soft knock on the door drew her attention.

"You want an invite to the pity party?" she asked.

It was Leon, not Wes who poked his head through the door.

"Langston White's lawyer says he's willing to talk to us. Thought you might leave your pity party and see if we can get this guy to crack like a peanut."

Margot beamed at him. "Don't threaten me with a good time."

THIRTY-ONE

Langston White wanted to talk.

The problem was, Langston White only wanted to talk about how *not* guilty he was.

Margot and Leon sat together in a different interrogation room, with Leon taking the lead this time, while Langston and his lawyer sat across from them. His lawyer was a woman about Margot's age, maybe slightly older, with the physique of a linebacker, and her mousy brown hair parted severely and worn in a low bun at the nape of her neck. The woman's intense frown and unwavering eye contact said she would *not* stand for any shenanigans.

She kind of scared Margot.

"My client will not answer any questions regarding the death of Frederica Mercado."

Margot couldn't stop herself from letting out a snort of annoyance, which drew the fierce attention of the lawyer, whose incongruous name was Joy. Joy Larkin.

"Your client is a person of interest in multiple homicides," Leon said, his voice calm, unperturbed. His voice said, *I have all the time in the world.* "Perhaps he'd like to talk about some of those."

"*Multiple* homicides?" Langston's voice hitched up. "What the fuck?"

Joy rested her hand on his forearm, but rather than functioning as a gesture of comfort, Margot saw a vice-like squeeze pinch the firefighter's skin until he winced. "We agreed, you wouldn't say anything unless I approved it."

"They're accusing me of murder, I feel like it shouldn't be crazy for me to say *I didn't kill a bunch of bitches*," he shot back.

Joy briefly looked at Margot and behind the steely facial features was an expression that said, *Lord save me from mediocre, stupid men.*

Margot knew the expression well. It was one she made accidentally whenever she forgot to school her own features.

"My client will not be speaking about any active homicide investigations," Joy said, releasing her hold on Langston's arm.

"Then I'd love to know what you brought us here to talk about," Margot said.

Langston looked pleadingly at Joy, who after a visible war with her own good senses finally sighed and said, "Only what we talked about, though."

"I know you think I'm guilty because I knew Freddie was dead, but I promise you it wasn't what you think."

"Enlighten us," Leon prodded.

"The real reason Freddie and I broke up a few months back is that I found out she was a call girl, and I lost my mind. I said some really fucked-up things to her and she dumped my ass."

Margot was dying to ask more questions about Frederica's supposed profession, but Leon was taking lead here and she needed to let him run this interrogation the way he wanted to. His way might be slower than hers, but it had been well-honed over the decades. He'd get them what they wanted.

"Can you explain what you mean about Frederica's job?" he asked.

"She had a normal nine to five situation, but sometimes she'd be busy at night and wouldn't tell me why. So, one night I decided to see if what my gut was telling me was right and I ended up seeing her out with another guy. That turned into a big fight, you can imagine, but then she told me it wasn't cheating because it was work. Like somehow getting *paid* to fuck some ugly old man was better than her cheating on me."

Joy tapped his arm, giving her head a slight shake.

"Sorry. Anyway, she told me she was working for this company that does very exclusive dating services. That when someone wanted a no strings attached date for an event, someone who wouldn't embarrass them, they would call up a girl like Freddie. She said more than half the time they didn't even want sex, they just wanted to show off a hot girl on their arm."

"Did she tell you the name of the company?"

Langston shook his head. "No, and I didn't ask."

Margot could already sense a long day ahead of calling dating agencies and trying to unearth escort services from the bowels of the internet. If this place even had a web presence.

Leon gave an unamused smile. "As interesting as all of that is, Mr. White, it doesn't answer our most pressing question."

Langston seemed momentarily confused, but that also might have been the way his face looked all the time.

"Oh, how I knew Freddie was dead."

Margot did her best not to sigh and was mostly successful.

Langston looked at Joy again, who nodded.

"I got a call the night before that story hit the paper—it was a protected number, which can sometimes be work. When I answered they told me that Freddie was dead, and if they found out I had anything to do with it, I'd be dead, too. I thought it might be a prank at first, but then I saw that story about the Jane

Doe and I just fucking *knew* it was her. And if these weird people she worked for were going to pin the blame on me, I thought you guys might also end up at that conclusion, so I wanted to get ahead of the eight ball, y'know?"

"And the people on the phone didn't say who they were?" Margot asked.

Langston shook his head. "They said *one of our best girls*, so it had to be the company she was working for. But that's all I know."

Margot stared at him, his standardized good looks, his hangdog expression, and she wondered how often he had skated through life by leaning on this stupid jock persona that he had cultivated for himself.

"You realize how unbelievable that sounds, don't you?" she asked.

Joy looked as if she might interject, but Langston was quick to pull out his phone and slide it across the table to Margot. The call history was open, and she could see an incoming call the previous day from a number simply marked *Private*, and the call had lasted three minutes.

After that Langston had made several calls to a number labeled *Freddie*, but none of them appeared to have connected. While the call log could obviously have been staged to his benefit, it also loaned some credence to his story. Margot would get a copy of the records from the phone company to confirm what he was showing her, but it was compelling, especially considering his stupid mess up this morning. Someone who had killed Frederica wouldn't pretend the newspaper had broken the story to them.

Leon glanced down at the call history then up at Langston. The expression he wore was stoic, not cruel but not warm either. It was a subtle, unnerving expression that Margot hadn't yet been able to hone for herself.

Margot felt her own phone buzz in her pocket, the surprise

vibration making her jump slightly, but she made no move to retrieve it. She had voicemail for a reason.

"Mr. White, I have just one more question for you," Leon said smoothly. "If you believed there was even a slight chance that caller was telling you the truth, why didn't you do something about it? Especially after..." He scrolled through the phone screen. "Fifteen unanswered calls to your former girlfriend?"

Langston shifted uneasily. "They said she was already dead, I'm not sure what calling the cops, or filing a missing person's report would have done to help. And I *did* call, didn't I? I called this morning as soon as I saw the paper and knew they were right."

Margot gritted her teeth. "Yeah, you called when you decided it was time to cover your own ass. How gallant."

Joy cleared her throat loudly. "We won't be dissecting the actions my client *didn't* take, detectives. He is here of his own free will and I think he's done more than enough to be useful to you today. Now, Detective Telly said that was his final question, so if that's everything, we'll be leaving."

Margot wanted to outright ask him if he'd killed Frederica, but she knew Joy would shut that down immediately. She also knew he'd lie.

"I do have one more question, actually," Margot said, staring at Langston until he broke eye contact and looked down at the table.

Margot opened up her phone, flipping through pictures until she found the image she'd taken of the tiny mark they'd found on Frederica's body. She slipped the phone across the table to Langston.

"Do you recognize that mark?" she asked.

Langston picked up the phone, holding it close to his face and then pinching the screen to zoom in. "Oh, yeah, that's Freddie's weird tattoo." He then seemed to realize he was looking at a photo of his dead girlfriend and set the phone down with a clatter, pushing it away.

"Do you know what it's meant to be?"

Langston shook his head as he wiped his hands on his pants. "I thought it was a birthmark, but she told me it was a tattoo. When I asked what it was, because it's kind of small and stupid, she totally shut down, wouldn't talk about it. That kind of annoyed me, because, like, what's the point in getting a tattoo if you don't want to blab endlessly about the deep personal connection you have to, like, hummingbirds or whatever? She never did tell me."

She let his words sink in, then gave a nod to Joy. "If we have any other questions, we'll let you know."

"And I don't need to remind you both that visiting my client without my presence would be a stupid idea, do I?"

Leon snorted. "We're in no hurry to talk to him again."

Joy and Langston left, leaving Margot and Leon sitting side by side in the empty interrogation room.

"What do you think?" he asked, after they'd had a moment to mull things over.

"I think I'm sick of talking to stuck-up assholes today."

"Present company excluded, I hope." He winked at her, which succeeded in making her smile.

"I think he's putting on an act, making himself look dumber than he actually is, but I think he *is* pretty dumb. Probably too dumb to pull off a triple homicide."

"Let's not think about it in terms of the other two. Let's just focus on Frederica. Do you think he's capable of killing his girlfriend and leaving her out there?"

Margot thought about this for a moment and nodded. "I think he was physically capable of it. I think he intentionally gave us reasons for his DNA—including semen—to be on her body. I absolutely believe he could have carried her out there. But... and it's a big but... it doesn't feel right, does it?"

Leon settled back in his chair, resting his hands on the slight curve of his belly. "I can see so many reasons why he makes sense as the killer. He has the motivation, especially after seeing her with another man and finding out about her profession. He had a good foot in height and at least a hundred pound of muscle on her, could have easily incapacitated her. But you're right. Something in my gut is telling me we need to keep looking. I do think we need to keep an eye on him, though."

"Well, you work on the warrant to have him surveilled. I'll start digging into the escort angle, see if I can find this company she worked for. If there's anything to that angle, it feels worth digging into."

"Agreed."

Margot's phone buzzed again, vibrating on the wooden tabletop. The number wasn't one she was familiar with, so for the time being she let it go to voicemail. Normally she'd answer unfamiliar calls, but her focus was elsewhere right now. She'd call them back.

She had two different interrogations she needed to unpack, and two different women demanding justice.

She only wished she had the final piece of the puzzle to give those women what they deserved.

THIRTY-TWO

Oakland, CA

Eddie found himself thinking about Miss Shirley a lot. There was a funny sort of feeling down in his belly when he recalled the way she'd looked at him, and the venom in her words when she said *I really don't think you are, Eddie.* It was so quiet but so vicious.

Because she knew.
She knew who he was.
She knew what he'd done.

The feeling wasn't guilt, because he'd heard people talk about guilt a lot, and it just wasn't something he felt. People told him it was a queasy feeling in the belly and heart when you knew you'd done something wrong. Guilt, they told him, was our mind's way of keeping us in check, of telling us good from bad.

Eddie knew when the things he did were considered wrong by others, and *that* was why he didn't do them, because of how it made other people look at him and treat him. But what he did when no one was watching had no such restriction.

Because Eddie didn't care.

When he thought about Miss Shirley, he didn't feel guilt, but he did feel a rush of unease about having been discovered. He needed to be more careful, more calculated.

Miss Shirley didn't matter anymore. Because she was gone, and she had taken her knowledge with her. But he knew he had to be mindful going forward, because there were people watching him who might not be as stupid as he'd thought. Those people could be problems.

He lay awake in bed that night, letting himself feel the twisting unease, letting himself learn the signs of warning it brought with it. He'd learn to listen to those little internal warning bells. He'd keep himself safe.

When the house fell into its usual nighttime slumber, the loud snores of Mama floating down the hall along with the laugh track of whatever terrible sitcom she'd fallen asleep watching, Eddie clambered up onto his desk and out the bedroom window, a routine so well-honed he was out on the street within seconds.

He had a mission this time.

Next door, where all the lights were off, Eddie let himself do something he'd never done before, emboldened by the knowledge that Miss Shirley was gone, and the house was empty. He'd paid attention to the construction of his own window screen, and how a little jostling at the corners was all it took to pop them out of the window well.

The next step was harder, because it depended on someone forgetting to close or lock an interior window, but he'd smelled the fresh paint coming from inside the house even as the movers were hauling out boxes. Fresh paint meant open windows, and sometimes people forgot to lock those windows after closing them.

He held the screen aloft as he pushed the window firmly with his fingertips, and there it was, a hushed sliding sound.

Once he was able to get his fingers into the gap, opening it the rest of the way was easy.

While he knew the house was empty, he crept in as quiet as a mouse, because this wasn't about *this* house, it was about learning how to do this at *other* houses. He thought about all the stops on his usual route, the way people dozed through the night with windows open a crack, letting the night breeze cool them as they slept.

He imagined coming inside, quieter than that breeze, and moving through those homes at night, when no one knew he was there. He thought about all the little secrets he could uncover, the things he could see and touch close up. They didn't belong to him, but they *could* be his if he moved like a ghost.

Miss Shirley's house smelled of fresh paint, but beneath that, deep in the bones of the carpet, were the scents of cigarette smoke, and the tiniest hint of ammonia that would tell new owners a cat had once lived here. It wasn't an overpowering stench, more the memory of a scent.

Houses could tell people a lot of things about those who had once lived in them, if people were only willing to listen.

Eddie didn't want to prowl empty houses, though.

He wanted to see what it was like to do this in a house still filled to the brim.

Moving through the empty rooms, he was surprised by how little remained of Miss Shirley. There were indents in the carpeting where her belongings had once been, the shape of a couch and a dining room table still embedded in the living room.

A cross remained nailed to the wall in the kitchen.

He drifted into her bedroom, where he sat in the middle of the four divots that had once been her bed legs, and laid down on the carpet, staring up at the ceiling.

He thought about that stupid cat of hers and a smile spread across his face as he ran his fingers through the short pile of the carpeting.

She was right.

He didn't feel sorry at all.

THIRTY-THREE

Whoever had called Margot during her interrogation didn't leave a message, which made her feel vindicated for not picking up. It was probably some scam artist or a telemarketer trying to get her to switch to a different internet provider.

She was looking through some files that had been sent to her by the vice squad, listing known escort and sex work groups that operated out of the Bay Area, and their web presence, wherever they had one.

A lot of these groups had gotten smart about hiding what they were doing. Some of them were masked as dating sites, where the girls available to hire were simply *hot singles*. The one Margot was looking at now was fashioned as the alumni page for a non-existent sorority.

She knew there had to be a code to the write-ups on the girls, something that would tell prospective clients what the girls were available for, but Margot wasn't sure she wanted to know what the finer points of *rush chair* and *events coordinator* meant in terms of sex work.

As she scrolled mindlessly through page after page of so-called alumni, it made her heart hurt to think about these women. Yes, working for an escort agency was probably miles safer than working a street corner, but they were still putting themselves on the line every night in order to make a living, and Margot wondered how they got to that point.

She'd read Frederica's file in the downtime following interviews and there were no red flags that would earmark Frederica to become a sex worker. She had a nine-to-five job, just as Langston had indicated, doing social media for a local chain of coffee shops popular around the Bay Area. Granted, that kind of work probably didn't pay a ton, but was that reason enough to start working with an escort service?

Perhaps there was more to this that Margot wasn't seeing, and it wouldn't become obvious until she figured out what agency was employing Frederica. Margot was also aware she had her own biases when it came to sex work because she was looking at it from the perspective of a cop, and that would skew things no matter what. There was no way for her to remove the element of judgment from her viewpoint, try as she might.

With the sorority site a bust, she leaned back in her chair and rubbed the bridge of her nose, blinking as the office came back into view. How long had she been looking at the smiling headshots and bikini-clad "dating" photos of hundreds of different women?

There was still no sign of Frederica among them.

Wes, at his own desk across from her, was likewise pinch-faced staring at a computer screen until she nudged his foot under the desk. He looked up at her. "Hey. End of day, Phalen. Let's pack it in."

Despite how much they'd done that day, she was still shocked that it was time to go home. Part of her wanted to stick around and keep going through vice's list of websites, but the list would still be there tomorrow. If she didn't sleep, she might miss something important.

"You want to go get some dim sum?" Wes asked, rubbing his

hands over his face and scratching at the fine dusting of stubble that had grown in since that morning. His coloring was fair enough that she hadn't even noticed it until his nails brushed over it.

"I don't know if my bustling social calendar has room for that."

Wes snorted. "I'm not going to force you. I know how you feel about eating out."

Margot wanted to correct him. It wasn't eating out that she avoided, necessarily. She had been known to join others for a bite to eat, or a quick beer, but the thing she simply *couldn't* do was develop a routine around a place. She loved a specific Thai restaurant, but she'd never once been there in person. It was simply the best and fastest place near her apartment, and even then, she had the desk manager at her apartment building call the orders in for her.

Margot couldn't establish routines outside the house.

She had a half dozen different routes to get to work, some that took much longer than she would have liked. She had nothing in her car to distinguish it from others, even the model and color were about as basic as they came. She had no bumper stickers, no seat covers, she didn't even have an air freshener. The FasTrak pass that would automatically pay her way on toll roads was so ubiquitous in the area that it didn't distinguish her car from a thousand others.

How could she explain any of this to him in a way that didn't make her sound insane? She looked at him as he packed up his stuff and felt a flash of affection. He *knew* her. Maybe he was trying to make her feel normal by turning it into a quirk rather than a deep-seated terror that forced her to evaluate every move she made in her life to wonder if it was an invitation to a killer or not. He knew why she had a thousand locks. Why she didn't walk alone at night.

"Dim sum sounds good. I could use some of those killer soup dumplings from Hon's Wun-Tun House."

"That's the place that makes them in the window out front, right?"

She nodded. "They're so good."

He slipped his jacket on and stretched his legs. "Yeah, I'm up for that, let's go."

They agreed to drive separately, since the restaurant was ridiculously close to Margot's apartment, making it silly for him to have to drive them back to the station afterwards so she could get her car.

As Margot headed into Chinatown the buzz was euphoric, and she soaked it up, letting it drown out the business of the day. Restaurants were open hours later than usual, music boomed up and down the streets, and people were out in droves celebrating early Lunar New Year festivities. The big event was the next day, but it was such an enormous celebration, especially in Chinatown, that there was live music and parties for days leading up to it. Part of that was to appeal to the tourists in town for the big day, but it was also just a warm and excited sense of a community coming together to celebrate.

On the street outside the restaurant, a family posed with a set of foo dog heads resting on the sidewalk. The heads were huge, covered in brightly colored paint and fur, and were a component of a traditional foo dog costume that would be worn as part of the lion dances that would take place up and down the street the following day.

Wes arrived a moment later, his jacket likely left behind in his car, and beamed at her. "This place is getting wild. We should come back tomorrow."

Margot wasn't sure if this was a friendly invitation, or something else, but the latter took too much mental and emotional energy to unpack at the moment.

"Yeah, I'd be down, this place is crazy for the Lunar New

Year. I can usually hear the firecrackers at my apartment the whole day." Despite everything that had happened over the last few days, and innumerable reasons she should be feeling like garbage, the idea of hanging out with Wes in Chinatown for the New Year filled her with an unusual sense of happiness.

She tended not to look forward to things so much as dread them, so this would be a nice change of pace for her.

They didn't need to wait long in the restaurant before being seated at a booth in the corner closest to the kitchen. Before Margot even had time to flip over a menu there was a full glass of water in front of her and an alert, beaming waitress ready to take her order.

Margot ordered the soup dumplings, tempted to make it a double order because she couldn't remember the last time she'd eaten, but also knowing that her stomach could be notoriously queasy when she worked a case. She could always get a second batch later. The restaurant churned them out with alarming efficiency. Wes ordered a barbeque pork noodle soup, and the Shanghai fried soup dumplings, and they both requested green tea.

Once the waitress was gone, Margot sat back in the booth, looking around the restaurant. Despite it being later than the place was usually open, the tables were mostly all full, and a surprising number of families with small children were sharing mixed plates as they laughed and joked together.

Try as she might, she simply couldn't muster up a single memory of her family laughing around a dinner table like that. She could barely recall an instance where she and her family had eaten at a restaurant. Ed was a very frugal man, and he believed it was a waste of money to go out to eat, especially with small children who were picky eaters. Justin had been deep into a frozen fish sticks phase for several years, while Margot as the first child had learned it was much safer to just eat what was in front of her to avoid making her father mad.

To this day, she couldn't leave food behind on her plate, even if she was full. She'd hear Ed in her mind, that low and menacing tone creeping in, saying *I don't work forty hours a week to see you waste perfectly good food, Megan. If you take it, you'll eat it.*

Never mind that she never loaded her own plate.

Arguing with him was a dangerous game. She'd only started to do it when she became a teenager and there was a dark kind of thrill to pushing his buttons. In retrospect, she realized what a foolish thing she'd been doing at the time, but even as an adult she kind of liked the rush she got when she pissed him off.

It took power to make someone mad.

And any time she could exert power over him, it felt like the tiniest win, a miniature victory for her former self.

Margot looked at Wes, weighing what she was about to ask next, then deciding to just go for it. "Don't take this invitation the wrong way, but do you want to come over after?" she asked as the waitress was setting teacups down in front of them.

Wes raised a brow but managed to avoid coming at her with any innuendo, so she was proud of him. "You need me to build IKEA furniture, don't you? You're buttering me up with dumplings, but you want me to build like a HAKVAART sofa or something." He made a deliberate face of suspicion that almost made her spit out her tea.

"One, you have seen my apartment enough times to know that there isn't a stick of IKEA furniture in it, thank you very much."

"No, it's all ancient grandma couches and mismatched end tables."

"Not all of us need our apartment to be ready for a spread in *Architectural Digest*. I happen to *like* my granny sofa and my curbside end tables."

Wes made a face, like he couldn't fathom the idea of second-hand furniture. And having seen his apartment, Margot now understood why.

"Two, no, the help I need is actually kind of..." She drifted off and let out a big sigh. "I want to go through the letters that my lawyer forwarded to me. The ones from Ed's fans to me. Maybe if I have enough gin in the cupboard, we can even look at some of the ones Ed sent me." She was stirring the little metal pot of chili crisp oil to give herself something to do.

As she waited for Wes to respond, the waitress brought out their orders, and fragrant steam filled up the space between them.

"Why do you want to do that, Margot?" Wes asked, barely acknowledging the soup sitting in front of him. His hands were folded on the table and his attention was entirely on her, concerned, but not judging.

"A couple of reasons. One personal, one professional. I want to see if there's anything in there that might hint at this case we've got going. You know, maybe some loon bragging about how he's going to make my daddy proud or something. Since the letters are sent to me and not Ed, the FBI doesn't catalog them. There could be something there that wasn't in their database."

"Assuming that's the professional reason, what's the personal one?" Something about his tone, which was calm and a little too reasonable, told Margot he already knew the answer.

"I want to see if she ever sent me anything."

"She?"

Margot pierced one of the dumplings with her chopstick, adding the chili oil to the broth that seeped out. She focused on the food, so she didn't need to see his face when she answered.

"Rhonda. Ed's wife."

THIRTY-FOUR

Wes did a good job of not judging her when Margot stopped at a liquor store before they went back to her car. She had cut back on her drinking considerably over the time she'd been his partner, and the time she'd been seeing her therapist, but there were still times she needed something to dull the roar of her thoughts, and anti-anxiety meds didn't always do the trick.

A bottle of Hendricks and a bag of pretzels later, they made the short drive to her apartment. Brody, the desk manager, gave her a nod of acknowledgment as she passed through the lobby.

The building was old, and the only reason she could afford a place with a doorman and a low-rent concierge was because the owner treated the place like a hobby rather than a business. If Lorenzo ever decided to sell, she'd be forced to move somewhere else, and the idea of that made her feel sick to her stomach.

They made their way to her apartment, a tense quiet hanging between them in the elevator and down the hall. Wes hadn't said much since they'd left the restaurant, and Margot wasn't sure if it was because he was waiting for her to speak first, or because he was worried what he had to say would upset her.

Inside, after she locked the door, she took two lowball glasses from the cupboard and filled each one with ice before mixing the gin with some Sprite she had in the fridge.

She plopped the glass down in front of him at the small dining table. "Voila. A lazy man's Tom Collins. Enjoy."

Wes toyed with the glass, clearly fighting the urge to say something. Finally, he took a sip from the drink, made a subtle expression of enjoyment, and as he set the glass down he said, "You don't have to do this, you know. None of it. It's not up to you to tear your personal life apart for a case. And I don't think anything good is going to come from you digging up information on this woman who was crazy enough to marry Ed fucking Finch even knowing everything he did."

Margot stayed standing, leaning against the peninsula that separated her kitchen from the tiny dining area. She sipped her own drink, pleased with the mix of sweetness from the pop and the botanical bite from the gin. It wasn't cold enough by far, but it would do.

"She believes in demons."

Wes choked on his second sip of drink, wiping little bits of gin from his cheeks. "What?"

Margot settled in across from him, handing him a paper towel. "I looked at one of the letters she sent him when I was going through the FBI's database the other day. She thinks his *body* committed the crimes, but that it was demons that made him do it."

"Yeah, she sounds *super* sound of mind." He was dabbing at a few marks on his shirt, but they seemed to already be drying. "Why would you want to give someone like that any of your time?"

Margot made a helpless gesture, fanning her hands out in front of her as she shrugged. "I don't know. I... I guess I wonder how someone could still see the good in him even though she knows what he did. But it's not just about that. I want to know what it is about *her* that would make him agree to marry her. You know how many fans guys like him end up with. Women who would do anything for an ounce of his attention. Women who genuinely think he's innocent, or that they can change him, or they don't *care*. Like the danger is part of the excitement, I don't know. But out of all the women like that, he picked this one. This woman who told him she thinks demons did it. Ed is many things, Wes, but he's not an idiot, and he's not fond of stupid people. So why her?"

She let out another sigh and picked up her drink, mostly to keep her hands from shaking. That had been a little *too* honest, and she wouldn't be surprised if he thought she was nuts herself now.

Then again, Wes had known her a long time, he'd seen her at some low lows. He hadn't run screaming from her yet.

"Well, all right then," he said after a long pause. "Let's go through these goddamn letters, shall we?"

Margot went to her closet to collect the banker's boxes she kept everything stored in, while Wes topped up their drinks, leaving the bottle of gin on the table alongside a full bowl of pretzels. Margot passed one of the boxes onto him and took one for herself. She had intentionally given him the one that had the scant few letters Ed had sent to her over the years.

She'd never even opened them, let alone read them. Reading Ed's words after she'd learned who he was had simply been an unbearable proposition. Two decades later, she had no idea what they said.

They each pulled out a stack of cards and letters and got to work as the ice melted in their glasses and their fingertips became wrinkly from the pretzel salt.

Two hours later, Wes thumped his hand on the table and practically made Margot jump out of her skin. They had found a few rabid fans who suggested they might *finish what Ed started*, but so far nothing from Rhonda, and nothing that seemed likely to point them to a real killer.

Wes handed her the letter in his hands without a word, making her stomach churn uneasily with mixed curiosity and fear.

She recognized Ed's sharp, slanted scrawl immediately, and her gut instinct on seeing it was to crumple the letter up into a ball and toss it across the room. But she needed to see this. At least Wes thought she did, and he'd gone through almost every Ed letter she had without once making her take one. Based on the expression he'd worn for the last two hours, he had done her a favor.

Buddy.

It's been a long time, kid, and I get the feeling you're sending your old man a message. Well, loud and clear, I know you're not coming to visit, but you could at least write back, let me know how you're doing. I know your name is different now, and no one will tell me what it is, but they tell me these will get to you at some point, so that means I know you're ignoring me out of spite.

Good job, you've sent the message. Now stop being an entitled little cunt and write me a letter. You owe me that much. You owe me more, if you're willing to really think about it. But one fucking letter won't kill you.

I wanted to tell you things in person, but you never gave me the chance, and since I've got nothing but time on my hands, maybe I can tell you a little bit of truth in a world filled with lies.

I met someone.

She's nothing like your mom, and I know you'll think that's an insult, but it's just a fact. Kim was a bitch, that's where you get it from, and she never really loved me. The real me. I couldn't be myself around her, it was just day after day of keeping up an act, and that gets exhausting.

But I suspect you know all about that, now, don't you? What is your life now, if not pretending to be normal, pretending you're not my daughter? And you are my daughter, Megan, I could see myself in you so much while you were growing up.

Not that you'll admit that to yourself now.

But this woman, her name is Rhonda, and she's unlike anyone I've ever met before. She sees me for what I am, but still wants to love me. There's power in that, in being loved for who you really are, not who someone wants or hopes you'll be one day.

I want you to know this, because you're the most important thing in my life. The one thing I ever got right. I don't know if love is something I'm capable of, maybe not the kind of love other people talk about. But you are the one thing I've ever loved.

And that's not worthless.

Tell me where you are, Megan. That shouldn't be too much to ask.

Love always,
Dad

Margot stared at the letter, her hand shaking as the words on the paper blurred, and she felt the first tear slip down her cheek. She didn't even know *why* she was crying. She dropped the letter and swiped the tears away from her face, trying to obliterate them before Wes saw them, but of course it was too late.

"That's the only one I've seen where he mentioned Rhonda, or a wife, in any capacity. The... um... well, the tone is pretty consistent in all of them."

Margot let out a little laugh. "Sorry you had to read a hundred letters of my own father calling me an *ungrateful cunt*. That can't have been fun."

Wes reached across the table and gently wiped away a tear she had missed. He held her chin in his hand and for one achingly long second, he stared at her, his eyes searching hers. "Margot, you don't have to make a joke."

"No, but if I don't there's a really good chance I'll start screaming and tearing my hair out, and to be honest with you, Wes, my hair is like my *one* redeeming feature."

He smiled like he couldn't help himself. "God, you're so fucked up."

Margot pulled away from his grip because the only other option was to lean into it. She caught the last few wayward tears and smiled. "I've been telling you that since the very beginning."

"Yeah, well, I thought you might be the endearing kind of fucked up. The daddy issues I usually deal with aren't quite the same."

She sipped the last of her cocktail and smiled, the weight of the letter not gone, but lighter. At the time she'd invited Wes to do this with her, she hadn't really understood her own motivations. Now, she knew why she'd invited him.

"I guess I found the answer to my question."

Wes took back the letter, reading it through again with his brows furrowed. "I don't know. This reads like manipulative bullshit. He doesn't care about being understood. He just wants your attention."

"He wouldn't get married to get my attention."

Wes reached over the pile of letters on the table, taking both her hands in his until she looked at him. "Margot. He has confessed to three different cold case murders just to get your attention. Marrying a woman he only has to interact with by letter seems like a pretty Ed-like thing to do. I'm surprised he didn't send you a wedding invitation."

Margot glanced down at the heap of papers still in both their boxes. "I guess anything is possible." She didn't pull away from him this time, because the warmth of his hands and the vaguely rough texture of his skin gave her something to focus on, something real. It helped.

She stared at his face, his beautiful face, and wondered how she'd found him. Amid all the assholes, the macho idiots, the guys she *could* have been saddled with as a partner, she'd found the one guy who wanted to understand her.

His eyes searched hers, and a sensation of yearning tugged in her belly, a magnetic draw that told her *lean in*.

Instead, she took her hands back, and looked away with a shuddering little breath, knowing what she was rejecting and hating herself for it. But this was Wes. This relationship *mattered*. And if she knew one thing about herself, it was that she was uniquely capable of ruining a good thing, especially when it came to sex.

So, desire needed to take a back seat to what she needed so much more right now.

A friend.

THIRTY-FIVE

When Margot woke the next morning Wes was already gone. She'd insisted he stay on her grandma couch because of all the gin they'd gone through. And because she wasn't nice enough to give up her bed. She'd spent most of the night staring at her ceiling, wondering if she should throw common sense to the wind and go back into the living room to climb on top of him.

But then the words in Ed's letter snuck in, and there was nothing quite as sobering as a vicious letter from her serial killer father to dampen the mood.

What would she have done if she'd read those letters when she received them? Wes had only given her the one, but he had told her there were letters for all her major milestones. Her birthdays, the month she graduated from high school. He told her they weren't worth reading, containing mostly anger masked as pride. She didn't think she wanted to read any more of them. The one he'd given her had been nasty enough to validate her decision to leave them in the box forevermore.

She'd wanted answers, but she wasn't sure she'd gotten any.

It was the same as the two interrogations from the previous day. They had two ideal suspects for two different crimes, and both of them had left without arrest. Margot only had more and more questions in both scenarios, and she hated letting good suspects walk away. But sometimes a good suspect didn't equal a killer, and she knew that despite her frustrations and personal feelings about both Langston and Ewan, her dislike didn't immediately make them guilty.

Even if she wished it worked that way sometimes.

She would continue to work the escort angle in Frederica's case, but she had another idea for Ewan's. He was overly confident, but she also got the sense that a lot of that was bravado. She expected that Ewan's only friends in the world were those seven kids in the robot club, and she was also willing to bet that his projection of superiority meant he might be prone to bragging about his achievements.

If he'd done something to Shuye, would he have told them? Maybe not a confession, but... something. Something she could use.

Margot touched the folded blanket Wes had left on the arm of the couch, then looked at the two banker's boxes on the table. He'd repacked them and left a note on the top of one. She picked it up.

Stop trying to find a reason to be a miserable bitch. You're at capacity.

Margot barked out a laugh. What a prick. She loved him.

She took the note to her fridge and stuck it to the door with a magnet. It seemed like a good reminder to see on a regular basis. He was right, too. She didn't need to dredge up the past; her present had more than enough going on to keep her busy.

After she'd put the boxes back in her closet and got herself ready for work, her phone started to buzz on the kitchen counter. Caller ID told her it was Greg.

"Hey Greg." She cradled the phone against her ear while

tying her hair into a ponytail. The glasses she and Wes had used the previous night were still sitting in the sink. The bottle of gin was missing, but she suspected he had put it in her fridge.

If that was the case, he would have witnessed her thoroughly embarrassing food situation, which consisted of fifteen kinds of condiments, five different bottles of booze, a container of leftover spring rolls, and a wildly unnecessary box of baking soda to keep her non-existent food fresh.

"Hey, Margot, sorry to call so early."

It seemed very on-brand for Greg to open a conversation with an apology.

"Don't worry, I've been up for ages. What's going on, you find anything?"

"OK, well, this is going to be a don't shoot the messenger situation, but I'm calling for two reasons."

"That's not the *best* opener, but I'm listening." She was hunting for her keys, which she had failed to leave in the dish by the door as usual.

She noted that the apartment door had been locked with the door handle lock, the only one that could be engaged by someone leaving. Good man.

The keys were back in the kitchen, where she'd apparently put them in a bowl of limes when they'd gotten in last night. Apparently, her brain thought one bowl was as good as another.

"Do you want the good thing first or the bad thing first?"

Margot paused, mulling over this question. She didn't want the bad thing at all, perhaps she could distract him and never have to hear it.

"Good thing first. Bad thing never."

He cleared his throat and laughed nervously. "OK, the good news is that I found a letter which might be useful to you. It's pretty generic, but I think when you read it, you'll understand why I flagged it. I'm going to email it to your work address if that's cool?"

"Yeah, that sounds great, Greg, thanks." While she was curious about the letter, him calling it *generic* made her think there wouldn't be anything useful in helping her track Shuye's killer.

She said nothing.

He said nothing.

Finally, he cleared his throat again, and she sighed. "*Fine.* Tell me the bad thing."

"Andrew wants you to go see Finch again. Like, tonight."

Margot grimaced. Two times in less than a week? She'd never gone to see Ed that frequently. Something must have happened—the lawyer must have said Ed was willing to give them more names. Whatever it was, it made her feel queasy, knowing she might need to listen to another grisly confession when she'd barely had enough time to recover mentally from her last visit.

"Is there a reason Andrew didn't tell me that himself?"

Greg sputtered out another apology before saying, "I mentioned I was going to call you, so he thought I might as well deliver the message."

In other words, Andrew knew she had a little soft spot for Greg and was less likely to yell at him than she would Andrew. Smart. And accurate.

"Thanks, Greg, tell him to text me the time and I'll make arrangements." She was working the day shift, so she didn't think there would be any conflict with her current schedule.

If she *had* to leave early, she knew she could make the captain understand.

Explaining it to Leon while they were making headway on the Redwood Killer case would be another thing. He would want her to stick around and chase down leads, and normally she would, but visiting Ed had to supersede that. Leon might know who she was, but he didn't know about her work with the FBI, something she didn't feel like advertising. He knew she had connections there, but not *why* they were so willing to help.

Margot caught herself thinking the name and groaned.

"Stupid goddamn Sebastian." It really *was* a catchy name.

She hated the thought of not being there to help, when she felt so deeply in her gut that they were on the cusp of something major with the Muir Woods case. Things were in good hands, but she'd rather they be in *her* hands.

Missing out on a big break in the case would kill her.

She grabbed her bag and headed out, knowing a stack of escort agency websites awaited her attention. She would head over to Ewan's school at lunch, and she wanted to arrange that visit with administrators before going. It was just a friendly little chat, hopefully they'd see it the same way.

It would have been easier to talk to them after school hours, but she had no idea how frequently the robot club met, and she wanted to be able to talk to the kids without Ewan looming in the background.

Wes was seated at his desk when she arrived and there was a coffee sitting in her place. She couldn't help but smile softly to herself to see that even when they nudged up against the safe borders of their friendship, things could still feel the same between them after.

She knew she hadn't made a mistake letting him into her life, and she was happy to have him there, no matter what the capacity.

Tossing her bag on the floor beside her and hanging up her jacket, she opened the file folder that was sitting precisely where she'd left it last, just waiting for her to fall down the rabbit hole again.

"You know, if you were really my friend, *you* would look at the hundreds of escort listings," she said with a sigh, taking a sip from her still-hot coffee. He couldn't have gotten here that much earlier than her, then.

Wes looked up from his screen. "As fun as that sounds, I have the dubious pleasure of reading through a ten-page report on the contents of a dumpster behind a restaurant in Chinatown, and frankly there are few things that I can imagine putting me off food more than knowing how many dead rats were present in there."

Margot raised a brow and Wes held up three fingers. She made a queasy face at him. "Anything actually useful to us?" she asked.

"So far, nothing out of the ordinary, but we *did* get some good news from forensics that there was a partial print on the knife. Smudged, so we may not have much luck with it, but it's something. I'm having them run it through AFIS to see if we get any hits."

"And then we have them compare it to the prints we got from Ewan," Margot said.

Wes nodded, looking thoughtful. "You think it's him?"

Margot typed in the address for a website pretending to be an all-women's rec soccer league and watched as dozens of smiling faces loaded on her screen.

"I don't *want* it to be a seventeen-year-old kid who likes robots and wants to go to Caltech, but I also know that where there's smoke there's fire, and aside from motive—and I still can't come up with anything better than she was an easy target for a first kill—the opportunity was there, plus he has no alibi. She would have let him walk right into her house." She scratched the back of her neck and stared at the computer monitor, as if the smiling women on the screen might be able to give her a better answer. "I just don't know."

Wes nodded grimly and continued reading through his report. Then Margot remembered that Greg had promised to send her a letter he'd found among Ed's correspondence.

She opened her email and found the attachment.

Dear Ed,

You don't know me, and that's OK. I feel like I've spent my whole life learning about you, hearing stories about you, and I bet you're thinking: if that's true, this kid must think I'm a monster. But that isn't what I think at all. I think you did something brave and bold by listening to what your instincts told you. We think that men who go into the woods to hunt helpless animals are tough and masculine, but what is more alpha male than killing your own species? You saw what you wanted and took it. And society might tell you that's wrong, they think a lot of things that are right are wrong, and a lot of things that are wrong are right. Fuck what society thinks. I want you to know that I feel like I know you, because I think I feel the same way you once did. And maybe still do. It doesn't ever go away, does it? The yearning? The hunger? I think that's the only thing that scares me, is that once I feed it, it won't stop. Anyway, I won't waste any more of your time, but I just wanted you to know that there are people out here who understand.

Sincerely,
A fan

The letter's envelope was also attached and while it had no return address in the corner, the postmark indicated it had been sent from Trenton, New Jersey. It was a few years old, obviously, and the handwriting was almost childlike in its messy loops and uncertain letters, like someone who wasn't accustomed to writing by hand.

It wasn't a beating heart in the floorboards, but it was interesting. While it didn't outright *say* the writer was planning to kill anyone, there were little turns of phrase that Margot caught easily. But a lot of people *considered* killing. Most of them never did. Margot's biggest question was if this fan had ever followed through.

A fan.

Her mouth felt thick and cottony, and she took another sip of her coffee, even though it tasted bitter on her tongue.

Closing the letter to stew on it later, she opened the soccer website again. She couldn't be certain but she assumed the dozen or so team names were the code on this one, indicating what the girls were available for. Bobcats and Lightning and Unicorns. She had a pretty good guess that the last one referred to women who would be willing to have sex with couples, since *unicorn* was a term most bisexual women were keenly aware of. She pulled a face.

On the third page, she stopped scrolling, her whole body freezing. There, brown eyes gleaming and perfectly white teeth exposed, was Frederica Mercado. On the website she was listed as Becky Harper, but all of the names were generic, wiping out any kind of ethnic ties. *Frederica* might have been a bit much for the white millionaires looking for a date. It also helped her maintain anonymity.

"I think I found her," Margot whispered, opening up the player profile for "Becky." It contained minimal information, probably most of it was code, and then Margot's gaze drifted to the team name.

The Larks. Their team logo was depicted in the corner of Becky's profile page. A little bird, the silhouette of a lark.

Exactly like the tattoo.

She cursed under her breath and sent the page to the printer, then opened up another tab, this one for the Internet Wayback Machine, a website that could find previous versions of websites, even after changes had been made. She popped in the link for the Larks' team page and picked a date a year earlier, before they'd started finding bodies.

Scrolling through the faces, she spotted Frederica again, still called Becky, but now she was looking for two different faces.

When she saw one of them, her heart stopped.

"Wes."

He looked up, and when she didn't say anything, he came around the desk to look over her shoulder. He smelled good, like fresh soap and something spicy. "What am I—" Before he even finished his sentence, Margot was pointing at the picture of Leanne Wu on the screen.

When they had found her body, she'd been so badly decomposed she barely had any face left.

This living version staring back at them with her bronzed skin and happy smile was named Olivia Miller.

Margot scrolled the Larks page for a good half hour, looking back several different years, but found no picture of Rebecca Watson, either before or after her big makeover. She checked different team pages, and nothing.

Two out of three, though, that was enough to take to Leon.

That was enough to say with certainty at least two of the dead women were connected.

They had a serial killer after all.

THIRTY-SIX

One of the most exhausting parts of being a homicide detective in a major metropolitan city was that one could never sit back and enjoy a minor victory. Margot was thrilled that she had discovered—at last—a connection between two of their Muir Woods victims.

But the Muir Woods women weren't technically even her case.

And she felt achingly close to uncovering the truth in another homicide, which meant leaving her revelation about Frederica and Leanne on Leon's desk and heading out the door to go back to Lowell High.

While she gathered her things, something fell out of her bag and onto the floor near her desk. When she stooped to pick it up, a cold chill went through her. It was the wedding photo of Ed and Rhonda. Margot had barely registered that Andrew had given it to her. She must have been in such a daze getting the news that she'd put it in her bag without thinking.

She never would have kept it under normal circumstances.

Her impulse was to crumple it into a ball and throw it in the trash, but she found herself staring at it, wondering if, the longer she looked at it, the blurry smear of Rhonda's face might resolve itself into a real picture. All Margot could make out was a white flash of teeth, the color of pink roses, and her father staring unflinchingly into the camera.

Her mouth felt dry.

Finally, she shook free of the stupor and shoved the photo back in her bag. Throwing it out at the office would risk someone finding it. Someone who might wonder why she had Ed Finch's wedding photo to begin with. She had enough questions of her own about the wedding, and Rhonda, she didn't also need to open up an invitation for people to question her.

She glanced at Wes, who was finishing going through the report on the contents of the dumpster, and saw his eyes go wide.

"Hold up, Margot, there's something interesting here."

She paused and looked at him expectantly.

The contents had been listed by item, with photos of each item added in a table at the back, making it a time-consuming process to go through page by page.

"Look at this." He handed her the thick report, a line highlighted near the end of the list: *Paper, torn, book page (?), blood present. Additional testing requested.*

Margot raised a brow at him, but he just nodded, urging her to go to the end of the report with the corresponding photos.

And there it was, another page from the Andrew Rhodes book, this one evidently used to wipe blood off something before it was put in the bin. This was marked as heading to the lab to be cross-checked against the partial print lifted off the knife. Margot was relieved to see the lab techs had already considered the evidence vital enough for testing. The problem was, even if they marked the evidence as priority, it would be weeks before it was even looked at by the lab, owing to an enormous backlog of requests.

They wouldn't have cold, hard evidence until then.

The additional evidence was good—it connected the knife in the dumpster to the Shuye crime scene more definitively—but still it wasn't something they could make an arrest on. Margot decided, rather than wait for test results, she'd go after the next best thing to physical evidence. A confession.

As she and Wes headed to the school, there was a buzzy excitement between them thanks to both the escort agency find and the extra piece of the book.

Things felt like they were falling into place, which was thrilling but also made Margot feel uneasy. No matter how much work, how much digging and searching and solving went into a case, sometimes it felt too simple and the answers, when they came, were underwhelming.

Margot wasn't sure if this was because she was waiting for some kind of *aha* moment that would tell her all this work had been worth it; the sins of the father were absolved, and she was finally free to go out and live her real life.

That moment never came.

And the older she got, the more she realized that moment might *never* come, which was its own kind of nightmare. Margot wasn't sure what she would even do with her life if she ever achieved peace with her past. She would definitely get a pet and move somewhere that didn't have a neighbor for miles. Maybe she would raise goats.

Rural Ireland with goats and a dozen orange cats. That sounded nice.

She parked in the visitor lot at the school again and led them confidently to the administration building.

After speaking to the receptionist and then the principal himself, it was agreed that the kids in the robot club—excluding

Ewan—could speak to the detectives of their own free will. The principal set Margot and Wes up in unoccupied offices and called the seven students out of class.

This would certainly set off some alarm bells for Ewan, but Margot didn't mind that so much. It was good for him to start sweating. He'd be more likely to slip up if he thought someone from his cohort might sell him out.

They needed to speak to the kids one-on-one, so to avoid dragging the interviews out for hours, she and Wes split up, each taking an open space—Margot was given the vice principal's office—and dividing up the students in the club to hopefully get answers faster.

The first student shown into the room was a tall, gawky boy who looked precisely like he belonged in a robot club. He wore a NASA T-shirt and cargo shorts, and when he sat in the chair across from Margot it seemed as if none of his limbs could agree on how to complete the process and he just sort of collapsed into place.

According to the list of students she'd been given, his name was James McCray.

"Good afternoon, James, my name is Detective Phalen, and I want to ask you a few questions about your friend Ewan."

James made a sound somewhere between a snort and a laugh and hunched his shoulders a little higher around his ears. Margot wasn't sure which part of her introduction he found worthy of derision, but he *was* a teenager, so it was probably a universally directed sneer at authority.

"How long have you known Ewan?"

He gave a one-shouldered shrug. "Since he transferred here? So I guess about a year, maybe?"

"Do you spend a lot of time together?"

"I guess so."

The kid wouldn't meet her eye, and while Margot often took that as a sign of guilt in the people she interrogated, she wasn't blind to the fact that James might have been ADHD or autistic, which could explain him avoiding her gaze. He reminded her a little of Justin, especially after Ed's arrest, when all of his signs started to manifest more assertively.

She tried to be patient with him, but as the interview progressed, she got mainly one-word answers and nothing very committal in any of them. Margot didn't know James was covering for Ewan, or if Ewan simply mattered so little to James that it never occurred to him to think about the other boy when he wasn't around.

James left, and the sole female member of the group came in after him. Where James had been aloof and showed no signs of concern or curiosity, the girl was already speaking nervously before she even sat down.

"This isn't going to go on my permanent record, is it? I've never even been late to class before, I really can't have this going on my record." She sat on the edge of the chair, a pleading expression steadfastly locked on Margot.

"No, Nora, this isn't going on your permanent record." Margot thought it was funny how her concerns were so similar to Ewan's when they'd spoken the previous day.

Margot set about asking Nora the same questions she'd lobbed at James, but the answers here were strikingly different. Where James was oblivious to whatever was going on with Ewan, Nora had a *lot* to say about him.

"I mean, he used to be a pretty nice kid when I first met him, but then he got really... I dunno, I don't want to say mean things about him, but he got to be kind of a dick? Over the last year he just started bossing us around more and being more demanding, and I sort of thought the project would help him work through all that, but so far, it hasn't."

"I'm sorry, the project? What project?" Margot felt odd, sitting behind the vice principal's desk, but it wasn't that much different from sitting across from someone at an interrogation table.

For Nora, it had obviously loaned a certain air of authority to Margot, beyond her badge.

"It's nothing." She looked down at her hands. "Sometimes he'd come up with these, like, logic games for us to solve, kind of like the Kobayashi Maru from *Star Trek*, you know?"

Margot stared blankly at the girl.

Nora sighed, like she was tired of trying to explain this to uneducated adults. "In *Star Trek*, when cadets attend Starfleet Academy, they would be put through a logic test called the Kobayashi Maru. Basically, it puts the cadets into a no-win scenario to see how they handle it. Ewan would make up his own little scenarios and then give them to us to see how we would all solve them. We'd get together once a month to discuss our solutions and compare them. But since Ewan came up with the problems, he always thought his own solutions were the best, which made the game kind of boring after a while."

While this was roughly fifty times more words than James had spoken, Margot wasn't sure any of it was actually helpful to her.

"Would you say you know Ewan pretty well?"

Nora thought about this then nodded. "Decently well. He doesn't talk about himself much. I think he feels like a bit of an outsider sometimes, which is kind of funny because we're some of the nerdiest kids in school, so we're all outsiders." She gave a little *what can you do* shrug.

Margot stared at the girl for a beat, then another. "Have you ever considered going into criminal psychology?" she mused. "Like, if the robotics stuff doesn't work out, I feel like the FBI could use you." The girl had great insight into Ewan, whether she realized it or not.

The quiet ones were always watching.

Nora blushed. "I never did before, but I recently... I mean, I think I notice stuff about people, like with Ewan, I know he kind of misses being on the east coast, but he doesn't really talk about the specifics. Like he doesn't say he misses a certain friend, or wishes he could eat at a certain restaurant, nothing like that." Margot wanted to hit a pause button as something tickled the inside of her brain, but Nora kept going. "And like, when we started this month—"

The door to the office opened without a knock, swinging hard enough to hit the back wall and causing both Margot and Nora to jump. A middle-aged woman with an asymmetrical black bob entered the room and grabbed Nora by the arm, yanking her up out of the chair.

"*Excuse me,*" Margot said, getting to her feet as if she might vault the desk to protect the girl.

"Yes, *excuse you*, officer—how *dare* you speak to my daughter without a parent or lawyer present?"

"Mom, they asked us if we were OK with it," Nora whined.

"You are a *child*," the woman snapped, dragging the poor girl in the direction of the door.

"Ma'am, we're working a homicide investigation, it would be very helpful if I could have just five more minutes of your daughter's time." She felt oddly desperate to go back to something Nora said before she lost the thread of it.

The woman spun around at the door, almost knocking Nora off balance. "This investigation of yours. Is a student dead?"

"No."

"Is my daughter a suspect in this homicide?" She said the words sarcastically. *Investigation. Homicide.* Like she thought Margot was making them up.

"No, but—"

"Then any further discussions can be coordinated through my lawyer, who you'll be hearing from shortly."

She disappeared into the hallway. Margot had to wonder if Ed Finch might be the *second* most insufferable parent she spoke with today.

THIRTY-SEVEN

Oakland, CA

At some point over the course of winter, Eddie lost the delight in looking into windows.

For one thing, people were drawing their blinds with more frequency, stymieing his attempts to peer into their lives. As if they were so special they couldn't show him. Like what they were doing was so goddamn interesting it needed to be privatized.

He started to loathe them for it.

The woman down the street who had spent all summer showering with her bathroom window ajar had closed it, and the frosted glass denied him access to that regular treat he so looked forward to. He tried, at night, to imagine the shape of her body as she stepped out of the shower and meticulously dried herself with a fluffy pink towel.

He tried to recall the curve of her breast, the heaviness of her bottom, but his imagination simply wasn't enough for him. He didn't *want* a fantasy; he wanted the real thing.

After weeks of being denied the woman in the bathroom,

the couple two blocks over who liked to fuck—a word he'd picked up at school and learned the ever-so-delicious meaning of only recently—started going to sleep at night instead. The regular haunts weren't working for him anymore.

So, he started going further.

He tried different blocks, different streets. It all looked the same. Dirty streets and poorly tended houses, the unmistakable trappings of poverty. Some people had bigger TVs, nicer cars, but none of that could hide the fact that they were living in a terrible area that people had stopped caring about a long time ago.

Here and there you could see signs of someone desperately clinging to the way the place had been twenty or thirty years earlier. Old women tended flowerbeds, tidy American flags were hung outside front doors. But even on those houses the paint peeled and the foundation cracked, because it was simply impossible to escape the creeping fingers of being on the wrong side of the tracks, even when there were no tracks.

On his walkabouts, he saw others like him. Solitary men at night, trying to scratch their own imperceptible itches. Eddie avoided them carefully, but their presence fascinated him. Did they peep through windows, too, or had they found a different means to satisfy their urges?

Some of them were just homeless, and harmless, rifling through garbage cans or sometimes finding an unlocked car door and going through it for loose change. These men didn't interest him.

There were others, whose cat-like footfalls and loose-limbed demeanor spoke of something more insidious, more intentional. He watched one night as one of those men slipped gloved fingertips into a nearly invisible window seam. The window slid up with a *shhhh* sound and the man wriggled his body through the opening.

Eddie moved closer, desperate to see what was going to happen. The enviable audacity of going into a house knowing people were in it was a step Eddie hadn't taken yet, though he'd thought about it endlessly, and he sometimes checked the locks on windows and doors, testing to see which of his neighbors were the most cavalier about their safety. He'd made mental notes of the first houses he would visit when he decided to be truly brave.

This man, though, he made it look easy, like the fear of being caught simply didn't exist for him.

Eddie crouched in the shadows near the house's garage where he could see the window but felt certain no one coming out would be able to spot him. He waited, but he didn't have to wait long.

From within the house there was a short scream that stopped as quickly as it had begun, followed by several thumping sounds, and a brittle crash, like a lamp or vase falling to the floor.

For a moment, Eddie was rooted in place, terrified but thrilled. Had the man been caught? Was someone beating him bloody with whatever furniture was available to them?

When no new sounds came, Eddie crept closer to the open window, hoping to hear something that might give him a clue. Perhaps a frantic phone call to the police, or the distant wail of sirens.

But when he settled beneath the window, he had to strain to hear anything, and when he did, it wasn't at all what he expected.

A low, masculine voice, speaking as if his teeth were gritted and his throat was raw, said, "You're going to be a good little girl for me, now, aren't you? No more fighting, because I know what room your baby is in, and if you so much as whisper a single word, I'll slit that kid's throat and leave you tied up in that room so you can watch him die. Nod if you understand me. Good girl.

Now you're going to take off your clothes, or I'm going to cut them off you. Your choice."

Eddie's body jerked the way it did when he got a strong static shock.

The words filled his mind, clouding anything else. His ears throbbed with the pulse of his heartbeat, and a stab of pure hunger shot through him. He was riveted, revolted, but more than anything, he was inspired.

He listened longer, to every whispered threat, every sharp intake of panicky breath, until the rising sun started to turn the sky pink, and Eddie knew he'd stayed too long. He ran home, barely paying attention to see if anyone was looking, the sky soon bright enough that it could only be called morning.

Climbing through his window, his thoughts were racing, full of what he'd heard that night, desperate to understand it, to relive it again and again. So his mind wasn't as sharp as it should have been. Which was why he didn't see that his bedroom light was on until he was already crouched on the desk.

When he turned to find Mama sitting on the bed, she didn't need to say a word.

Her red cheeks and wild-animal eyes told him there would be no talking his way out of this.

Still, even as she grabbed him by the arm and started slapping him on the cheeks, the only thing he was thinking about was those guttural, whispered words, and the threat held by, *or I'll cut them off you.*

Or I'll cut them off you.

Mama dragged Eddie to the bathroom, yanking his shirt over his head and screaming about how he reeked of sin. But tonight, Eddie didn't care.

Because that night he'd finally felt the euphoria people claim to experience in finding God, and he would go to hell and back to find it again.

Looking through windows was never going to be enough from now on.

THIRTY-EIGHT

Things had not gone at all according to plan in Margot's day so far.

She had felt so certain that morning that they were inching closer to answers in two of her cases, and now those answers felt further away than ever. It was turning her unease over visiting Ed into something more like resentment. If he hadn't insisted on seeing her, she could keep working until the answers in her case became clear. She felt like she was being jerked around by Ed, like this was all a powerplay to show that he could summon both her and the FBI at his slightest whim. He was dangling the promise of more victim names over them, but Margot was starting to wonder how long he planned to use that same ploy.

Indefinitely?

There had to be an end point to all this, otherwise it was going to make her crazy.

Was there a number of crimes solved that would make her feel as if she had done enough? Because at a certain point he might just start inventing murders if it meant keeping her at the end of his leash.

THE KILLER INSTINCT 249

Ted Bundy had tried to claim he had unknown victims right up until the bitter end, but ultimately, he was still executed.

Margot wished the state of California would make her life a little easier.

She was halfway through the lobby of the police station, on her way to make the drive to San Quentin, when a fierce-looking woman with a familiar dark bob haircut entered the building. Trailing behind the woman was the timid figure of Nora, shoulders hunched, head down.

Margot froze, wondering if this insane woman had really come all the way down here to file a complaint, something that would only eat up precious time in her evening. As much as she would love a reason to decline her meeting with Ed, she really didn't have that luxury at the moment.

The woman caught sight of her and there was a brief pause, the woman clearly struggling internally with what to do next, then she wrinkled her nose and drew Nora into the room, so they were standing directly in front of Margot.

"Ms. Phalen," the woman began.

"Detective Phalen," Margot corrected, because she didn't feel like this woman had earned the leeway to be intentionally rude to her.

A tight-lipped pause inflated the tension in the room before Nora's mother went on. "I'm sure you can understand the position I was in this afternoon when my daughter texted me to tell me that she would be speaking to the police."

Margot squared her shoulders, waiting for the yelling to begin, but so far, the woman's tone was calm, if somewhat peevish, as if she didn't enjoy saying what she was saying.

"Nora is a good girl, very smart, great future ahead of her, so naturally I was *concerned* about what might have driven the police to want to talk to her. And when you mentioned *homicide*, well, it triggered a protective urge in me, which I'm sure you can understand."

Margot wasn't sure if this was meant to be an understanding she had as a woman, or because Nora's mother assumed that Margot had children of her own, but either way she'd missed the mark. This time Margot didn't bother doing anything to correct her.

"Mrs...." Margot let the title trail off, hoping Nora's mother would supply the rest.

"Oh. Mrs. Olynyk, apologies, you can call me Kim."

Hearing her own mother's name come out of the woman's mouth made Margot's whole body go cold.

"Kim," she said with a forced smile. "I do know that you were trying to protect your daughter, I think that's a very natural response. But I was trying to do my job, and your daughter wasn't a suspect, she was someone we thought might be able to provide a little insight."

Kim's hand tightened on Nora's shoulder. "Yes, well, about that." She gave her daughter a little shove forward. "When we got home, I asked Nora why it was the police might be chatting with her, and she told me about a little *game* she and her friends had been working on. And I think we both realized it was something she needed to tell you more about. Nora?"

Margot realized for the first time that Nora was holding a slim folder in her hands, one that might be used to hand in a report, if those were even still done on paper. Nora handed it over to Margot.

After taking one look at the cover, Margot's heart sank, and she knew she was going to be late for her meeting with Andrew, despite all her good intentions to leave early.

Written on the cover sheet of the folder was the title *How to Commit the Perfect Murder*.

Margot glanced up at Nora. "What is this?"

"It was the logic puzzle I was telling you about. Ewan challenged us with certain parameters to see what we could come up with. That was mine."

"Nora, this looks like a fu— this looks like a book report."

Nora nodded, almost with a gleam of pride, then her face crumpled. "Detective Phalen, this was supposed to be a game. We never meant it to be anything serious. But..."

"But?" Margot glanced around the open space and realized this wasn't the place to have this discussion.

She showed Kim and Nora into an interrogation room, then went back to her own office, where Wes was still working on his computer.

He blinked in confusion when he saw her come in. "I thought you left."

"Yeah, well, that was until one of the robot club kids showed up in the lobby with this." She dropped the report in front of Wes, who stared at it like it was in a different language before he started to flip through it. When he was only a few pages in, he looked up at her, his color ashen.

"Margot..."

"I know."

"This is..."

"I know."

"She's still here?"

"Yeah, I'm about to talk to her and her mom, if you want to come with."

Wes didn't hesitate, he followed behind her and they entered the interrogation room, sitting across from the Olynyk mother and daughter. The two women looked remarkably alike when they were side by side, a similarity Margot hadn't noticed before.

Rather than taking her usual terse tone, Margot set the file on the table between them and looked at Nora, her expression about as close to kind as she could make it.

"Nora, can you tell me about this project?"

Nora once again explained how Ewan liked to initiate unsolvable problems for the club to work out. "This time around he told us he had a tricky problem and didn't think any of us would be able to solve it. He got us all to read *Killer in the Classifieds*, and then explained that we should use those murders as our template, but determine a theoretical way to do them better, because obviously Ed Finch got caught."

Margot ignored the sick feeling in her stomach and opened the folder to where there was a checklist.

"*First kill, select a victim you know but not too personally (no friends, no relatives), someone who wouldn't be surprised to see you.*"

Margot gave Nora a meaningful look. The girl continued, "I looked at the statistics for violent crime and knew that *most* homicides were committed by someone who knew their victim. But I also noted that they typically looked to people in the person's circle: a spouse, a boyfriend, someone they worked with. I hypothesized that someone who recognized you enough to open the door to you, but not someone you would regularly spend time with, would be the ideal victim profile. It could also give plausible deniability for fingerprints found at the scene."

Margot's pulse ticked up a few notches as she fully realized what the girl was telling her. "Nora, did you know what Ewan was planning to do?"

The girl started to cry. One moment she was explaining her report in a detached tone, the next there were tears pouring down her cheeks and she could barely catch her breath. "N-n-no. I sw-swear. But after... after he said, *Good work, Nora, but I think it could use a little tweaking for next time*, I thought he was *kidding*. And then you guys showed up and..." Nora looked at the folder in abject disgust, snot bubbling at the corner of her nose, which she hastily wiped away with the back of her hand. "Did I help kill that woman?" she asked, staring at Margot pleadingly.

Margot looked at her for a long moment, then set the folder

back on the table, where it sat untouched between the four of them.

"No, Nora. If he was going to kill someone, he was going to do it one way or another."

What she didn't say, and never would, was that the selection of Shuye Zhou so precisely matched the criteria from Nora's report, it was highly likely that, if Ewan had been left to pick a victim on his own, the old woman would still be alive.

That was a kind of truth that didn't help anyone.

"I have one more question, if you don't mind," Margot said.

Nora was wiping tears from her face, but she nodded.

"Do you still have your copy of *Killer in the Classifieds*?"

Nora shook her head and opened the folder to where there was a blank page. Margot looked closely and saw that there were little clear sticker squares, like the old photo album mounts, stuck to an otherwise empty page.

"Mine was an old copy, basically falling apart, it was even missing pages when he gave it to me. He must have gotten it at a thrift store or Little Free Library or something. But I had taken out the page on Finch's first victim and put it here." She tapped the page. "Visuals really help a presentation."

Realizing what she had said, tears began to well in her eyes again.

"Mrs. Olynyk, Nora, we're going to need to get Nora's fingerprints, just to eliminate them," Wes said gently.

"Why?" Kim asked, ready to go into protective mode all over again.

"Because she might have touched evidence."

Nora took a look at both of them, then got to her feet and made it only as far as the tiny garbage can before she threw up.

THIRTY-NINE

Margot's mind was racing as she drove over the Golden Gate Bridge and tried to slot together everything she'd just learned. The police had a crew, led by Wes, heading out to pick up Ewan, and while she desperately wanted to stay and participate, she was already twenty minutes late and she wasn't going to *gain* time fighting against San Francisco traffic.

After firing off a quick text to Andrew on her way out the door, she was alone with her thoughts for the rest of the drive.

A game?

It had been a *game*?

Margot could imagine a great number of horrific scenarios that ended with someone dead. Passion, rage, jealousy, hunger, fear, there were reasons both terrible and understandable that resulted in a body resting on a slab in Evelyn's office.

But a game?

That was more than she could bear.

Whether or not those kids had known what they were participating in—and from what she'd learned from Nora, they were oblivious—their little puzzle-solving club had gotten a woman killed.

And what was worse, if they had done things just slightly different—slightly better—Ewan might have actually gotten away with it.

With the distraction of the game on her mind, the trip from the precinct to prison went faster than she expected. It was only when she pulled into the lot that she realized she was still wearing the jeans she had put on that morning. Jeans she wasn't allowed to wear into the prison.

"*Fuck*," she screamed, slamming her palms against the steering wheel.

She blamed Andrew for this. Andrew, for deciding to slot a last-minute prison trip into her day. She had better things to do today. She was supposed to be meeting Wes in Chinatown to celebrate the Lunar New Year, but now with the prison trip and Ewan's pending arrest, that plan might be on ice indefinitely.

She went into the trunk of her car and kicked off her leather ankle boots as she rifled through a bag she'd tossed in the previous week, pulling out a pair of pants. They weren't khakis, but a pair of mustard yellow corduroy pants that she'd planned to dump in a donation bin would have to do the trick. They clashed horribly with the mauve shirt she was wearing, but there was no one here she wanted to impress.

Casting a quick glance around the parking lot, which was as empty as it was going to get, she moved back to the driver's side door for a modicum of privacy, stripped off her jeans and slipped into the pants.

"Fucking prison rules. Fucking Ed fucking Finch. Fucking goddamn Andrew Rhodes," she cursed as she fumbled with the zipper and remembered why she'd decided to get rid of these pants in the first place.

"Wardrobe malfunction?" a familiar voice asked.

Margot froze and looked to her left, where Goddamn Andrew Rhodes was standing behind her car, a bemused expression on his face telling her he had seen the whole thing.

"Not one single word from you," she said, tossing her jeans on the front passenger seat.

"A pantsuit solves a whole world of life's problems," he replied, smirking.

"Yeah, but then we'd be matching, and what a terrible fashion faux pas that would be."

Andrew scratched his beard as he looked over her mauve-and-mustard combo. He was wise enough not to say anything else about it.

She locked her gun and personal items in the trunk, and they went through the routine of clearing security. It was later in the afternoon than when she usually visited, and she was surprised by how quiet it was. She wondered if this was a scenario where Andrew had needed to pull some strings, because she was struck by the funny feeling they weren't actually supposed to be here right now.

Once she was settled into her usual uncomfortable seat at the table, a thought struck Margot, something that Nora had said earlier, the first time they met.

He misses the east coast.

Of course. Ewan and his mother were transplants, they weren't from the Bay Area originally. While Nora hadn't specified a city or even a state, Margot wondered about the fan letter to Ed from a kid in Trenton, New Jersey.

It was one of those things that seemed to be too implausible to be real, and yet it was like a puzzle piece falling into place. Ewan could be that kid. Why not? He'd already proven that his obsession had pushed him to follow in Ed's footsteps, something he'd hinted at doing in the letter.

Margot wondered if Ed even remembered that letter.

She realized she'd been so distracted thinking about the case —almost buzzing—she hadn't had time to feel nervous about seeing him.

And then the door opened. As Ed Finch shuffled into the

room, he was smiling, which made her instantly so mad she tasted blood in her mouth from biting down on her tongue. The guards helped get Ed settled across from her and the entire time he was grinning from ear to ear.

He gave her a quick once-over, leaning to the side to see under the table, before straightening up even as the guards had begun to inch forward to correct him.

"That is certainly a choice."

She stared at him in his navy prison-issue uniform and his hand-knit cardigan with sleeves that were a little too long. Rather than answer, she raised her eyebrow and gestured in the general direction of his ensemble.

"I wasn't trying to be rude," he countered. "I'm just so used to you wearing the same thing every time. This is interesting. A choice. It was you who took it to mean I was implying a *bad* choice."

Margot sighed. All at once she felt bone weary, tired down to her soul, as all the adrenaline she'd felt since Nora's lead at the station left her body.

Normally she had time to go through the anxiety, and get her mind right, to do some meditation in her car, or simply try to turn off the parts of her brain that felt anything before seeing Ed. Tonight she was totally unprepared and she had no patience.

Patience was not a good thing to be lacking in this scenario.

Before she'd left the station, she had quickly reviewed the names that Andrew and the team believed to be the most likely candidates for Ed's summer killing spree. She needed to stay focused so she could get out of here as quickly as possible. Anything off the path of the investigation, and she was likely to snap.

"I'm not here to get input on my fashion choices, Ed."

He looked mock-offended. "No, but you came all this way,

didn't you? A little small talk with your old man couldn't hurt, could it?"

"Physically?" She sighed. "Psychologically?" She touched a finger to her nose.

"Oh, come now. Are you really paying some stranger to lie on their couch and tell you that your dear old dad is the root of all your problems?" He clucked his tongue. "Megan Finch, I thought you were a tougher girl than that."

She remembered a joke Wes had made at her expense earlier in the week, and the words were out of her mouth before she could think better of saying them. "Well, you know what they say, don't you? Ten out of ten times, dads are to blame for daddy issues."

One of the guards stifled a laugh, but Margot couldn't turn to see who it was without looking away from Ed, and that would have meant missing the way his smile faded away as he internalized her words.

She couldn't help but look at his face, taking in the color of his eyes, the set of his nose, all the details she caught when she looked at herself in the mirror, at her brother.

"I was a good father to you."

"Beg to differ."

Ed slammed his fists down onto the table, and though Margot jumped, she quickly held up a hand to stop the guards from getting closer. They paused, and then stepped back—but their trigger fingers were all a tiny bit closer than they'd been a moment earlier.

She had worried she'd be the one to lose it, yet it seemed his patience with her was also starting to wear thin. That might have been the only thing that pleased her about this interaction.

Margot didn't want to give Ed *any* satisfaction from these visits.

When Ed spoke again spit flecked his lips, as if he had to fight against his own anger to get the words out.

"You ungrateful little cunt," he snarled.

Out of the corner of her eye she saw Andrew shift in his seat, as if he might get up and call this to a stop. With her hand beside her on the edge of her seat where he could see it but Ed couldn't, she held her fingers up, keeping him in place.

There wasn't anything Ed could say to hurt her anymore.

Words were just words.

These words weren't even original by his standards. She'd read them in his letter not long ago, and they'd barely stung then.

Margot had had enough.

She had done this time and time again, giving up little bits of herself, little shards of her soul, of her well-being, of her very sanity, all for the sake of justice. But what was justice? Was it a name crossed off a list? Was it a body dug from the ground that could finally be buried with a proper headstone? Maybe a family sleeping better at night?

There'd been a time when those fragmented, distant versions of justice had been enough to keep this going, because she'd told herself it was important. It mattered.

But now, looking at the curl of her father's lip, the white-knuckled tension of his clawed hands, shackled and harmless, she didn't think justice was a real thing anymore.

The monster had been pulled out from under the bed.

The girls were never coming home.

She didn't need to pay for his sins.

"I want you to listen to me," she said quickly, leaning closer, though still out of reach in case he grabbed for her. "I know this is fun for you. You love to see if I'll come running at the drop of a hat. One word from Daddy Dearest and here she is, ready to beg for her scraps and say thank you. But Ed, I didn't come here today to play quid pro quo to find out who else you killed."

He stared at her, his eyes so like hers it was a stark reminder that they *were* cut from the same cloth. She hoped there was light in her eyes, where his were flat and dull.

She went on, now that she had his full attention. "You've had a real good time, playing with me, playing with the FBI, telling us when you'll bless us with another name, another grave, but it stops here. Today."

In truth, she'd been planning to ask about the girls. She'd felt certain she would keep showing up here, keep chipping away at herself as long as it was for a good cause.

But he was getting off on it.

And she was *done* giving killers a single ounce of gratification.

She was positively *over* this. The way he got to pick and choose what bits of information to feed them. The way he got to drag her away from cases that genuinely needed her attention, because the lives of other *living* women could be at stake if she didn't find those killers.

The way kids were making a game out of murder the same way Ed did every time he made her come back to this godforsaken place.

The seething rage etched on his features had faded, replaced with confusion.

"Ma—" Andrew caught himself, even as the name came to the tip of his tongue. "Maybe," he course-corrected, "we could get what we came here for."

"Leigh Keller and Ruby Goldberg. You killed them both, didn't you?" She looked at Ed, only now she was looking right through him.

He ground his teeth together before finally giving a tight nod.

"And Ginny Hubert?"

"Yes."

"Great. My work here is done." She pushed herself up out

of the seat, but Ed rose at the same time, causing all the guards to surge forward as one.

Margot and Ed stood like that, as the world moved in slow motion around them, staring at each other. In her heeled boots, she was taller than him. For some reason that made her feel good.

"There are more," he said finally. "Come again. Come once a month. I'll give you all the names. There are so many more, Buddy."

Margot looked at him but couldn't see the man who had called her that name so long ago.

"You can tell them to someone else." She turned to leave, not waiting to see if Andrew was on her tail. She didn't care.

She was all the way to the door, waiting for a guard to let her out when she heard Ed yell, always desperate for the last word.

"This isn't over yet. You and me, we'll talk again real soon, just you wait."

FORTY

Margot was not willing to wear corduroy pants for the rest of the night. This time, she got her jeans from the car and brought them into the security check-in building, to change somewhere other than the middle of the parking lot.

The whole time, as she balled the yellow pants up into a ball, she was only distracting herself from what had happened with Ed.

They had finally pushed each other past their own breaking points.

She hadn't said anything to Andrew, and he hadn't said anything to her. There seemed to be a mutual understanding that now was not the time for lectures, or for him to ask her to change her mind. Now was the time to leave her alone.

When she got back into her car and retrieved her phone from the glove compartment, there were several missed texts and calls from Wes.

Ewan Willingham was not at school, and not at home. His mother had let the police thoroughly search the apartment, and she claimed to have no idea where he was.

Meet at the Dragon Gate? was his last text.

Their prime suspect was in the wind, and she wasn't entirely sure if Wes was asking her to go look for him, or if he was sticking with their plan to enjoy the Lunar New Year festivities. Considering Ewan lived in Chinatown, perhaps this was intended to be a two-birds-one-stone offering.

Margot fired off a text letting him know her ETA, then headed back into the city. For the first time ever when driving away from the prison, she turned on the radio.

For once, she didn't feel like being alone with her thoughts.

An oldies station played "Tusk" by Fleetwood Mac, and while the grungy rhythm of the song had her tapping her fingers on the steering wheel, she felt a growing sense of dread in her stomach, something that she couldn't quantify. Maybe it was nerves about finding Ewan. Maybe she was just now beginning to realize what she'd done by severing ties with Ed.

She'd made statements like that before. Even *she* wasn't sure she meant it.

But she wanted to mean it.

She switched to a pop station the rest of the way home, because it was impossible to feel bad while singing along to "I Want It That Way" by the Backstreet Boys, and that was the kind of disassociation she was craving.

Back in San Francisco she left her car at the apartment and quickly changed clothes, as if the shirt being in the same air as Ed Finch had tainted it.

The air outside was cool, so she slipped on a green sweater, something she could wear without a coat, but brought her jacket anyway because she was keeping her shoulder holster and badge with her.

She was halfway through putting on lip gloss when she realized she was *primping* and was horrified with herself. But it was too late to undo it now, so the cherry-flavored gloss got to stay.

Fifteen minutes later, she was at the Dragon Gate entry to Chinatown. While she normally avoided walking alone at night, the streets were thronged with tourists and locals participating in the night's events, and that gave her enough semblance of security to make the short walk.

She kept an eye on her surroundings, though, always.

Never let your guard down, Ed said once.

And Margot never had. Not since the day the FBI hauled him away.

Despite everything that had happened over the course of the day, all the bullshit weighing so heavily on her soul, when she saw Wes waiting near the gate her heart immediately lifted. He was still wearing his suit from work, though he had abandoned the coat somewhere along the line, and two fewer buttons were done up than when she'd previously seen him.

He looked tired, and Margot knew this day hadn't been a fun one for him either.

"You lose your buttons?" she asked, poking him in the exposed patch of bare skin on his chest.

"Someone stole them, would you believe it? Major Crimes informs me they're too busy to look for the person who did it, so I guess I'm just a deep-V guy now."

"I'm not sure if you impressed the importance of this on Major Crimes, Wesley. They're not going to have to look at you."

He smirked, jostling her with a quick one-armed hug as they headed up the incline into Chinatown, and it felt good and comforting to have his arm around her.

Whatever he was about to say next was obliterated by the ear-splitting sound of shots. Margot, still mentally recovering from the recent sniper attacks on the city the previous fall, froze in place, her hands flying to her ears and her head ducking against Wes's chest.

A cloud of fragrant smoke, stinking of sulfur, wafted past them, and Margot saw that on the ground there was a veritable confetti of red paper and lettuce leaves. Even as her pulse pounded, she blushed, feeling stupid. The paper was from the hundreds of firecrackers being set off up and down the street all day long. The tradition was meant to usher in good fortune and prosperity by scaring off evil spirits. The lettuce was a part of the lion dances, as it was meant to be spat up by the lion at a business owner to bring them wealth in the coming year. The streets were a disaster for days after, but it was all part of the tradition, something that Margot normally relished being part of.

She straightened up and pressed her hand to her chest, taking deep, concentrated breaths until her pulse was back to normal. She gave Wes a sheepish smile.

"Don't you dare make fun of me," she warned.

The look on his face was hard to read; it was concern, but with a hint of faked amusement. In the background she could hear the steady beat of drums and it took her a moment to realize it wasn't her heart.

Up and down the street, which was closed to traffic for the festivities, people were going in and out of shops that normally shuttered around six, but were enjoying that Lunar New Year prosperity in a very active way by staying open hours later than usual.

More firecrackers went off further up the hill, but Margot was ready for them this time, only jumping slightly.

"Tell me what happened with the kid," she asked, wanting any excuse to move the topic away from her reaction.

Wes, ever gracious, went along with it. "We sent a unit to the school, but there was no sign of him and according to his record he has no extracurriculars today, so he had no reason to be there. I went with the crew to his house with a warrant, but his mom didn't even ask to see it, she just let us in and stood out in the hall. She didn't seem the least bit surprised to see us, but she also didn't give us much to go on. She said he hadn't been home since that morning. Said she saw him briefly before he left for school."

"You think she knew what he was up to." Margot had suspected as much. Toni gave her Mommie Dearest vibes from the get-go. Margot's calves burned as they climbed upward to the next stop light, letting the regularly scheduled trolley cross. Tourists snapped photos and selfies as the tram moved up the hill, but Margot knew what it was like to be stuck behind one in rush hour when it became disconnected from the power cables, and they needed to wait for someone with a special pole to reattach it.

The trams had long ago lost their luster for Margot, but she did get a kick out of seeing how others reacted to them.

The drumming got louder as they moved up the hill, as did the scent of BBQ duck and any number of other delightful foodstuffs. A lineup had formed outside the Golden Gate Bakery—or more likely had been ongoing since morning—as people hoped to get their hands on celebratory mooncakes and custard tarts. Margot had learned previously that the mooncakes were not actually a traditional part of the Lunar New Year celebration and were traditionally for the Mid-Autumn Festival, but they had become so popular during times of celebration in Chinatown that most local bakeries stocked them for both holidays.

She was thinking about baked goods when a blond head passed by in the thick crowd, heading back down the hill.

At first, she was certain she was imagining him, because it seemed too convenient for him to be here, but at the same time, it made perfect sense. They were only a block past Washington Street, right on his home turf, and there was a chance he was cocky enough to believe that no one would be able to find him in this melee.

She grabbed Wes by the arm, but as she called him her voice was lost to more firecrackers, and the smoke that floated out into the street in their wake. Margot craned her neck as the surging crowd jostled them from both sides, and tried to keep an eye on the head to get a positive ID.

The smoke cleared on a light breeze, and there he was, looking back at her, possibly as startled by the crackers as she had been.

Ewan locked eyes with her, and for a moment the whole street was frozen, and a dead silence fell around her as the sound of her heartbeat filled her ears.

"*Wes*," she screamed, squeezing his arm and pointing. There was no need to be subtle now, Ewan had seen her. Wes realized what she was pointing at and grabbed for his phone even as Margot started to push through the crowd. She tried to tell them she was police, but no one was listening and she kept getting bounced around as people pushed forward.

The only positive was that Ewan was also locked in by the bodies around him and although he was running, it was like a chase through molasses. Wes caught up to her quickly, bodies parting around him like Moses in the Red Sea thanks to his tall figure and apparently more commanding presence. She pushed him ahead and they moved in the direction Ewan had been going, though she could no longer see him among all the other bodies.

Their one stroke of luck was that all the side streets off Grant were teeming with police, on hand in case anything got out of control. When Margot got to the corner of Grant and Jackson, she knew where Ewan was headed.

He might be a killer, but he was also still a kid. He had no money, nowhere to hide himself except the one place he knew best. Home.

A squad car on Jackson had just engaged its lights, getting the BOLO from the call Wes had placed. Margot ran up to them, flashing her badge. She pointed up the block to the alley running between Jackson and Washington. "Get cars on both ends of that alley and block it off. He lives in one of those apartments," she instructed.

The officer acted quickly, getting into the squad car and navigating the short distance up the hill to the mouth of the alley, blocking it off. Multiple shouts of annoyance could be heard, as they were effectively cutting off access to the Golden Gate Fortune Cookie Factory. No one seemed to care why the car was there, otherwise.

Margot and Wes followed it up on foot, and she waited until they were in the alley before drawing her weapon.

Lights bounced off the alley walls from both directions as two uniformed officers moved in their direction from the opposite end. They reached the end of Ross and the group pivoted together down the narrow alley between the restaurant and Ewan's apartment.

Margot was half convinced Ewan was going to pop out of one of the small alcoves in the alley brandishing a knife at her, but instead they closed ranks in the little courtyard she'd found during her first visit.

Ewan was sitting in one of the plastic chairs playing a game on his phone, the blue glow lighting his face and mingling with the lights from the nearby squad cars.

He looked up, seeming only to see Margot, and gave her a smile that could freeze mercury.

"I'm glad you're the one who figured it out," he said, still grinning. "He promised me you were smart enough to do it, I just didn't believe him."

FORTY-ONE

He looked so normal.

Margot and Wes stood in the interrogation viewing area into the room where Ewan was seated. There was an unopened can of Coke sitting in front of him and he was leaned back in his chair, arms dangling down at his sides, while he studied the ceiling, the mirror, the space around him, all with an air of indulgent curiosity.

He didn't seem at all concerned about where he was.

Margot watched as Ewan rocked backwards on the chair, then forwards, like he was having the goddamn time of his life.

"What did he mean?" Wes asked.

"What do you think he meant?" she replied.

He promised me you were smart enough to do it.

Wes frowned. "But you had the FBI go through Finch's letters. There was nothing they found, nothing they confiscated to suggest he was sending instructions to someone on the outside, or even that he was humoring some demented kid."

Margot just shook her head and shrugged. "Maybe they missed something. Maybe I missed something. We don't know if they were using code. We'd have to go through at least a decade of letters to know if this kid has been writing to him and getting anything in return."

Ultimately, they'd have to do that anyway, but there wasn't time to do it before talking to Ewan.

"You want me to take this?" Wes asked.

Her shoulders tensed, creeping together and pinching the nerves at the back of her neck. "Let's do it together. If anything starts to feel like it's crossing a line... if *I* start to cross a line, then you take over, OK? I won't fight you on it." Considering she had just been sitting across from Ed Finch himself a few hours earlier, she figured she could manage his little acolyte.

But things hadn't exactly gone smoothly with Ed, either, so there was no telling how things might unfold.

Margot and Wes entered the interrogation room together. She had Nora's report in an evidence bag, along with the page from Andrew's book that they'd found at the crime scene.

Ewan smiled when they entered, shark teeth flashing. It was an eerie kind of déjà vu.

"Detectives," he said cheerily. "A real treat. What an experience."

"Be sure to leave a review on Yelp," Wes said, leaning in the corner.

Ewan snapped his fingers and winked at the tall detective. "You got it, Buddy."

Margot's eye twitched at the unexpected use of the nickname, even though it wasn't aimed at her. She had to steady herself with a deep breath before she set her items down on the table, arranging them so they faced Ewan. Then she put down a photo from Shuye Zhou's crime scene and placed it neatly in between them.

Ewan didn't even flinch.

"Tell me something, Ewan. Who was your first choice?"

He stared at the three items in front of him, then reached out and adjusted the photo so it was properly centered.

"Here's what I think I might have done. If I was the one doing it, you know, not saying I did. Just hypothetically."

Margot wanted to laugh out loud. "Hypothetically, of course."

"See, with Ed's first kill, it seems obvious to me he picked someone who was available. I know he has this creepy reputation for stalking his victims and finding them through classified ads, or whatever, but that's not really the whole story, is it? Because if you really *learn* about his crimes, it becomes pretty apparent that Ed wasn't a killer, exactly, he was a *predator*. That's what makes him so scary. And, like, sure, sometimes a lion will hunt the same lame gazelle for days before going in for the kill, but an apex predator also isn't going to ignore the opportunity for an easy meal when it's right in front of them."

Margot schooled her features, but it was difficult. Despite sounding like a teenager—and a little bit like a member of a cult—so much of what Ewan was saying and how he was saying it made her think of Ed. She found herself looking at his face, wondering. Even though she knew it wasn't possible, she still couldn't *help* but wonder if this might be the son Ed wished her brother Justin had been.

A chip off the old block.

"So, you wanted to prove you were the same. A predator."

"*Hypothetically*," Ewan corrected. "If I wanted to mirror Ed's process, I should have found someone at random."

"Or through a personal ad," Wes said from the corner of the room.

Ewan shrugged. "Sure, but like, no one really *does* that anymore, do they? Like the pickings are going to be pretty slim if I went looking for someone that way. *If* I was looking. But then Nora nailed it." He tapped the report. "Someone you know, but don't know *well*. Someone it wouldn't necessarily be easy to connect you to. And man, my first thought when I read that was one of the kids who hung out behind the restaurant. So maybe, if that was the best option, I start hanging out back there a little more, start getting to know them, share a smoke, make it so they don't feel weird if I happen to be there. And maybe I wait for the right time for one of them to be alone out there at night."

"Sure, but then they're never alone when you need them to be, right?"

"I mean, this is just a thought exercise. So, then the brain starts going, gears spinning, and you start to wonder, *who would be alone?* And maybe you're thinking that when an old lady shows up with a cart of groceries. Or a load of laundry. Or needs her newspaper brought upstairs." He scooted the chair forward, folding his elbows on the table, nudging the Coke out of the way. He rested his chin on his arm and looked at the grisly photo of Shuye almost fondly. "And maybe one day she says *Why don't you come in so I can give you something to take home for dinner?*" He affected a mock Chinese accent for this which made Margot's formerly impassive face twist into a grimace.

He looked up at her, chin still rested on his hands, and smirked.

He was intentionally trying to push buttons to see which ones got him a reaction, and he'd succeeded.

"You know what I bet would be the hardest part?" he said, looking back down at the photo.

"Why don't you tell us?" she said through gritted teeth.

"I bet I can guess what you think I'm going to say. And *hypothetically* I bet you'd think the hardest part would be getting a knife through someone's skull, because bones are hard as shit. But when I ran through this whole totally made-up encounter in my head, I found something else was even harder."

She didn't *want* to give in to his obvious prompt, especially since he'd already implicated himself past the point of no return. The stab wound to the head had never been made public knowledge.

So, it didn't matter if she let him have things his way.

"What was the hardest part?" she asked.

"Stopping at twenty-two." Ewan sat up, holding Margot's gaze. He was practically *begging* for a response from her. But if he thought he had pushed her past her breaking point, he was a few hours too late.

Margot started to collect the items off the table and Ewan's face fell. "That's it?"

"It's been a very long day, Ewan, and I don't feel like playing games with little boys." She pushed her chair back and was about to stand when he stopped her.

"Don't you want to know *why?*"

"Why doesn't matter in a hypothetical."

"Why *always* matters."

They stared at each other. She wasn't even sure if Wes was breathing behind her.

"Why did you do it?" she asked him.

Ewan gripped the edge of the table, smiling. "Why do you do what *you* do, Detective Phalen?"

"My *why* got lost a very long time ago," she said, surprising herself with the honesty that tumbled so easily off her tongue.

Ewan shook his head. "I don't think that's true. I think the reason you do what you do, and the reason I did what I did... hypothetically... are the exact same reason."

She looked at him and once again couldn't help but overanalyze the shape of his nose, the color of his eyes, the feral turn of his smile. And sure, she was probably projecting it all considering how recently she'd seen Ed, but she couldn't help it.

Not when they sounded so much alike.

"I don't care why you did it." She pushed herself up from the chair.

"Well, that's not true."

She rolled her eyes. "Then tell me why, since you're obviously dying to."

"I think we both did it to prove something to our dad."

FORTY-TWO

Oakland, CA

Eddie really didn't know why Sarah was crying.

Red and blue lights bounced off nearby houses, and every time Eddie looked around, it seemed a new neighbor had come to their front stoop or had parted their curtains to look out at what was happening.

Overhead, it was a rare night where the stars were visible, despite the glow from the city lights, because the new moon was letting them peep through. Eddie chewed on his thumbnail and stared up at the stars, trying to remember where the Big Dipper was.

Sarah wouldn't stop crying.

They had both been wrapped in scratchy wool blankets that the paramedics had brought with them, which was funny because it wasn't even particularly cold out, so why did they need blankets? But it seemed that the paramedics and cops either weren't parents or left most of the hard parenting to their wives, because none of the men standing on Eddie's lawn seemed to be able to shut Sarah up.

They were all watching her the way he imagined the crew of an old Greek ship might watch a siren, knowing if they got too close, she would drag them down to their deaths. So, everyone let Sarah go on crying.

And then they looked at Eddie and wondered why he wasn't.

They were sitting on the top of Miss Shirley's stoop—the house still vacant after all these months—because people were coming and going from their own house at a steady pace, and because no one knew who to call to take the kids somewhere else.

"You don't have your dad's work number?" one cop had asked, several times.

Each time Eddie replied, "We don't have a dad." This concept, however, seemed not to be sticking. Finally, when asked the third time, he simply amended it to, "Our dad is dead." This, at last, made the cop stop asking. Eddie didn't have any other suggestions for him either. Mama never had visitors, never talked about family except to declare them all useless sinners who would be in Hell soon if they weren't yet.

Eddie hoped she'd say hi to them for him.

Their front door opened, and a metal gurney came out, requiring four different uniformed men to carry it down the few steps. It hit the concrete with a heavy *thud* and Eddie briefly wondered if the whole gurney might collapse under Mama's considerable girth, sending her body rolling down the street for all to see.

That would have delighted him.

Instead, her body was covered with two of the same scratchy wool blankets the kids had been given, and belted to the gurney so it wouldn't budge. As soon as Sarah saw the gurney her wailing reached fever pitch, tears streaming down her face as she rocked back and forth.

"You are making a spectacle of yourself," Eddie said

coldly, a phrase their mother had liked to use any time either of them had dared to raise their voice at her within earshot of others.

Sarah, on hearing Mama's words come from his mouth, sobered enough to look at him, her face puffy and eyes red. "She's *dead*, Eddie, don't you understand that? Mama's *dead*."

He looked at her like she was stupid, because she was. "I know."

"Don't you care?"

Eddie didn't reply, and it was probably better he didn't. A cop stopped to talk to the two paramedics and while they kept their voices low, Eddie heard everything they were saying.

"—in the shower?"

"Looks like she slipped. Smashed her head. She was probably out cold instantly, don't think she felt much of anything at all."

Eddie rested his chin in his hands and smiled to himself.

They were wrong.

She'd been very much awake when she realized what was happening to her.

A brown station wagon pulled up behind the ambulance, and a woman wearing a tweed skirt suit, her hair pulled back into a precise bun, emerged from the front seat. She spotted Eddie and Sarah immediately but stopped to speak to an officer first. The officer pointed to the kids, his face so clearly relieved Eddie understood immediately what the woman was doing there.

She crossed over to them and stood at the bottom of the stoop. Unlike most adults, when she spoke to them it wasn't in a dumbed-down tone. She was no-nonsense and meant business right away.

"My name is Mrs. Fitzsimmons. I'll be keeping an eye on you until we can make contact with a suitable relative. If there's anything in the house you need, you have five minutes and one bag." She stood waiting for a moment, taking in Sarah's tear-soaked idiocy and Eddie's nonchalant disregard.

"Sarah. Eddie. I'm very sorry for your loss, but there will be time to discuss it later, and somewhere more suitable. Now let's go." She clapped her hands twice and gestured to their own front door where a uniformed officer waited.

Sarah got up first, moving into the house like she was a ghost about to start haunting it.

Eddie pushed himself off the steps and looked at Mrs. Fitzsimmons, trying to size her up. He suspected this was not someone he wanted to trifle with.

"Ed," he said finally.

"Pardon?" She squinted down at him as if he'd just spoken to her in Pashto.

"My name. It's not Eddie. It's Ed." And without waiting for her to reply he headed straight for her car and climbed in the back seat.

There was nothing left for him in that house anyway.

FORTY-THREE

Toni Willingham hadn't bothered to lock her apartment door, so when Margot knocked, a raspy, "Just come in," was the reply she got.

Wes had offered to come up with her, but Margot felt like this was something she needed to do alone.

Inside, the curtains were drawn and cigarette smoke hung in the air, giving the place the same vibe as a seedy cocktail lounge.

Toni was sitting on the couch in the living room, but the TV wasn't on, nor were any of the lamps. She was staring straight ahead, periodically bringing the cigarette to her lips before exhaling a plume of smoke into the air.

Margot wrinkled her nose but managed not to cough. She didn't want to be here, didn't want to speak to this woman, because she *knew* that somehow, either by hiding the truth or ignoring it, Toni was responsible for everything Ewan had done.

Being here made Margot feel queasy, because she felt like there was something else left, something only Toni might know.

Like how Ewan had known who she was.

Who her father was.

Because Ewan wasn't saying.

"Ms. Willingham, I'm surprised we didn't see you with Ewan down at the station."

Toni let out a rough little laugh. "He'll be eighteen in three weeks, you know that? They'll try him as an adult. And they should." She continued to stare at the wall, and when Margot followed her gaze, there was a small family portrait hanging across from Toni that depicted her and Ewan sitting together, the New York skyline in the background.

They were both smiling, but there was something so familiar in the emptiness in Ewan's grin it made Margot feel sick to her stomach.

She glanced down at a stack of mail sitting next to the door. Her own business card was lying next to it, the number circled in blue pen as if someone had wanted to call but simply never had.

Margot picked up the mail and Toni did nothing to stop her, and as she flipped through the bills and flyers her pulse sped up as the other shoe she'd been waiting for finally dropped.

The last letter in the pile, with a mail forwarding sticker on it and the name she'd been hoping not to see.

Rhonda Reese.

Rhonda.

Margot looked up from the letter to Toni, who was still smoking, still staring off into nothingness.

"You followed him here?" Margot asked, her voice cracking.

Toni didn't bother to pretend, or lie, and Margot was grateful to her for that one small thing. "He asked me to go ahead of him, and I did. It pissed Ethan off to no end." Toni finally flicked a glance in Margot's direction. "That's his real name. Ethan. He didn't want to change it, but I changed mine. Thought we would get a fresh start here, be new people. I just wanted to be someone different. But you can't become someone different by changing your name, can you?"

Margot had lived that exact life—moving across the country and changing her name—and understood how difficult it could be for a kid.

"What were you running from?" Margot set the letters back down. While part of her wanted to get closer, she stayed rooted in one spot.

"It wasn't me who had things to leave behind. Ed's suggestion... well... it came at the right time to get a clean break for Ethan. Things weren't going well for us. When Ed said he thought he might be going somewhere else soon, he implied it might be nice to have a friendly face on the other side. He knew all about Ethan, of course. I tell him everything."

She stubbed out the cigarette.

"Ewan... Ethan..." Margot struggled to find the right words to ask what she needed to know, mostly because she was terrified of the answer. Ewan had spelled out what he *wanted* her to believe. She'd done the mental math, and unless the FBI had totally messed up the timeline, she *knew* in her soul that Ewan was a liar, but she desperately needed that to be backed up by the one person who would know the truth. "He's not..."

Toni hiccupped out a sound that was either laughter or a sob. "Ed's?" She shook her head. "No, honey, he's not Ed's. Ed and I, I mean... No. That's not possible at all. Ethan was born before I met Ed. He didn't need the genes to turn him into what he is."

"Just the inspiration," Margot whispered. Ewan either wanted *her* to believe he was Ed's son, or had convinced himself that was the case. She wasn't sure which option was more depressing.

"I guess you're proof the genes don't always turn out all bad, though, aren't you?" Toni got up and went to the window, parting the curtains enough to let light in. Despite the new brightness, Margot felt like the room had gotten darker with Toni's words. It was early still, but to Margot, who hadn't slept, it felt late. But right now, she was wide awake and chilled to the bone. Toni continued, oblivious to what one sentence had done to change the room. "I think I'm to blame for a lot of this. For Ethan looking at Ed and thinking... oh, who knows what he thought? But I talked about Ed a lot, about the better man under the demons, about a good soul who just did terrible things. And I can't help but wonder if that encouraged Ethan, gave him permission to like him... to want to be like him." She stared out the window into the surprisingly bright morning.

It was the dawn of a new year in Chinatown.

Margot wanted to ask how Toni had known who she was, because there was nothing in Ed's letters about his daughter being a cop—that would have gotten pulled—but knowing Rhonda visited Ed, or had in the past, it wasn't beyond reason he could have said something in person.

Putting the pieces together when Margot showed up asking about Ed's book wouldn't have been all that difficult. Now that she knew who Toni... Rhonda... who she really was, the rest didn't feel like such a mystery anymore. But one thing still bothered her more than anything else.

"Why did you marry him?" Margot asked, because if Ed wasn't going to explain it, then maybe Toni could.

"I don't know. I saw something in him during the trials on TV. He was sort of magnetic, I don't know how to explain it, but it was like a voice in my head was telling me, *You can help him, you can heal him.*"

Margot didn't interrupt, though she knew she wasn't doing anything to school the disgusted expression on her face.

Toni went on, almost wistfully, like Margot wasn't even there. "The first time he replied to my letters it was like someone had really seen me. He was so kind, and he'd really paid attention to every word. I wasn't used to that, to people actually listening to me. He really listened to me. And when I finally got to see him face to face, he really *saw* me. And I like to think I saw the real him."

Margot had sat across from the *real* Ed Finch, and she had an awfully hard time imagining it would be love at first sight for a mentally well woman.

"Did you really think demons made him do it?"

Toni was looking down, and Margot's pulse sped up as she let her gaze drift to the top of the window, checking to see if the lock was engaged.

"I think about jumping, sometimes," Toni said, as if reading Margot's mind. "When they found Susie's body, you know, right after you came to my door that first time, I thought about opening the window and throwing myself right out. Because no one would believe I didn't know. But it's not far enough. The fall, it's just not far enough. And where would that leave me? In traction somewhere, with *him* being the one to make those decisions."

Margot wasn't sure which *him* Toni meant, if it was her serial killer husband or her psychopath son. She understood that neither option would provide much comfort. Even if she believed that demons were piloting the ship and good men lived within Ethan and Ed, how can you trust someone with a demon inside them?

"Why didn't you say anything then?"

"Because I didn't want to believe it. And I hoped, I prayed, that maybe it wasn't him. That he hadn't finally taken that step. But of course it was him. It was always going to be him."

Toni fingered the lock on the top of the window and Margot did the mental math of how quickly she could clear the coffee table and couch to stop the woman if she suddenly decided to open it up and toss herself out.

A tiny, horrible part of her wondered if she'd even try.

Toni turned to Margot. "That's why you're here, isn't it? To see if I knew? I guess I always knew he was capable of it. Maybe

I always knew it was inevitable. But when you showed up at my door that day, I wanted to believe it couldn't be true. For him. For me."

Margot hesitated, thinking about how broken Toni had become, and how little she seemed to care who Margot really was. Maybe Ewan was the one who had worked out the truth first, with his ungodly gift for logic puzzles and obsession with all things Ed. If that was the case, the repercussions could be catastrophic for her carefully constructed lie of a life, and Margot would need to talk to Andrew about what to do about it. But there was a chance it was at least contained.

Margot nodded, mostly to herself. "I guess I only have one last question, then," she said, when Toni stepped away from the window and the room fell back into darkness. "After all this, are you still going to see Ed?"

Toni picked up the cigarettes in front of her and lifted one to her mouth, lighting it easily and blowing a plume of smoke into the air before she answered.

"You tell me who I have left in this world aside from him, Detective Phalen. Ed Finch and Ethan are the only family I have."

Margot gaped at the woman, a sick pit of guilt and rage mingling in her stomach.

Then maybe you need to find a taller building, she thought, but couldn't make herself villain enough to say it.

Instead, she shook her head and said, "Then I feel sorry for you, because you've got nothing at all."

FORTY-FOUR
ONE WEEK LATER

February had overstayed its welcome.

The short run of nice weather had turned into day after day of rain and chilly fog. By nightfall, the streets were nearly empty, making the city feel like a ghost town as people stayed indoors, huddled under blankets. Everyone was catching up on TV shows they'd missed when it was nice enough to be outside.

Margot and Wes were back on night shifts, and it seemed that at least for a day or two, everyone in San Francisco had decided to stop killing each other, so they'd been granted a brief reprieve.

Margot wasn't going to complain, she didn't want to hunch under an umbrella and watch as the constant rain washed away her evidence.

She was also tired to her bones after the week she'd had and felt like the lull was a gift from the universe, telling her she deserved one tiny moment of peace before the next barrage came in.

Wes had gone to get them dinner, as it was after midnight, and they had foolishly decided it was a good time to clean their office and review some background evidence on a few cold cases lingering in the precinct.

Her phone buzzed, Wes's name on the screen making her smile in a way that was not entirely friendship-related, but also didn't mean anything more. Just a smile for her.

In the week since the case had closed, he'd been such a rock for her, not protective necessarily, but also more keenly attuned to her. He, more than anyone else she knew, understood the implications of what Ewan had tried to make her believe in that interrogation room, and he knew how much it had shaken her.

Even with logic on her side, there had been moments Margot couldn't help but wonder... *what if?*

Wes had been around to make sure she stopped those questions in their tracks.

Likewise, Andrew had been surprisingly gentle with her following her blow-up at the prison. He gave her a few days to calm down before he checked in, and even then it had been to ask how she was doing. He'd told her they were looking into Ewan knowing who she was, to see if he'd shared the information at all, but so far it seemed to only be something he had used to toy with her.

Just like Ed.

She knew Andrew well enough to know he wasn't going to let her off without a fight when it came to working the cold cases, but for the time being, she had no intention of ever setting foot in that prison again.

Wes's text read,

> They're out of corned beef, you're going to have to make a sacrifice.

> How very dare they.

> I tried to tell them you wouldn't stand for it, but they said I get what I get after midnight and I should be grateful for it.

> Turkey?

I can make turkey happen for you.

> My hero.

Gyro out of the question.

> I'm ignoring you now until you bring me a sandwich.

She set her phone down on her desk, glad no one was around to see her grinning like a fool, and she turned her attention back to the organization project they'd started an hour earlier.

Their case board for the Shuye Zhou murder was still up, and while there was still evidence to be gathered to satisfy the district attorney's office, the case itself was closed. Ewan—or Ethan—hadn't outright confessed, but they had him on record sharing details no one but the killer could possibly know, and his mother's account of him had helped.

He hadn't exactly been hiding his guilt.

The FBI had someone going through all of Ed's letters, both in and out, trying to figure out how he'd been communicating with Ewan, but so far there was nothing, which bothered Margot.

It was possible, she supposed, that Ewan had imagined a relationship with Ed that simply did not exist, but given that Toni was Rhonda, and Rhonda was married to Ed, Margot didn't think it was likely that Ed wasn't involved *somehow*. Margot needed to know.

They just weren't seeing the connection yet. Once they did, the kid would probably be joining his hero in San Quentin.

Margot took down all the items from the board and put them in a banker's box with Shuye's name and case number on the outside. They'd eventually go into storage with the rest of the physical evidence from the case, but for now they would wait beside the couch until everything was resolved.

Nora and all the other robot club kids had made official statements, and the others had provided copies of their own perfect murder reports. Based on everything they had worked on, if Ewan hadn't been caught, Margot suspected he would have moved on to some of the other suggestions in the projects.

Ewan, as it turned out, was not a criminal genius, but he was very good at having other people do his homework for him.

The kids, for their part, were all horrified by what they had participated in. Even one-syllable-answer James had come close to tears when he realized what their group had been party to.

None of them would face any legal consequences, but they would likely need to testify if Ewan's case ever went to trial. But as minors their names would never be made public. No one but Ewan should see their future ruined as a result of a game.

With the board now empty, Margot needed something to focus on. She pulled out the Muir Woods documents, a case which now felt much more active than it had a few months earlier, and put her three victims' photos on the board, along with crime scene images, and the pictures of Frederica and Leanne from the escort website.

They were having trouble tracking down the owner of the site, so vice was working on an op to help them book a date with one of the girls and hopefully work their way back to whoever was in charge. Margot could practically *feel* a break in the case coming, but they weren't there yet.

She thumbed through the files, including autopsy notes and interview records, looking for anything that might be important enough to put up on the board.

Spotting a photo of Rebecca Watson before she had all her plastic surgery, she pulled it out and found a magnet to attach it next to the others, when something in the photo caught her eye.

The picture had been taken off Rebecca's Instagram page

and hadn't been the clearest quality to begin with, but as Margot squinted, she looked more closely at the necklace Rebecca wore.

It was simple, gold, and could have been anything, which is why it never stood out before. But as Margot grabbed the printed image from the Larks player page on the escort site and held it beside the picture of Rebecca, she let out a sharp gasp.

The necklace and the logo were the same.

On her desk, her phone started to vibrate. Wes certainly had a good sense of timing.

She picked it up without looking. "You are *never* going to believe what I just found."

Silence, and then an inhale of breath were all that came from the other end of the phone, and Margot pulled her cell back to look at the screen.

It was the unknown number that had been calling her for weeks, that she had assumed was simply a very motivated scammer.

She brought the phone back to her ear and while common sense told her to hang up, something kept her fingers from moving to the *End Call* button.

Finally, the breathing turned into a chuckle, a self-satisfied, mean kind of chuckle that made Margot's stomach turn and forced her to sit down on the sagging couch in their office.

"You know," came the familiar voice. "I was getting so tired of having to use that godforsaken lawyer every time I wanted to talk to you. And you could say this was overkill..." He laughed at his own joke. "But I knew there had to be *some* way to get your attention."

Margot's mouth went dry. In her hand, the one still holding the Larks' logo, the paper began to shake.

This had to be a bad dream. She'd fallen asleep on the couch and any minute now Wes was going to come in and wake her up. Any minute. She closed her eyes and tried counting to ten, but by two, he was speaking again.

"What, you have nothing to say to your dear old dad? After I went to all this trouble? Had the boy do something right out of the Ed Finch handbook. What do you think of him, by the way? A bit overzealous, but a lot of promise. Shame to waste it all so early."

"What do you want?" she whispered, barely able to make the words form.

"Your attention, I thought I made that clear. Is it clear now?"

Margot was trying to be analytical. If this was real, he had gotten a cell phone somehow. Prison pipeline, things from the outside got in. Maybe he bribed a guard. That would explain how Ewan had been communicating with him without leaving a paper trail.

They'd need to check phone records, text records, CCTV. Now that she had the number, that had to give them a leg up.

"Don't ignore me," the voice said.

"I'm not." Because how do you ignore a knife buried six inches deep between your ribs? How do you ignore a gloved hand in the night? How do you ignore the shadow of a man in your doorway?

You can't ignore a living nightmare.

"Good girl. Now I want you to promise me something."

She stayed quiet, but that didn't seem to matter.

"I want you to promise you'll visit me again. I have so much I want to tell you, and your little outburst was very unbecoming. You need to behave like the daughter I raised."

Margot couldn't help herself, she let out a sharp, humorless laugh. "You went to all this effort just to get me to see you?"

He clucked his tongue. "You forget. I went to all this effort long before you said you'd never come back."

The chill of that sucked the wind from her lungs. And she

had to ask the question that Ewan had practically begged her to ask.

"Why?"

"I wanted something even simpler. Something you wouldn't give to me."

She stayed dead quiet, the paper in her hand crumpled and damp with sweat, fighting back a wave of nausea. She closed her eyes like that could make him go away.

Instead, he said three simple words, his voice as raspy as fingernails on a rusty screen door.

"Detective. Margot. Phalen."

A LETTER FROM THE AUTHOR

Huge thanks for reading *The Killer Instinct*, I hope you are continuing to enjoy Margot's journey.

If you want to join other readers in hearing all about my Storm new releases and bonus content, you can sign up for my newsletter:

www.stormpublishing.co/kate-wiley

And if you want to keep up to date with all my other publications, you can sign up to my mailing list:

eepurl.com/ASoIz

Reviews mean the world to authors, as they can help new readers decide what to pick up next. If you've enjoyed Margot's books, I would be so grateful if you would leave a review. Even a short review can make all the difference in encouraging a reader to discover my books for the first time. Thank you so much!

These books have been such a risk for me, but something I was so excited to do. This world I've created is meant to keep you up at night, and if I've made you put a book in the freezer, I've done my job right. Every new Margot book I'll be looking for ways to move her story forward and keep you on the edge of your seat.

Thanks again for being part of this amazing journey with

me and I hope you'll stay in touch—I have a lot more planned, and if you keep reading, I'll keep writing!

Kate Wiley

www.katewiley.com

facebook.com/SierraDeanAuthor
x.com/sierradean
instagram.com/sierradeanauthor

ACKNOWLEDGMENTS

Thank you so much for reading this book. It's hard to believe we're already three books into this series (and by the time you read these words I'll be sending the first draft of book four to my editor). This series was never supposed to happen, if you believe the agent rejections, the publisher rejections, all the things that led me to set it aside for almost two years.

I have to thank one person, unexpectedly, and that's Ellie Alexander. Ellie (who writes marvelous cozy mysteries) announced on her Instagram one day that she'd signed a new series with Storm Publishing, and my brain went "who are they?" Less than a week later I'd submitted the draft of *The Killer's Daughter* (then known as *In the Blood*) and less than two weeks after that, my editor (who also happens to be Ellie's editor) emailed me back with interest.

Publishing usually doesn't work like that, but when the stars align, you have to dive in with both feet.

Thank you to Vicky Blunden. I've been blessed in my life to have some amazing editors, but I've never had one who so liberally peppers my drafts with the word "Brilliant!" You are almost too good for my ego. To Alexandra, Elka, Anna, Oliver, and I'm sure dozens of others behind the scenes at Storm Publishing for all they do. It's a rare treat to feel so seen by your publisher, and I'm grateful to you all on a daily basis.

This book was a labor of love in a lot of ways. I have been to San Francisco many times, but this year I was able to go *just* to do on-site research for Margot's books. The time I spent in

Chinatown over Lunar New Year, the vibes of the city, the tour of Muir Woods (shout out to Gray Line Tours and my amazing tour guide Doug, who was incredibly knowledgeable – and if I name-dropped a million plants in here you can blame him). Also, if you head to San Francisco hit up their local indie bookseller Borderlands, they are lovely. There's nothing better for a book than getting to visit the settings in person, and getting to immerse myself in Margot's universe (without the danger) was a real boon to the texture of this book. I hope you'll agree.

To all the readers and reviewers who have grabbed hold of this series with both hands, thank you. To anyone who read it on KU and bought the paperback: you are the MVP and have my eternal devotion.

To Lauryn Allman, my amazing audiobook narrator, you are such an angel of a person, a fellow Canadian baddie, and I'm so, so happy to have you as the audio voice of my books.

And last but never least to my family and friends. To my mom, who started watching true crime documentaries so that she might psyche herself up to read my book. To Auntie Shirley, who is a ceaseless cheerleader of all my work. To my besties Rachel, Jessica, Jessica, Jessica (yes, I know), Kristyn, Carol, Catriona, Jamie, and Kevin: thank you for your years of support and celebration. I love you to the ends of the earth. I'm sorry I'm always on my computer.

Printed in Great Britain
by Amazon